D1142375

PAGAN VOYAGER

Also by Simon Finch:

GOLDEN VOYAGER

PAGAN VOYAGER

by

SIMON FINCH

SOUVENIR PRESS

First published 1979 by Souvenir Press Ltd,
43 Great Russell Street, London WC1B 3PA
and simultaneously in Canada

ISBN 0 285 62405 9

Printed in Great Britain by
Bristol Typesetting Co. Ltd,
Barton Manor, St. Philips, Bristol

CONTENTS

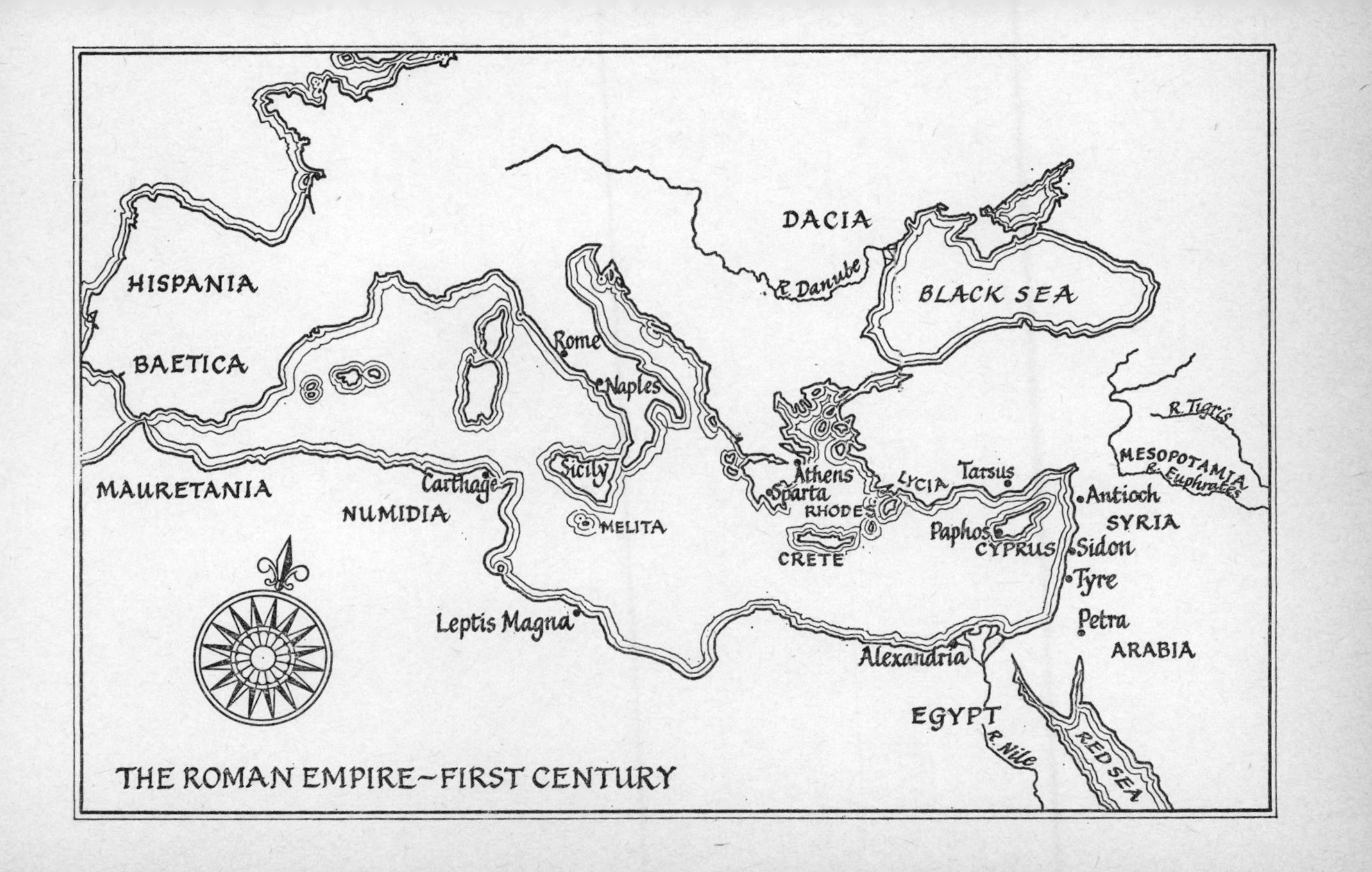

THE ROMAN EMPIRE—FIRST CENTURY

BOOK ONE

THE BATHS OF NERO

1

Vesuvio kicked off his canvas slippers, dropped the muslin bath sheet from his perspiration-soaked body, and sat down by the edge of the large blue mosaic pool in the Baths of Nero called the *tepidarium*. He hoped to find more peace here than he had been able to enjoy in the steam rooms and, again, he wished that he were not visiting this dissolute city – Rome.

Dangling his bare legs in the pool, Vesuvio was still rankled about the sexual approaches which had been made to him in the steam rooms. He asked himself if a man could not go anywhere in the city of Rome – Rome the *urbs* – without being propositioned like a whore or approached by slobbering panderers.

The year was 863 according to Roman calculations; 110 A.D. by the Christians' calendar. Nine emperors had ruled since the establishment of the Empire – four since Nero – and each emperor had built a bath to be used by Rome's populace. But the baths which Nero had built on Campus Martius were still the best equipped Imperial *thermae* in the city.

The Baths of Nero were also the most lascivious. Nevertheless, they were located nearby the bureaus where Vesuvio had business to attend to later today and he had mistakingly thought that he could relax for a few hours in the baths before resuming the work which had brought him to the city. He now regretted that he had not gone to sit in a wine shop until the official bureaus reopened.

A few moments earlier, Vesuvio had been pacing back and forth through banks of mist, working up a fine perspiration on his arms and chest and legs in the steamy *calidarium* as he mulled over his problems. Young men began to emerge like phantoms from the vaporous shadows, persistently following him through the clouds of steam, darting their tongues rapidly in and out of their mouths, making lewd proposals with their hands and buttocks, reaching to grope the linen cincture knotted around his groin.

An obese man had rushed from a far corner of the steam room to chase away the young men with the edges of his bath sheet as if they were a flock of bothersome geese. But then the fat man also began to shuffle around Vesuvio, jangling a leather pouch of coins and whispering that – for a small percentage – he could find bedwork for Vesuvio with love-starved ladies who lived nearby on the Capitoline Hill.

Reminding himself that today was not the first time that he had been mistaken for a burly soldier or athlete who gladly sold himself to catamites and unfaithful wives for a few *sesterces*, Vesuvio leaned back on his arms by the edge of the bathing pool and gazed at the naked and semi-naked people cavorting in the water.

Males were not required to wear clothing in the pools at the Baths of Nero. Females were now also refraining from covering their bodies. And the women who did wear clothing donned only diaphanous scarves which clung to their nipples with the water and moulded over the dark patches between their legs.

Vesuvio sat on the pool's edge and looked at a bare-breasted woman standing nearby in the water, hearing her strident laughter echo across the hall as a man dived between her legs and nibbled at her groin like a fish.

Looking to the far end of the pool, Vesuvio noticed an old man with oyster-white skin grope a pimply faced boy. He watched two females embrace and kiss like lovers. He saw groups of nude bathers bunched together in threes and fours, rubbing, touching, fondling one another in the pool.

Nero had built these baths forty-five years ago. Trajan

reigned as Emperor now and Vesuvio had heard that he was commissioning a larger, more magnificent edifice than the Baths of Nero, that Trajan was erecting a monument to himself on the Equiline befitting the emperor who had pushed the boundaries of the Roman Empire to their greatest extent in history.

Stories were spreading, though, that mixed bathing would be prohibited at the new Baths of Trajan – or, as people gossiped, that was the wish of Trajan's priggish wife, the Empress Plotina.

Gazing overhead at the sunlight filtering onto the pool through squares of mica set into the domed ceiling like transparent jewels, Vesuvio thought about the Empress Plotina, sexual abandonment, and the reasons why he personally felt uncomfortable in the city of Rome.

Vesuvio's parents were dead but they too had not enjoyed leaving their home in southern Italy to visit the capital city. He wondered if he had inherited more from them than the ancient family name of Macrinus, a light Etruscan colouring, and the rich estate in Campania – Had he been bequeathed his parents' strict Republican attitudes? A conservative way of life now rapidly disappearing in the Empire.

Am I a misfit amongst my own countrymen? he thought as he sat by the pool and half-listened to the loud squeals and prurient calls reverberating around him in the marble columned hall. I am not yet thirty years old but I conduct myself like a much older man. I do not go wenching. Boys hold no interest for me. I do not enjoy bragging in taverns about cuckolding husbands.

Love. Vesuvio wondered how much love had altered his life in the last two years. But then he had not been promiscuous before he had fallen in love with Miranda. He had been raised from boyhood both to honour and anticipate the responsibilities of being a *paterfamilias*.

The only fact which differed from Vesuvio's preparations for becoming a father and the present reality of his adult years was that the mother of his son did not come from his own class. Miranda was a slave girl. Also, he had not yet married her.

* * *

Vesuvio had ridden north three days ago on the Ostian Road from his home in Campania, coming to the capital to conclude the final proceedings by which he would legally adopt his ten-month-old son and finalise the purchase of the child's mother. Roman law allowed a citizen of Rome to marry a slave only when he owned her.

Miranda was still the property of the Athenian physician, Menecrates, who had trained her from childhood in the healing sciences and leased her to Vesuvio two years ago to attend the aged and infirmed slaves on his estate.

Menecrates had only recently agreed to sell Miranda to Vesuvio but, according to information which Vesuvio had learned today at the *Tabularium,* the physician had not yet signed the final agreement of sale and sent it from Athens to be officially recorded.

Foreseeing no trouble arising from this matter, Vesuvio nevertheless feared that he might have to spend a longer amount of time in the city than he had intended. That he might again have to postpone his marriage for legal reasons. He disliked city life and was growing to hate the Roman slave system more and more with every single document he had to file to prove that Miranda – by law – was worthy to marry a citizen of Rome.

Cursing all the demeaning aspects of slavery, thinking how he would have married Miranda long ago if it had not been more difficult for men of the senatorial class than males from lower orders to marry slave girls, Vesuvio took a deep sigh and began to wipe the beads of perspiration from his body and to comb his fingers through the tangle of his blond hair.

Running the flat of his hand over the ripples of his stomach muscles and around the definition of his chest, Vesuvio considered the possibility of taking Miranda as his bride by an ancient form of marriage long-ago abandoned, the law called *usus* which bound a man and woman together who had been living for a year as a man and wife.

Suddenly, Vesuvio's thoughts were disturbed by a cascade of water from the pool. He jolted upright and saw that the person who had splashed him was a young girl. She was standing shoulder-deep in the pool and smiling at him.

'Why are you looking so glum?' she called.

'I'm not glum,' he answered, relaxing back onto his arms. 'Only thinking.'

'Thinking? About your sweetheart? Is she here today with you?'

Vesuvio shook his head and studied the olive-skinned girl moving toward him from the depths of the pool. He guessed that she could be no more than seventeen or eighteen years old. As she began fanning her hands across the sparkling blue water, he noticed that she wore costly gold bracelets around her wrists and upper arms, twin bands on each arm connected by thin gold chains. He doubted if a daughter of a senatorial family would bedeck herself in gold at a public baths – if a high-born girl would even come to the Baths of Nero. He suspected that the girl belonged to the Equestrian class, a Patrician rank lower than the Senatorial orders but citizens who were gaining in wealth and power in the fastly changing Empire.

Not wanting to talk about Miranda to a stranger, especially unwilling to answer questions about his beloved to someone whom he suspected would scoff at the idea of an aristocratic landowner being in love with a slave, he asked, 'What is your name?'

'Livia,' she answered as she waded closer to him. She was unashamed that she wore no *bandulum*, that her breasts bobbed like two small melons in the water.

Vesuvio wondered if he might have been wrong about the girl, that in fact she might be a prostitute. He knew that many such women came here from the Street of The Lanterns in Subura to ply their trade in the afternoons.

'Why do you cover yourself with a cincture?' she asked, falling back into the water and gently fluttering her arms to keep afloat. 'Are you embarrassed by being built small? Or don't you like to . . . boast?'

Vesuvio could not resist grinning at the outrageous question as he looked at the girl thrusting her furry patch upwards in the blueness of the pool. She floated so close to him – so unabashedly – that he could see the hairs turned into the cleft of her feminine mound.

Standing, planting her feet on the tiled floor of the pool, she called, 'You think I'm bold, don't you?'

Vesuvio slowly nodded. 'Yes, I do.'

'Where do you live? You're not from the city.'

'I live in Campania.'

'Campania! Ah, if you live in Campania then you must go often to Baiae! I love the beaches at Baiae. I meet so many people in the summer there. So many Praetorian guards go to Baiae. And the parties they have! Ah!' She held out her arms, twisting her wrists like an Egyptian dancer, and laughed.

Vesuvio decided that his first instinct had been correct. The girl did belong to the Equestrian class. Baiae was a resort in the Bay of Naples which was popular with the Equestrian families from Rome who brought their corrupt ways south in the summer – along with their wide-brimmed straw hats, filigree ivory fans, and thin clothing made from Cosian weave.

'I do not go to Baiae,' Vesuvio answered.

The girl looked aghast. 'You live in Campania and never go to Baiae?'

He did not want to sound arrogant but neither did he want to lie. He said flatly, 'I do not enjoy the life there.'

Tilting her head to one side, she looked at him quizzically and said, 'I can tell by your accent that you are educated. That you are more than a free man. I would say that you are what my Papa calls a "Republican". Papa says that the citizens who live in the country are all Republicans. That Republicans spend their time reading the poets, singing Homer, and counting their . . . debts!'

Vesuvio reached for his bath sheet. Romans were obsessed with social castes and he did not want to tell his life story – or listen to abuse about Republicans – from a spoiled rich girl.

Seeing that he was abandoning her, the girl named Livia waved both hands and shrilled, 'No! No! Do not leave the pool! Not yet! Not without me! Let us go upstairs to the shade terrace. I will recite poetry to you. We can argue about the philosophers. And then if you still think that I'm too bold, too crass for your musty old Republican ways, you can always move yourself to a bench by the railing and watch the procession on Via Neronis.'

Again tilting her head to one side, Livia asked, 'You do know that the funny old priestess from the Temple of Vesta is passing through the Martian Gates today, don't you? The priestess and her ridiculous band of jangling virgins? They should interest you very much if you find *me* boring!'

Vesuvio stood by the edge of the pool and wrapped the bath sheet around him. He tried to muster all his civility. 'Thank you for the invitation, Livia, but, no, I won't join you. And if you go to the shade terrace yourself, let me give you a little . . . brotherly advice. Try to speak with more respect for the high priestess of Vesta. I know that Eastern gods are fashionable these days in Rome. But you must not forget that Vesta is our country's most important diety. That the high priestess has Imperial protection. That you can be arrested for the slightest blasphemy against her. Take that as a friendly word of advice.' He turned to walk away.

'Wait!' she called. 'You haven't even told me your name.'

Vesuvio kept walking.

'If you are going to chastise me, at least tell me your name!'

Having as little time for spoiled rich girls as he had for perfumed catamites, Vesuvio continued toward the archway which opened onto an arcade.

'I'm sorry I made fun of Vesta and the Republicans,' Livia shouted. 'I am even willing to take the chance that you are built . . . small!'

Vesuvio exited from the *tepidarium*.

* * *

The Baths of Nero sprawled over an area larger than even the Circus Maximus, the largest amphitheatre in Rome; it was a pleasure centre composed of vaulted halls, marble colonnades, and a seemingly endless variety of health baths, swimming pools, and decorative fountains. Vesuvio's canvas bath sandals slap, slap, slapped against the tessalated marble floor of a wide arcade which connected the *tepidarium* to the recreation halls. He glanced disinterestedly at the small shops in the arcade selling fruit, perfumes, and religious amulets. He passed through the wafting scents of cinnamon, civet, and myrrh. He saw piles of oranges, osier baskets spilling yellow grapes, large oriental palm trees suspended from the ceiling by brass chains, their drooping fronds lit by the sunlight shining through the translucent domes.

Ignoring a vendor's call to inspect a monkey skull from India, brushing off the hand of another salesman who tugged at his bath sheet and whispered that he had recently received a shipment of an aphrodisiac from Leptis Magna concocted from ground rhinocerous tusks, Vesuvio continued walking down the long arcade of shops and tented stalls.

Not only had he forgotten how sexually oriented the Baths of Nero were but he also had not remembered them being this commercial, that a visitor could virtually buy anything here on any day of the week.

More than a place to cleanse your body, the Baths of Nero were a marketplace, a melting pot, a spot where the poor people from the *insulae* – the city's tenement blocks – could mingle with privileged citizens who came here attended by retinues of slaves. The price of admission to the baths was the coin of the lowest domination – one *quadran*.

Passing from the hubbub of the commercial arcade, Vesuvio proceeded to the more quiet wing of the recreation halls. He slowed by a walled garden planted with dwarf palms and heard a poet reading his work to a small group of attentive listeners. He continued walking and saw the library, a pillared room where ivory-rolled scrolls set stacked in tall mahogany recepticles built along the gleaming white marble walls. Then he glanced into a small games field opened to the sky where men and boys knelt in circles tossing dice and knucklebones onto the sand.

Vesuvio kept scuffing along this second arcade until he reached two Doric columns. He stopped again to look. He saw a large group of men gathered in one of the many gymnasiums here called a *palestra*.

Remembering how his father had taken him as a boy to see wrestling matches in a bath-house, Vesuvio slowly edged his way through the crowd.

As Vesuvio drew closer to the sand pit, though, he could only see one wrestler inside the circle of men. He also noticed that the athlete was wearing a loosely fitting tunic, a garment too fulsome for a wrestler normally to wear. Vesuvio next saw the man raise a wooden *gladus* in one hand – the type of blunt sword given to gladiators in training schools.

Still not seeing the athlete's opponent, Vesuvio noticed the wrestler's arms tensing with muscle, that he was struggling with something, someone whom Vesuvio could not yet see.

Then, as the wrestler turned, Vesuvio realised that the man was not fighting another man but was grappling with a python which coiled to attack him, a long and thick snake which . . . yes, the butt of the snake was somehow attached between the wrestler's legs!

Trying to grip the twisting python with one hand, the wrestler used the other hand to stab his wooden sword at the snake to keep it from wrapping around his neck.

Vesuvio asked the man standing alongside him, 'What kind of match is this?'

'He is supposed to be Priapus,' the man answered, keeping his eyes on the struggle. 'You know, the god Priapus with the big prick. Now he's fighting his prick like a gladiator!'

Priapus? But Priapus was the deity of the garden, Vesuvio thought. Priapus was an ancient symbol of fertility always depicted with outsize genitals whom many Romans planted in their gardens for good luck. Farmers often put a straw replica of Priapus in the fields to protect their crops from crows. Never before had Vesuvio seen the god Priapus depicted in this way, fighting his own fabled phallus!

Watching the wrestler strain against the reptile coiling up from his groin, Vesuvio now understood why the man wore such a loosely fitting tunic. He caught sight of a leather girdle which had been strapped between his legs to encase the serpent's base. The python's slickness – as it arched up from the wrestler's groin – did look like a grotesque rendition of a curving, bending, uncontrollable phallus.

Both impressed by the ingenuity with which this public entertainment had been devised, and repelled by the vulgarity with which the Romans were beginning to treat their familiar gods, Vesuvio soon realised what complete thoroughness had gone into this bout to give a new interpretation of Priapus.

By legend, Priapus not only had enormous genitals but he also was an extremely ugly god. And this 'Priapus' fighting his 'phallus' had a severely pocked face. One eye was missing. His hairline grew down to his bushy black eyebrows. Vesuvio had never seen such an unfortunate looking man.

But the wrestler's physical imperfections only added to the audience's amusement. Some of the crowd cheered for 'Priapus' to conquer the python whilst others called instead to the 'phallus'.

'Go on, get him, you big prick!' one man shouted.

'Wrap yourself across that ugly face!' another urged.

'The throat! The throat! Drive down the throat and suck yourself, Priapus! Suck yourself!'

Feeling someone tap him on the shoulder, Vesuvio thought that another observer had come to the *palestra* and wanted to know the details of this sham athletic contest as he had done.

Turning to explain about Priapus battling his own penis, Vesuvio saw a man with a shaved head and a notched ear facing him. He recognised him as a slave, the same bath attendant with whom he had left his clothes in the dressing-room.

The slave asked '*Domine,* excuse me but are you addressed as "Aurelius Macrinus"?'

Vesuvio nodded. People rarely called him by his formal family name. He wondered if someone had come from the *Tabularium* with news of Miranda's manumission.

The slave explained, 'There is a traveller from Campania asking to see you, *domine*. He is waiting upstairs on the shade terrace.'

'Campania?' Vesuvio asked, puzzled. 'Did he give his name?'

Holding his head loftily, the bath slave answered with the smugness used by most city dwellers – regardless of their class – when they referred to people from the country. He said, 'The traveller is only a farmer, *domine*. If you wish, I can easily send him away. He claims his news is grave but he's probably drunk. You know those peasants from Campania. They stink so much from animal manure you cannot smell the wine!'

Turning away from the sandpit, Vesuvio said, 'Lead me to the man. I come from Campania, too.'

2

A warm afternoon breeze gently blew across the shade terrace of the Baths of Nero, a flat-topped roof covered with a saffron awning and lined by a marble balustrade on which set potted tropical ferns alternating with busts of Nero. Vesuvio preceded the bath attendant up the stone steps to the terrace, anxiously looking for a familiar face from home amongst the people gathered here with their body slaves soberly bearing fringed sun umbrellas and dipping ostrich fans attached to bamboo handles.

Having racked his brain for any trouble which would bring a messenger this great distance, Vesuvio remembered the recent problem between his bailiff, Galba, and the man's adulterous wife. He wondered if the situation had become more delicate in his absence, if the time had come for punishment to be delivered to the promiscuous woman and her Sicilian lover.

But would someone travel all the way from Campania to tell me that? Vesuvio asked himself. To report that adulterous lovers have become so blatant that they finally must be caned or whipped? He next thought about sickness, about the malaria rumoured to be spreading in southern Italy. Had it crept toward Villa Vesuvio?

The bath attendant moved alongside Vesuvio and pointed to a stooped figure cowering in a far corner of the terrace. He said, 'That is the man there, *domine*.'

Although not recognising the person, Vesuvio pressed a *quadran* into the attendant's hand and pushed his way through the crowd of people drinking wine from silver goblets and nibbling sausages, nuts, and sweet seeds from plates and wicker baskets.

He asked, 'Are you the man wishing to see Aurelius Macrinus?'

The farmer nervously gripped a pointed *peperino* cap in his hands and eyed the sophisticated city people standing around him on the shade terrace. He began to explain in murmurs, 'My name is Tuto, *domine*. I live near Stabaie with my wife and children. I was returning home last evening and came across a man lying by the side of the public road.'

'Was the man from my estate?' Vesuvio asked.

Shaking his head, the farmer explained, 'The man had little breath left in his body, *domine*. He whispered your name to me. He begged me to ride to Rome. To look for you in the building here called the *Tabul*. . . .' The farmer faltered, struggling to pronounce the name correctly in his coarse dialect.

'The *Tabularium*,' Vesuvio said anxiously.

Nodding, the farmer continued, 'I rode here but, reaching the gates called "Porta Capena", I was not allowed to bring my animal into the city. I did not know that carts and work animals were forbidden to travel within the city during the day. I had no idea that the foot traffic was so thick in Rome. The streets so narrow. But I managed to walk to the . . . *Tabularium*. I found a man there who . . .'

'Yes, good friend. Yes,' Vesuvio said. 'But tell me about the man you found alongside the road. What was his name? Had he been thrown from his horse?'

Shaking his head, the farmer said, 'No, *domine*, he was not thrown by his animal. He was set upon by ruffians . . . or thieves.'

'Thieves? Thieves attacking a harmless field slave? But there are few people in our part of Campania who do not live there. The only strangers have been the herbalists gathering plants and kelp from the . . . sea!'

The farmer shrugged. 'I do not know who the men were nor the reason they attacked the poor man. Nor did he tell me. He only pleaded that I come to Rome and bring you immediately home.'

Shuffling his feet, the farmer respectfully added, 'I know of you, *domine*. I know that you are one of the largest slave-owners in our district. But I also know that you are the *padrone* of many men and women who once served under you as slaves. Now most of those people work plots of land you've given them. I know the good that you have done for the countryside. I am honoured to be of service to a *padrone* such as you. And how—' He shrugged. ' – how could I turn a deaf ear to a dying man?'

Vesuvio admired this simple farmer's integrity. He also knew that the ride to Rome must be an unparallelled adventure for him. He insisted that the farmer take some wine and food, telling him to wait here in the corner of the terrace whilst he went downstairs to dress. They would ride back to Campania together.

When Vesuvio was ordering wine, barley cakes, and sausages for the farmer to eat, he heard the first jangling of bells on the street below the terrace. When the sound grew louder, he glanced down at the small sienna-washed buildings pressed together on Via Neronis – food shops, taverns, public stables – and saw a white curtained wagon passing on the street. Four snow-white asses pulled the simple wagon and veiled maidens rang silver bells as they walked in sober attendance in front of and behind the jogging cart.

Remembering that the girl in the pool had told him that the high priestess of Vesta was passing along Via Neronis this afternoon, Vesuvio quickly beckoned the farmer to his side. He said, 'Look, my friend. See the virgins from the Temple of Vesta. That is the one cart allowed in Rome during daylight hours.'

The farmer quickly moved alongside Vesuvio and stared in awe at the four white asses pulling the holy cart. He whispered, 'The sacred priestess of the hearth! Who would have thought that I, Tuto, would come this close to Vesta and her maidens? *Domine,* you do not know how pleased my wife will be. And my children!'

Vesuvio and the farmer soberly watched the Vestal cart pass beneath the terrace. But the other Romans around them took no notice of the religious procession passing on the street. They continued chattering to one another, drinking wine and nibbling sunflower seeds as the sound of the virgins' bells proceeded down the street.

Ashamed of the wealthy Romans for ignoring Vesta's priestess, Vesuvio said to the farmer, 'This augurs well for you, my friend. You have the spirit of Rome's ancient hearth. Your home and children will be blessed by this.'

The farmer hung farther out over the marble balustrade to stare at the curtained wagon disappearing through the narrow buildings. He said, 'May the goddess Vesta also protect you, *domine,* and the woman you plan to make the mistress of your home.'

Surprised that the peasants in the district had already learned of his plans to marry Miranda, Vesuvio thanked the farmer for his good wishes.

The farmer added, 'May Vesta also protect you from whatever bad news is waiting for you at home, *domine.*'

Despite the good intentions of the farmer's wishes, the words strangely chilled Vesuvio. He wondered if the bailiff's profligate wife was indeed the trouble on his estate. Or had a slave been riding to Rome to deliver more important news? Perhaps malaria had spread to Villa Vesuvio. Or some troublemaker was planting discontent amongst the slaves, telling them that Vesuvio was like all the other Roman landowners. That he had no intent ever to free them, that his philosophy of equality amongst men was only a ploy to exact harder work from them.

Whatever the trouble was, though, Vesuvio knew that he must quickly dress himself and ride south to Campania. He doubted if his presence would be required at home longer than two or three days but he dreaded the prospect of returning to Rome in a few days' time to embark again on the complicated legalities at the *Tabularium* to make Miranda his lawful bride and official mother of his infant son.

3

The sun cast a golden glow over the rolling wheat fields of Campania the following morning when Vesuvio and the farmer, Tuto, arrived at a crossroads five miles east of Misenum. They had ridden throughout the night from Rome, stopping only to take fresh mounts at stations along the Ostian Road.

Vesuvio rewarded the farmer with a pouch of coins for bringing the message to him in Rome and promised to send a butchered sheep to his family and a pig for cured meat and sausages to enjoy in the wintertime. Then, again wishing him the gods' protection, Vesuvio took the road leading southwest to Villa Vesuvio.

Riding at a slower pace than he and the farmer had done in the last hours, Vesuvio tried to collect his thoughts as a cool morning wind tossed the yellow hair back from his forehead.

Remembering the farmer's description of a slave lying near death on a roadside, he again puzzled not only about who the man might be but also why he should be trying to reach him in Rome in the first place. And why should a slave not only be set upon by thieves but also murdered? What valuables had he been carrying? Or had it been only news? But what news?

Vesuvio slowed his horse to a trot when he came in sight of the fieldstone walls which divided his property from the public road. He saw familiar wisps of smoke curling in the distance from the white chimneys of the slave complex. He recognised the carts outside his stables. The iron gates stood solidly by the roadside. His bronze *nomens* was still intact on the travertine pillars, not ripped away or smeared with dung as villains would have done if they had come to cause damage within his walls.

Opening the gates and remounting his horse, Vesuvio cantered down between the cypress trees lining the gravel drive which led to the pillared portico of his sprawling home.

The air became sharper, turning into a biting breeze as Vesuvio rode closer to his villa's position on the cliffs high above the sea. He could already hear the distant crash of waves breaking against the rocks far below the front terraces of the house.

But, still, he saw no activity around the yard or the covered portico, nothing unusual except for wooden tables arranged in one long line across the gravel. He had left instructions for the tables to be brought there, though, long trestle tables on which he would pile sheafs of wheat, baskets of fruit, *amphorae* of wine, all token gifts from him – the *padrone* of this district – to the slaves whom he had freed in the last two years, and to his tenant farmers when they came to celebrate with him and Miranda at their wedding feast.

Reining his horse in front of the villa, Vesuvio saw no groom rushing to take his animal. But that did not surprise him either. He was not expected to arrive home at such an early hour. And no guests called in Campania at this time of morning.

Dismounting, Vesuvio brushed the dust of the road from his tunic and wondered if he would find Miranda in the house or had she already gone to the slave quarters to attend the woman who had birthed a son on the night before he left for Rome.

He still saw no one, heard nothing but the familiar cluck of chickens, the pounding of hammers in a faraway shed, the faint laughter of children already playing in a field. He walked across a mosaic of Mount Vesuvius erupting, a design of small blue, green, and red tiles laid on the floor of the portico.

Suddenly, he heard a loud shriek behind him. He spun around at the sound of the piercing cry and saw an old woman dressed in black. She dashed toward the portico, flapping her mantle back and forth like the wings of an ominous bird.

'Tia!' he called to the old woman, a superstitious crone whom he trusted to be the mistress of his household in place of a wife, sister, or mother.

'*Domine*!' Tia cried, rushing to Vesuvio. '*Domine*! Thank the gods you have returned!' She threw herself at his feet, wailing like a funereal mourner, rocking to and fro on her haunches in front of him.

Lowering his hand to steady the old woman, Vesuvio demanded, 'Tia! Calm yourself! Tell me what has been happening here! A farmer came all the way to Rome to find me. He told me one of our men was killed along the roadside. Who was it?'

Falling facedown on the ground, Tia began clawing fistfuls of dirt with her nails and throwing them over her shoulders. She wailed, 'Oh, Vesta! Jove! Sacred Janus of the hearth! Thank you for sending our master home!'

'Control yourself, Tia,' Vesuvio commanded, shaking her by the shoulders. 'Save your sacrifices for the *lares*. Tell me what happened here in my absence.'

Crouching on the ground in front of him, Tia cried, 'Your betrothed, *domine*! The Greeks came the day you left for Rome. The Greeks came and took away your betrothed!'

'Miranda?' Vesuvio gasped. 'What Greeks? Who took Miranda away? Why?'

'Oh, a mystery has been happening here, *domine*! A dreadful mystery has been happening since you left. Look! The earth appears the same. Smell! The winds seem as sweet. Behold! The sun rose this morning. The moon shone last night, *domine*. But a mystery confuses this land since the

Greeks came to Villa Vesuvio and took away Miranda!'

'Tia, speak slowly. Tell me exactly what happened.'

'Oh, *domine,* Pico left to take the news to you in Rome. But his body was brought back in a dung cart!'

'Pico?' Vesuvio asked. 'Is he the man who's dead?'

Falling facedown onto the ground again and scraping at the dirt, Tia moaned, 'Pico! Poor Pico's spirit! He was found dead in a ditch! Dead without even a coin on his tongue to pay the ferryman to take him across the River Styx to the nether-world.'

Seeing that he must be firm with the old woman, Vesuvio grabbed her by both arms and lifted her to her feet. He began to walk her across the mosaic floor of the portico, demanding, 'Calm yourself, good Tia. Calm yourself and tell me exactly what happened. You say that Greeks came here and took away Miranda. Who were these Greeks? Did you recognise their faces? Did they leave their names? What was the reason they gave for seizing Miranda? Were they from the physician in Athens who owns Miranda? Was one of the men called Menecrates? The physician himself?'

'Oh, *domine*!' Tia sobbed. 'We know nothing. We know nothing except that a mystery hangs over this land. A mystery as black as night! Black as death, *domine*! There is death here!'

'My son?' Vesuvio asked anxiously. 'Is young Aurelius safe?'

Throwing up both hands, Tia shrilled, 'Oh, the poor babe! The poor babe has no mother now! Who will care for him? Who will prepare him for the world? Teach him about the gods? Sing to him of heroes?'

Standing with his arm around Tia's frail shoulders, Vesuvio felt her old body convulse with sobs against his chest and he thought that if the words she said were true – that if Miranda had indeed been taken away from Villa Vesuvio – who not only would be the mother of their son but, also, who would be his wife?

Looking at the wooden tables already erected for their wedding feast, he thought, No, this is not true. Miranda can not be gone. *Greeks? Menecrates? But he agreed to sell her to me!*

* * *

Settling himself on a divan in the *triclinium* a few hours later for a light midday meal, Vesuvio held his infant son alongside him on the cushion and listened to Tia explain how the child no longer suckled on his mother's breast, that there was no need to send for a woman to come from the slave quarters and nurse him.

Vesuvio listened soberly to this and other domestic facts. He struggled with himself not to reprimand Tia – and his bailiff, Galba, and any of the other servants who had been around the house when Miranda had been taken away – for not keeping the Greek strangers here until officials were contacted in the nearby town of Puteoli to examine any documents which claimed a right on her.

Understanding the slaves' timidity in the face of firm authority, though, Vesuvio again cursed the bondage system which gave unlimited power to some men and rendered others as helpless as sheep, often incapacitating them even to use their minds. He was lumbered with the slave system as an economic fact of Roman life. He was trying to find some way to work his inherited lands without slavery. He tried never to forget that his slaves were human like himself, that they were not chattel. And now he told himself that he must not blame them for allowing strangers to take away Miranda without providing proof of their rightful claim to her.

Instead, Vesuvio tried to weigh the stories the slaves had been telling him all morning, that Menecrates had indeed demanded Miranda to be returned to Athens. A deputation of three men had claimed they had been sent to escort her to the physician's home there.

Before coming into the *triclinium* to eat his midday meal, Vesuvio had locked himself in his library to examine the contract which he had signed for Miranda's original position here. He carefully noted the condition of the contract which stated that Miranda could work for him as a medical attendant on his estate until he or Menecrates chose to end the agreement. The contract was to run for a duration of three years, six months of that time had yet to pass before the contract could be renewed or terminated by either party.

Vesuvio remembered that he had written a letter to Menecrates stating that he wished to buy Miranda and to make her his wife. He also knew that Menecrates had received the letter because not only had he quickly answered, submitting the price he wished for her sale, but also he had sent felicitations for their future happiness. Vesuvio had readily agreed on the sum which Menecrates asked; the papers were to be sent to be recorded in Rome.

Remembering how Miranda's manumission papers had not been processed at the *Tabularium* when he had been in Rome, Vesuvio wondered if that had been no mere oversight. Nor a fault due to slow communications. He wondered if Menecrates had changed his mind since their last correspondence. But, if so, why had the physician not notified him? There was no enmity between them. Menecrates was a respected and honourable man. And Vesuvio knew that in the event that the old man had suddenly died since their last communication, his will would be processed by the Roman Government – the same rules holding in Athens as here in Italy – and the contract would be as binding as if Menecrates were still alive.

Vesuvio was still troubled with these thoughts as he tried to eat his midday meal of lamb and fruit. The press of his son's small body against him only increased his frustration. The child was too young to know his mother had gone. He chewed on an ivory teat which old Tia had given him a few moments earlier, a nursemaid's object called an 'Aphrodite's

Thumb', as he crawled happily over his father's recumbent body.

Trying to play with the chubby infant, Vesuvio heard the sound of footsteps approach along the walkway of the central courtyard. He raised his eyes and saw his bailiff standing between the marble columns flanking the entrance to the room. He motioned for Tia to take the child and beckoned for the bailiff, Galba, to come toward the couch.

Galba was a tall, strong-framed man, with a mop of curly black hair. His large brown eyes were sad and downcast as he moved slowly across the room. Vesuvio guessed that Galba was not only troubled about his wife's shameless conduct but also was still embarrassed for not having sent for officials to question the Greeks who had taken away Miranda.

Vesuvio pointed for Galba to take a place on the divan opposite him, pushing the wine urn across the table and deciding to talk later about Galba's wife. He wanted to speak first about Miranda's disappearance.

He calmly began, 'You above anybody else should understand my feelings, Galba. You yourself are a married man.'

Shaking his head as he poured himself a goblet of wine and watered it, Galba said, 'My shameful wife, Catalia, is not worthy to be compared to your Miranda, *domine*.'

'We will come back to the matter of your wife, Galba. I am talking about being married. Siring children. You enjoyed all that once. You can understand my love. And now my loss.'

Hanging his head, Galba said, 'I see now we did wrong in your absence, *domine*. We should have not trusted the stranger's words. Letting them take Miranda without showing proof. But. . . .'

Shrugging his broad shoulders, Galba continued, 'I can not read, *domine*. I understand numbers. I supervise your crops. I oversee the slaves and tenant workers. But to read legal documents . . .' He gestured helplessly.

Vesuvio tried to contain his impatience. He said, 'But you heard me talk about the man who owns Miranda. We discussed the fact before I left for Rome that Menecrates is a just and honest man. That he upholds the laws of the Empire as if he were born a natural Roman. That he treats his slaves well. That he honours family codes. How he disapproves of unfaithfulness in marriage. Menecrates even acts as a counsellor in Athens on adultery and so why do you think that he. . . .'

Vesuvio stopped. He was becoming riled again. He realised its uselessness. Setting his goblet down on the table, he confided to Galba in a flat voice, 'I do not think Menecrates would break his promise to me. I cannot accept that. But I do not know why somebody would lie to take her away. I do not know why but I cannot help from thinking that someone is lying to me.'

'*Domine*!' Galba gasped. 'I would cut out my tongue before I would tell a lie to you.'

'No, no, no. I do not mean you. Not Tia. No one here.'

'Your people love you, *domine*. You buy slaves for the fields and mills only when you cannot find labourers to work. You are good to your slaves. You make them freedmen. Many rich people in the district despise you for freeing your slaves so easily. But your critics are all landlords who spend most of their time in Rome. There is not a single, hard-working person in the whole of this district, *domine*, who would lie to you. Not one man or woman who would even wish you harm.'

Vesuvio shook his head. He said, 'I am still too dazed to make sense even to myself about this situation, Galba. I do not know what to think. What course of action to take. I do not know anyone who would wish to keep Miranda from marrying me. I do not believe in my heart that Menecrates would break his word to me. No, Galba, I must have more time to think about this.'

Sitting on the edge of the divan, Galba stared at his large

red hands. He said helplessly, 'I am only sorry that I did not act more wisely, *domine*.'

'Do not blame yourself, Galba. I understand that you have many personal things on your mind.' Vesuvio studied the pitiful expression on his bailiff's face, saying more softly, 'Now tell me about Catalia. Is it still the same man?'

Galba nodded.

'Does she meet him in the hut where they were last found together?'

'Hut. Loft. Field. Anyplace where they can make love . . . and a mockery of our marriage vows.'

'His name is Rocco, true?'

Again, Galba nodded.

'The Sicilian from the flour mill?'

His face reddening, Galba asked in a fury, 'Has she no pride? Married to a freedman, the wife of someone who has distinguished himself by becoming bailiff to one of the largest estates in southern Italy? But yet she chooses to rut with a common slave from Sicily?'

'Galba! Do not be so prejudiced!' Vesuvio thundered at him. 'Would your pain be less if the man were free? Would your wife be less faithful if her lover were not a slave? Answer me honestly.'

Lowering his head onto his hands, Galba buried his eyes and said, 'I am sorry, *domine*. I speak in anger.'

'And an anger I can understand, Galba. But you must control it. We are both in a difficult situation. The bailiff would normally punish a slave who breaks a law on the estate. But as you are the offended man . . .'

'I would gladly whip them both, *domine*. Whip her and that Rocco. I would lash them until their pain would be so fierce that they could not even lay together on a bed of . . . feathers to make their accursed love!'

'That is exactly what I fear, Galba. That your punishment would go too far. That is why I do not think I can trust you with a whip.'

Raising his head, Galba focused his liquid brown eyes on Vesuvio and asked, 'Will you whip them, *domine?*'

'You know I do not participate in punishment. That I do not even approve of it unless it is absolutely necessary.'

'But this *is* necessary,' Galba shouted. 'You will not let them go free, *domine!*'

Shaking his head, Vesuvio said, 'That would be as unwise as punishing them too severely. Punishment is necessary for their actions. Adultery threatens the happiness of many families here. We cannot chance other men meeting secretly with the wives of good men like you. We cannot risk women flirting with an unmarried slave when their husbands are in the fields. That is why I must demand your complete co-operation.'

'I will do anything, *domine,*' Galba promised. 'I will do anything to see that they receive their due.'

'They will both have the cane, Galba. Not the whip but the cane. You will stand to cane Catalia but I will allow you the satisfaction of taking running strokes to beat the man who has cuckolded you. You must not exceed the number of strokes I tell you. And you must not strike to break his bones or cause him any severe injuries.'

'It will be difficult for me, *domine.* A deadly anger rages inside me. A deadly anger and injured pride.'

'If you do not promise to obey me, Galba, then I will have to send them both to Puteoli.'

'Not Puteoli, *domine.* It would be worse for me if the mother of my children was punished by town officials. I want to keep this as far away as possible from district gossip. I do not want my children to grow up and have people pointing at them, saying, "Their mother was caned in Puteoli for being a slut". No, *domine,* I promise to obey all your stipulations.'

Vesuvio nodded, telling Galba that if he promised to obey his instructions, the caning would take place this evening when the workers came in from the fields.

He said, 'I also understand your wish to keep this matter as private as possible. But your wife has conducted her shameful actions in public. All the people on the estate know about her and Rocco. Every adult man and woman on Villa Vesuvio, free or slave, must witness this punishment. I am sorry, Galba, but I have the welfare of other families to consider, too.'

Nodding his head, Galba said, 'I understand, *domine*, that you must make the others observe. But I do not want the mother of my children to be sent to Puteoli. What happens here on this estate is our business . . . your business, *domine*.'

Galba listened attentively then as Vesuvio told him that the caning would take place this evening in the dirt yard in front of the stables, explaining the exact method of delivering the punishment which he wanted him to follow.

4

It was rare for a slave to be physically punished on Villa Vesuvio. The slaves and the freed tenant workers who broke rules and were lazy at their jobs were barred from celebrations and parties, did not receive bonuses of produce, were made to work extra hours at their chores. The fact that the bailiff's wife and a Sicilian male were being caned meant that their offence was of the lowest order.

The men and women collected in the dirt yard in front of the stables at the sunset hour. They were still dressed in the roughly woven clothes they wore to till the fields and work the mills, grind wheat into flour and press olives into oil. They stood in sober groups in front of the stables, speaking amongst themselves in voices no louder than whispers.

Word quickly spread through the slaves and tenant workers that, because Catalia was a mother, she would receive a lesser amount of strokes than her lover. She would be the first to be given the cane. Also, because she was a woman, she would be caned in a standing position, not placed on a guard's back and struck like a male criminal.

A hush fell over the assembled workers as an old man led short, statuesque Catalia to the post in the middle of the dirt yard. She held her head high, not looking to the left nor right.

The old man moved to take Catalia's robe from her shoulder but, shoving him aside, she untied the cord from around her waist and dropped the garment to the ground, standing unashamed in her nakedness in front of her neighbours from the slave complex.

Next, yanking a thong from the nape of her neck, Catalia

shook her head and a mane of coarse black hair unfurled around her shoulders. She then lifted her hands to the post and held them there for the old man to bind with leather cords. She still showed no shame nor repentance.

Whispers spread amongst the crowd as Galba pushed his way through the onlookers and slowly strode across the dirt yard. He gripped the five-foot length of cane in one hand and walked sober-faced toward his naked wife tied to the wooden post.

Pausing a few feet away from the post, Galba studied Catalia's bare back and buttocks. His left hand toyed with the supple cane as he coldly scrutinised her, ignoring the blasphemies she was beginning to hiss at him.

'Does the cane make my husband feel stronger?'

Solemn-faced, Galba transferred the cane from his left hand to his right.

Catalia jeered, 'That is the only stiff thing you've waved at me in years, impotent pig!'

Galba stepped back a few paces, keeping his eyes on his wife's naked body.

'Go on! Show everybody how strong you are! That you are the big bailiff!'

Galba heaved his chest and spat. But not at his wife. He moved to stand upon the spot where his spittle had fallen – a markation for himself – and made his first idle swings of the cane in the air whilst moving his feet to find the correct position.

Catalia called louder, 'I'm not the only woman on this land who's strayed. I know many women who sneak away into the wheat fields. Do you want to hear names? I'll tell you names! What about . . .'

Quickly pivoting on one leg, Galba swung the cane through the air and landed a resounding crack against his wife's naked back.

Catalia's scream pierced the air. Galba drew back the cane and bent his knees to swing the cane a second time. He struck slightly below his first mark which already showed a dark line across her tender flesh.

His face remaining immobile, Galba kept turning to swing the cane, maintaining a steady rhythm of his strokes, striking Catalia again and again on her back until a ladder of dark bruises and rising welts ran down from her shoulders to her waist.

Many women watching the punishment winced in sympathy for Catalia as she plaintively began to beg for mercy. The men soberly studied Galba maintaining his calculated aims, knowing that Vesuvio had given him permission to administer thirty strokes. Dark red rivulets of blood were beginning to pour down from her back and Galba struck for the first time on her fleshy buttocks.

. . . twenty-two . . . twenty-three . . . twenty-four. . . .

Proceeding to smite his wife's buttocks, Galba centred the cane to stripe Catalia with the same sharp precision as he had marked her back. Welts began to form on her buttocks with the twenty-seventh strike and, by the time that Galba reached the count of thirty, blood now was also pouring down her thighs and calves.

Turning his back to the post after he had caned Catalia the last time, Galba waited for the old man to untie her body from the post. A woman moved from the crowd to help walk Catalia to the stable but a man stopped her. Two other males stepped forward to catch Catalia's fainting body.

As one man grabbed her hands and another took her feet, the old man picked up her robe from the ground and spread it across her naked breasts and midsection.

Slowly, Catalia's limp body was carried from the stable yard whilst two guards led Rocco towards the post. The slim-hipped Sicilian stopped when he saw Catalia. He looked nervously around him at the assembled workers. He held up his arms. He opened his mouth to speak. But the guards prodded him toward the centre of the yard.

The onlookers had less sympathy for Rocco than they had shown for Catalia. He was not married, not a father of children. And being a culprit in their eyes, they began to speak derisively about him, calling to Galba that he should show no mercy for him, even that his testicles should be sliced from his groin and fed to the crows.

Rocco began to resist the guards as they bound his hands together with leather thongs. They grabbed him by his wavy black hair and pushed him to straddle the back of a guard who stood in front of him.

Galba stood soberly watching Rocco's bound hands being placed over the guard's head and, when the guard leaned forward with Rocco on his back, Galba again began to cut the cane idly through the air.

Waiting until the guard was crouched into the correct position, watching until Rocco was bent in a way by which the striking cane would not cause any damage to his spine, Galba began to look around him for a standing.

He moved toward Rocco's naked body spread upon the guard's stooped back and, turning, he walked away for ten paces. He stopped. He turned to look at Rocco. He moved back three more paces and made a markation in the dirt, this time with the heel of his sandal.

Standing soberly at the end of his marking, Galba raised the cane in the air. He twisted it momentarily above his shoulder and, then, suddenly dashed forward. He gripped the base of the cane with both hands a few feet before he reached Rocco's body and made the first aim against his back.

Galba stopped his run a short distance beyond his target. He turned. He walked past Rocco now screaming astride the guard's stooped back.

Reaching his markation in the dirt, Galba turned. He raised the cane. And, again dashing forward, he gripped the cane with both fists only a few feet behind Rocco's back and hit him a second time, repeating the same action again and again until Rocco's back and buttocks were smeared with blood, his legs stained with his own excrement, when a total of fifty whistling strokes had been delivered for committing adultery.

5

Vesuvio walked along the western boundaries of Villa Vesuvio that evening, soberly pacing a marble chip path which wound high above the waves crashing against the craggy coastline of Campania. His mind was a maelstrom of images and sounds from the last few hours – the vision of Catalia's limp body being carried from the stableyard, of Rocco soiling himself whilst being flogged, the sight of Galba crying in the stables after completing the punishment.

Galba was a strong man with a keen sense of loyalty. Also, like many brawny men whom Vesuvio had known, Galba possessed a childlike sensitivity and his emotions had burst once he had finished caning his unfaithful wife and her lover. He had not been able to continue showing a calm veneer.

Vesuvio believed that Galba deserved a much better woman than Catalia for his wife. He remembered how the slatternly woman had taunted Galba from the post, trying to embarrass him in front of other people. Galba had borne up under her jeers, only bringing his first bite of the cane down upon Catalia when she was threatening to accuse other women of profligacy.

Now it was over. Galba had carried Catalia back to their small fieldstone hut. Rocco lay in the men's dormitory. Vesuvio had sent Tia with a pot of herbal salve to rub upon their wounds.

Vesuvio thought of the healing salve and realised that if Miranda were here she would be rubbing the unguent into the broken skin herself at this very hour, comforting Catalia in her pain, inventing games to divert the attention of Galba's three small children.

Miranda.

Vesuvio still could not believe that her rightful master had called her back to Athens. Menecrates would not dissolve a contract without warning. But Vesuvio still could not think of anyone else who would take Miranda away from here in the name of Menecrates.

Standing on a promontory of land jutting out over the silver-capped sea, Vesuvio listened to the waves crashing below him and pictured Miranda in his mind. He saw her lively black eyes, her raven hair falling in soft ringlets around her oval face, the curvacious hips which had given him a son, the woman whom he loved.

There were more than seven hundred women on the estate he could choose from. As their master, he could demand privileges with their bodies. But he did not believe in that kind of slavery. He did not believe in inflicting himself on a slave woman who did not want him – or whom he did not want after she had provided him with her feminine pleasures.

Cursing the fact that there were slaves in the world, that a young woman so considerate as Miranda should be treated like a mere bauble in a marketplace, Vesuvio hurled a rock at the sea and continued to pace along the marble path.

He thought of love and marriage and unfaithfulness. He considered the irony of how simple it had been for Galba to marry Catalia and the unhappiness they now suffered, and the difficulty which he was having to make Miranda his bride but the joy they always shared.

Miranda.

Vesuvio held his hands behind his back and walked farther up the path. He was remembering the last time he had seen Miranda. The last time he had held her in his arms. How he had been the one leaving and she was staying . . . home.

* * *

Vesuvio had been asleep when Miranda had finally crept into the bed the night before he left for Rome. He turned when he felt her cool nakedness beside him and wrapped his arm around her, asking about the woman whom she had been tending in childbirth, Lipa who worked in the flour press and was too old to bear children in comfort.

Snuggling closer into the warmth of Vesuvio's body, Miranda whispered, 'Lipa gave birth to a son. Her husband is sitting with her now.' Kissing Vesuvio gently on the cheek, Miranda lay her head on his shoulder and said, 'I love seeing your people happy.'

'They are yours, too,' he said, wrapping his arm around her neck.

'Shhh now,' she urged. 'You must go back to sleep. You have to rise early in the morning.'

Vesuvio did not fall immediately back to sleep. He lay awake, idly fingering the softness of Miranda's hair spreading across his shoulder. He smelt the familiar scent of verbenna on her skin.

Thinking how the people on the estate often forgot that Miranda was a slave, Vesuvio smiled to himself and was pleased that they already saw her as their mistress.

He heard her whisper, 'I love you.'

Surprised that she had not already fallen asleep, he urged, 'Rest, my love. You are tired.'

Snuggling closer against him, she said, 'How can I?'

Vesuvio did not know at first what she meant. Then realising that his manhood had become firm as he had been laying here in the darkness thinking about her, he drowsily teased, 'I spend my days like this. Just thinking about you.'

'I shall miss you.'

Vesuvio still remembered how Miranda had brought her lips to his mouth that night, how she had parted her lips to accept his probing tongue, had spread her legs to hold him when he rolled on top of her.

As she continued whispering her love for him, Vesuvio held her slim body beneath him, spreading his kisses across her face as he gently cradled her head in his hands.

Miranda nibbled on the squareness of his chin as he kissed her eyes. She arched her back to press her breasts against the hardness of his chest, whispering her need for him as he slowly inched into the feminine warmth between her legs.

Locked into a twisting embrace, they launched further into an exchange not only of softly spoken words – passionate kisses, tender fondlings – but also of souls.

Accepting his increasing drives. Miranda gasped her need for him, reassuring him louder and louder as he stirred deeper inside her that she could love no one else.

They clung together in this way, talking, praising one another, maintaining a continuous rhythm, moving toward a crest of passion until they were both gasping, forming a pliant ridge as male and female – emotions and words which bound them closer than husband and wife.

* * *

Staring despondently down at the waves licking the precipitous cliffs in the darkening sunset, Vesuvio thought of slavery and freedom, lovers and wives, the son which Miranda had given him.

Now Miranda was gone. But where? Why?

Vesuvio had once before lost the spiritual centre of his entire world. He had been taken away from his family. He himself had once been enslaved. He had been kidnapped by an Arab called Sheik Bakir only to return to this land to find his family dead or also enslaved. A political conspiracy had threatened this estate when his father was the master here and the land was called Villa Macrinus. Vesuvio had returned to find the only home he had ever known in shambles.

He had changed the estate not only in name but also he had been trying since those bleak days to work a farming system here which did not misuse people as slaves, a system which gave people a share of the land they toiled. His own days in slavery had reinforced his suspicions that there was a way to till, harvest, and produce without a slave system.

During the days in which Vesuvio had dedicated himself to building Villa Vesuvio into an example of how landowners need not depend on slave labour, Vesuvio's personal life was empty and lonely. He had often thought in that time he might have been happier remaining a palace slave in Mesopotamia, or even a pirate on the Mediterranean.

But he believed in freedom. His own freedom and the freedom of other men. He threw himself further into the task of creating order out of the shambles of his family's ruined estate.

Then Miranda had come to work here as a contract slave, assisting in birthing children and attending the infirm in the slave quarters. Their instant friendship soon turned to love and, then from love to spiritual dependency.

Thinking about how his love for Miranda had grown in the last year, Vesuvio turned on the cliffside path and slowly began to stride toward the house. He knew he had to do something about bringing her home. This was her home, too. They agreed on the inhumanity of slavery. They had worked together to give shape to a disordered life. He was not going to lose all that now.

Also, Miranda had given him a son. He considered her to be his wife despite the fact that Roman law did not yet recognise her as the mistress of his household. Miranda was his family and he was not willing to lose his family. Not again.

Walking faster along the path now, Vesuvio knew that he would be wasting his time returning to Rome and arguing with the lawyers and bureaucrats in the *Tabularium*. What could they do? Only he could do something.

Yes, he thought, the matter is entirely in my hands.

Beginning to run down the incline toward the overhanging terraces of the seaside villa, Vesuvio saw what he must do. And how wrong he had been to chastise his people for not sending for the officials in Puteoli to question the Greeks who had come to take Miranda back to Athens.

Athens! He would go to Athens himself! He would confront Menecrates. He would demand Miranda back by his legal contract. And if there was some stipulation in the contract which he had overlooked, he would pay an additional sum toward her purchase.

Dashing into the house, Vesuvio thought how he would pay a fortune for Miranda. But if Menecrates did not want more money, he would not hesitate to take her away from him by force!

Vesuvio suddenly stopped when he saw a figure bundled in black moving across the *atrium* carrying a clay lamp. It was Tia returning from the slave-quarters.

'Tia,' he said excitedly. 'I am going to Athens to bring Miranda home. I am leaving tonight.'

The old woman paused on the edge of the central courtyard, the lamp's flame lightning her wrinkled face.

Vesuvio ordered, 'Pack me food for a ride to Brundisium. I shall ride across Italy tonight and catch the first ship sailing from Brundisium to Greece.'

Tia stared at him suspiciously. She narrowed one eye and began to chew her toothless gums.

Vesuvio had expected the old woman to shriek and wail at his announcement. He was surprised to see her studying him so placidly.

'Tia? Your face makes a strange mask. Is there something you want to say to me?'

'Your noble parents nick-named you in honour of a mighty volcano, *domine*. You were born in the year that volcano broke forth fire and destroyed rich towns and many people.'

Vesuvio asked, 'Why do you mention that now, good Tia?'

'Like your namesake, *domine*, catastrophes start with a small rumble which grows louder and soon shakes an entire district. Troubles build upon trouble, *domine*, as storms of ashes and tidal waves followed the first rumblings of Mount Vesuvius.'

'What are you saying?' Vesuvio asked.

'I shall guard your son with my own life in your absence, *domine*. Have no fear for him. It is your own life you must protect. The first trouble which boils from rocks can carry a man down a crevice which he does not know exists. May the gods, protect you, *domine*, in the many lands through which you may travel beyond Italy.'

'I am only sailing to Athens, Tia! A short journey to bring back Miranda!'

Bowing her head, Tia held her hand in front of the sputtering flame and moved toward the pillars surrounding the *atrium*, saying respectfully, 'I shall prepare you food, *domine*.'

Vesuvio stood motionless, watching her bent body disappearing into the dark shadows. He knew that the riddles which old peasant women spoke often hid more truth than the harangues of learned statesmen. He told himself at that moment that, wherever he went beyond Italy, he must remember Tia's warning.

BOOK TWO

ATHENS

6

Vesuvio sailed from Brundisium late the following day on the *Galatia*, a merchant vessel which was ostensibly transporting bundles of cowhides from Italy to Greece. But straying from its course only a few hours out of port, the freighter first diverted south to take on crocks of honey at Melita, next stopping at Corfu to load barrels of salted fish, and then sailing to Actium to unload rolls of hemp.

Finally, on the morning of the eighth day, the *Galatia* entered the wide-mouthed harbour of Piraeus, a bustling commercial harbour on the Aegean Sea which also served as the port to Athens.

Both the military quays to the left of the Piraeus harbour, and the long commercial colonnades on the right, were filled with vessels quartered tightly against one another. The tall Roman triremes-of-war creaked in their moorings, their triple banks of oaken oars firmly locked in harbour position, their ornately carved mastheads depicting goddesses and sirens pushing against the stone paved wharf like a battalion of stern-faced Amazons.

An equally diverse representation of commercial ships crowded the warehouse docks: Cilician ships carrying lumber from Tarsus, Palestinian freighters packed with *amphorae* of sparkling Judean wine, sleek Egyptian boats laden with cotton from the Nile region, a congestion of freighters as different from one another as their cargo. There were forty-two provinces in the Roman Empire now under Emperor Trajan's expansive reign and nearly as many varied ships criss-crossing the Mediterranean with supplies.

The *Galatia* dropped anchor in the last available mooring

at a wharf fronting the commercial colonnades. The gangplank was thrown down to the dock and the Harbour Master came aboard to collect his entry tax, explaining that the congestion here was due to bad omens.

The Harbour Master told how successive sacrifices made to Poseidon, the Greek god of water, had not been favourable and no ship could sail from Piraeus until the blood of a sacrificed lamb formed conjoining pools of redness on the water.

Vesuvio listened half-interestedly to this report but, deciding that the present religious misfortunes of this Greek port had little to do with his own mission, he tossed his travelling pack over his shoulder and moved quickly down the gangplank.

He pushed his way through grain dealers gathered on the quay and passed the shrilling money-changers seated behind their wooden tables on the wharf. He finally found a harbour cart to drive him the four mile distance from Piraeus to the city of Athens.

Athens served both as the government capital and trading centre of Achea, the province of Rome which included the whole of southern Greece and the islands of Salamis, Chios, Lemnos, Imbros, Skiros, and Delos.

Vesuvio stood in the back of the jostling cart and shaded his eyes against the burning sun to catch his first glimpse of the Parthenon, the gleaming white temple of Pentelic marble columns which set upon the rocky hillsite above Athens called the Acropolis.

Telling the driver to leave him by an entrance to the main marketplace which lay to the west of the Acropolis, Vesuvio paid his fare from the *drachm* he carried in his money pouch – a coin with an owl stamped upon its back which singled it out as the symbol of Athen's patron goddess, Athena, and the most sound of Rome's provincial currencies.

Turning into the east gates of Athen's *agora*, Vesuvio

looked around the busy marketplace. He saw striped awnings, covered carts, donkeys laden with panniers of clay pots, melons, and cheeses.

The *agora* at first appeared no different to Vesuvio than so many marketplaces in southern Italy. Merchants sold the same produce here as they did at home – figs, olives, mespila, round loaves of goat's cheese. Women in black shawls crouched on the ground behind their baskets, shrieking the names of a variety of familiar herbs – mint, parsley, thyme, bay leaves, and garlic. Vesuvio also saw slave-dealers exhibiting sad-faced men, women, and children, the inferior class of slaves always sold in a marketplace anyplace in the world, people who would fetch low prices because of physical defects, ailments, or a history of being troublesome.

Vesuvio sniffed the air and caught the pungent smell of smoke rising from braziers on which *koubes* were being fried, pieces of cracked wheat filled with chopped meat, onions, and parsley.

Catching the tempting aroma, Vesuvio stood inside the east gate of the *agora* and noticed another odour which would be alien in southern Italy.

The Greeks preferred sweeter, more sticky cakes than the Romans, and a piquant redolence wafted from vendor's trays of syrupy honeycakes.

Momentarily enjoying these smells, Vesuvio listened to the voices chattering around him. He noticed that the Achean accent which the people spoke in the *agora* was similar to the peasant dialect in southern Italy. He recalled from school-boy days that Greece and southern Italy had been united in the past. But Greece had been the ruler at that time and Rome no more than a collection of mud huts on the River Tiber.

Although Greece had fallen to Roman power almost two-hundred-and-fifty years ago, Vesuvio looked around the teaming marketplace and saw that one difference between the two nations still remained the same.

The Athenians stepped aside for white-robed scholars and their pupils here in the *agora*. But Romans showed deference in their market-places only for obvious power, conspicuous wealth, and persons of sexual desirability.

*   *   *

Stopping a clean shaven man wearing a *chlamys*, a short wrap worn by Athenian professional men over the shoulders of longer robes, Vesuvio asked in Greek, 'Could you direct me to the house of a physician called Menecrates?'

The man did not immediately reply. He studied Vesuvio's simple tunic and, looking at the kidskin travelling pack, he said, 'Your Greek is fluent but your clothing and equipment say you are foreign.'

Vesuvio had spoken Greek since his tutor had taught him in childhood. Knowing the Athenian dialect better than those of the islands, he answered in the drawl particular to that city, 'I arrived less than an hour ago in Piraeus. I am Roman, sailing from Brundisium for the sole reason of visiting Menecrates in this city.'

The man said soberly, 'Then I am sorry to tell you that the person for whom you ask is dead. Menecrates passed to the netherworld only a few days before the feast of Athene Nike.'

Vesuvio's face tightened. He remembered that he had considered the fact that Miranda might have been recalled to Athens because of her master's death. But he also remembered thinking that, if Menecrates had died, the contract would still be binding.

The Greek said, 'I see the news upsets you. I am sorry you must learn it in a public place from a stranger. Was Menecrates a close friend of yours?'

'We had business dealings,' Vesuvio answered soberly.

'Ah now,' the Greek said, his voice brightening. 'If it is business you wish to settle, you can still call upon the house of Menecrates. His last testament still sets in the Temple of Diana waiting to be read. His household has not yet been disassembled. You can speak to his steward, a Thracian called Cleomenes.'

Vesuvio remembered the name, Cleomenes, from previous dealings with Menecrates but had never been in contact directly with this Thracian. Hoping to find out more about the physician's death, he asked, 'Were *you* a friend of Menecrates?'

'I counted Menecrates as one of my closest friends,' the Greek proudly announced. 'I am also a physician. And I am only sorry that it was not I who attended Menecrates on his death bed.'

'What was the nature of his illness?'

'If you've had business dealings with Menecrates, you might well know that he owned slaves whom he trained as medical attendants and let out their services for fees by contract. Such attendants nursed Menecrates at his death. No inquiries have been made into the reasons of his death but rumours are rife that his. . . .'

Stopping himself, the physician in the *chalmys* said, 'Forgive me. You asked for directions to the house of Menecrates. I must supply you with your request and hold my tongue. Please forgive a man who has taken the noble oath of Hippocrates for gossiping like a harbour boy.'

Pointing across the busy marketplace, the physician said, 'You must go there to the outside *stola* of this square, taking the gate beyond the Supervisor's Office, and then go to the Tower of the Winds. I trust you'll recognise that famous landmark. And, from there, you will see a small street which climbs the hillside. If you follow that street, you cannot fail to find the house you wish. The portal is still marked for mourning.'

Thanking the physician for his helpfulness, Vesuvio turned toward the arcade which housed the offices for the market-place. The arcade had been recently built by Romans, constructed in a style which they had obviously felt fit into the architecture indigenous to Athens. Vesuvio noticed that the marble columns were intricately fluted, their capitals too florid and not of a design which Pericles – the architect of the Parthenon – would have ever used.

The physician called after him, 'One last thing. Perhaps I *am* guilty this time of gossiping but there is one fact I think I should warn you about.'

Beckoning Vesuvio closer to him, the physician said guardedly, 'There is word in the *agora* that Menecrates's steward, Cleomenes, has already begun selling property which belonged to his late master. I am not saying that this is true but it is the gossip here. Such practise is forbidden by law, as you probably know – no property or effects can be sold until the deceased's testament is taken from the Temple of Diana and made public. I only tell you this fact because you are a foreigner. A party of foreigners passed through Athens only a week or so ago, Persians who bragged of making business dealings with the steward, Cleomenes. Now, I realise that deeds of sale can easily be back-dated, yes. But . . .'

Shaking his head, the physician said, 'I warn you of this only because such practises are very dangerous in Athens at the moment. Your Emperor has sent a very difficult man to govern us, a man who looks for people trying to escape Roman taxes.'

Raising one finger to his lips, the physician said, 'Merely a warning!' He turned to disappear into the crowd but was suddenly stopped by a small procession which neither he nor Vesuvio had see moving across the marketplace.

Four dark-skinned men dressed only in cinctures, their chest muscles gleaming with oil, carried a litter on their shoulders, a gilded platform on which sat a hammered silver representation of a vagina. A line of maidens followed the richly decorated bier, the young girls' faces veiled with spangled Indian scarves but the front of their himations tucked into the waist chains to give full view of their patches of furry femininity.

The physician looked at the silver oval being carried by the male bearers, glanced at the exposed midsections of the female attendants, and then turned to Vesuvio. He said with sudden irritation, 'I do not mind you Romans adopting every religion in the world but I do wish you would not contaminate the favourite city of Athena.'

The physician disappeared before Vesuvio could speak, before he could confide that they shared a mutual dislike for this fashionable rush to new religions, the frenzied embracing of secret cults which Roman's were beginning to call '*paganus*'.

7

The octagonal Tower of the Winds had served both as public clock and a gauge for the winds in Athens since ancient days. The top of each stone wall was decorated with a frieze illustrating a zephyr, with lines running down the lower sections of the sides to correspond with the lines of a sundial. Its sloping roof was topped with a bronze statue of a Triton holding a wand which revolved with the force of the wind, pointing in the direction from which it blew.

Vesuvio passed this popular landmark but he was too sober now to enjoy the frivolity of its design. Finding the narrow steps which led to a shady street, he considered the news about Menecrates being dead and the warning about the steward, Cleomenes, selling his master's property before the last testament was made public.

Knowing that Menecrates had grown rich in recent years, that investments he had made abroad had necessitated him to use a steward to oversee his household as well as business interests, Vesuvio walked pensively between bright purple sprays of bougainvillea festooning from the stone walls which lined both sides of this sloping street. He wondered how much authority this Cleomenes now had over Menecrates's medical slaves. If he indeed might have been the person who – in the name of Menecrates – had summoned Miranda back to Athens.

Approaching a dark blue door decorated with a spray of dried myrtle leaves to denote a death within, Vesuvio hesitated before pulling a bell rope and debated whether or not he should divulge his identity; he wondered if he should disclose the fact that he knew that Menecrates was dead.

Telling himself that he would not hide anything, that he would state his intentions of taking Miranda back to Italy and not accept any argument to the contrary, he pulled the rope and heard the bell clang deep inside the white stucco walls.

He was about to pull the rope again when bolts rattled on the opposite side of the thick wooden door. He was soon standing face-to-face with a surly porter.

He asked, 'Is this the house of Menecrates?'

The porter nodded.

'I am told that I can find his steward, Cleomenes, residing at this house. Tell him that . . . Aurelius Macrinus is here . . . from Italy.' He held out a coin, suspecting that Greek porters were no different from those in Italy.

Taking the coin and, seeing that it was a *drachm,* the porter beckoned Vesuvio into a courtyard. He motioned for him to wait upon a stone bench and then disappeared behind a curtain of jasmine hanging from an arched porch.

The serenity and sweet aromas in the small garden impressed Vesuvio. The branches of flowering trees formed an overhead trellis against the sun. Geraniums were planted in earthen pots. The few lemon trees were neatly pruned and a fig tree was heavy with small green bulbs waiting to ripen. A circular pond glistened with schools of silver fish swimming back and forth under the white-blossoming lily pads.

Vesuvio tried to picture Miranda in this peaceful courtyard, imagining her here as a young girl, probably sitting on this stone bench by the pond, learning the properties of cumin, tannis, eucalyptus from her master, acquiring the knowledge for making nostrums and possets to be used later in the outside world.

Miranda seldom spoke about her past to Vesuvio but he knew that Menecrates had bought her as a young girl from parents who could not afford to raise their children. Vesuvio also knew that Menecrates was exceedingly proud of Miranda, holding her above all his other female slaves.

Vesuvio's thoughts were suddenly disturbed by a pebble landing nearby him on the flagstone paving. He glanced overhead and, staring at whom he saw, he gasped, 'Miranda!'

* * *

Standing on a stone balcony which overhung the courtyard, Miranda beckoned to Vesuvio, motioning for him to take a narrow staircase lined with potted plants which led up to her from the end of the garden. She was dressed in a Greek-style *chiton* with gold clasps forming generously proportioned sleeves, a garment unlike any she had ever worn in Italy. Also, her shiny black hair was arranged on the top of her head which slightly altered her appearance – but not enough to make her unrecognisable.

Darting toward the stone stairs, Vesuvio took them three at a time, not believing that he had been so lucky. He reached the balcony and looked toward the low doorway where he saw Miranda now beckoning him into a room.

Having no care if anyone was observing him from the courtyard below or a room across the way, he rushed into the room and threw his arms around her.

Miranda struggled to free herself from his grasp and quickly moved to shut the louvred door.

'Are you being held here?' Vesuvio whispered anxiously, immediately sensing that something was wrong.

The room was small and dark with only faint shafts of daylight slanting through the louvred door. Seeing Miranda move back toward him in the room's dim light, Vesuvio held out his arms to her again and whispered, 'We must get you out of here. You can explain everything to me later. I only learned in the last hour that Menecrates is dead. That. . . .'

Holding one finger to her lips, Miranda signalled for him to be quiet and reached to unfasten the top brooch which held the *chiton* to her shoulders.

The garment fell quickly to the floor and displayed her

naked body. And as she stepped from the clump of linen, she reached to lift the hem of Vesuvio's dusty tunic.

'Miranda! Oh, Miranda,' he said, wrapping his arms around her smooth body. 'I want nothing more than to hold you, to tell you about little Aurelius, the fright you gave old Tia, how I had to leave Rome suddenly . . .'

Shaking her head for Vesuvio not to talk, Miranda lifted both hands to his face and parted her lips as she raised her mouth to his.

Feeling her breasts press against him, becoming more confused by her desire to make love so soon, Vesuvio nevertheless responded to the sweetness of her mouth. His manhood hardened as she pressed herself more persistently against his groin.

Pulling back her head from the kiss, Miranda nodded at a divan placed against the white-washed wall and began removing the golden pins from her pile of newly coiffed curls.

Vesuvio had never before seen her wear such adornments. But, then, when her raven hair tumbled down over her shoulders, she looked more like he was used to seeing her.

'I am dusty from the road, my love,' he began to plead again in whispers. 'I have only this morning arrived in Piraeus. This ship . . .'

Miranda was not listening to him. She had fallen onto the divan and, holding her slim arms out to him, she wiggled her fingers, calling, '. . . Vesuvio!'

Unable to restrain himself any longer, Vesuvio lifted the tunic over his head, untied the cords of his dusty sandals, and hurriedly pulled the cincture from his midsection, his phallus now bobbing with excitement.

Soon, he lay upon Miranda's familiar body, forgetting about the danger which only moments ago had worried him, now cradling her in his arms, kissing her lips and throat, whispering his love for her, repeating his fears for her safety, saying how anxious the *Tabularium* in Rome had made him about her manumission.

Unlike on previous occasions, though, Miranda did not return Vesuvio's words of love. She did not speak to him in the same considerate manner he spoke to her. When she did speak, it was only in coarse whispers, drawing attention to the parts of her body which Vesuvio kissed, touched, or kneaded.

He held her breasts in his hands and pressed her nipples between his index and middle finger.

Miranda smiled as she watched the pink buds becoming erect at his touch, saying . . . *kitaxte tis ibakoves roghes mou* – 'Look at my obedient nipples.'

He probed the lips of her vagina with his phallus.

She raised herself on her elbows to watch and murmured . . . *oson megalonis, toson vrehome* – 'The larger you grow, the wetter I become.'

He sank the first of his thickness into her moist slit.

Miranda lay back onto the divan, ordering . . . *meane akinitos via va mithisto monahi mou* – 'You hold still and I'll twist myself on you.'

Then, soon, pressing her eyes shut, Miranda spread her thin legs wide apart and thrust her groin for him to sink deeper and deeper inside her, stirring her hips to catch the crown of his erect phallus.

Vesuvio had never seen Miranda so desirous of sex yet showing no emotion, no concern for him. He fleetingly wondered if she had been drugged by Cleomenes. He considered the possibility of an aphrodisiac being administered to her. He knew that a stimulant herb such a satyrian would not be unknown in a physician's house. He wondered if it had been mixed into Miranda's food. He had never seen her so uncaring for his feelings in an act of love, putting sensual passions above all else, and having been so oblivious about the welfare of their son, his concern for her well-being . . .

Feeling her warm body eagerly pumping beneath him, though, Vesuvio obligingly planted his hands on the divan beside her shoulders and began to drive deeper – and harder inside her to increase her satisfaction.

But working now to sate this unusual lust – and to complete this act as quickly as possible so he could speak about returning home – he only heard her cry for him to continue, to increase his rhythm. She was beginning to toss her head from side to side. Her body was becoming beaded with perspiration as she pleaded for him not to stop.

Vesuvio intensified his pressure, driving still deeper, more relentlessly into her until he finally began to feel a liquid heat pressing around his manhood. Yet Miranda cried for him to expand, thicken, swell, distend his phallus still deeper inside her.

Vesuvio fought himself from exploding once, twice, three times, but, finally when he heard her gasping, and sensed an enflamed softness contracting around him, he unleashed his flood of excitement, feeling as if the jet of seed was surging from his very spine.

Miranda cried. She gasped. She thrust her groin harder against him to take each drop from him. She dug her fingernails into his back and blood formed in furrows across his shoulder blades.

As Vesuvio felt Miranda's nails rake down his back, he again thought of an aphrodisiac – she had never before scratched her fingernails across him at the peak of an orgasm.

It was not until they lay side-by-side on the narrow divan, when Vesuvio finally relaxed beside Miranda, gently stroking her hair, that he asked, 'My love, are you truly safe here? Are you perhaps suffering from a . . . drug?'

A brittle voice answered him, a voice which Vesuvio had never before heard. It said, 'My name is Despo. Miranda is my . . . sister.'

8

The physical likeness between Despo and Miranda was astonishing at first to Vesuvio's eye; he could discern no visible difference. Despo's nose was short and pert but, then, so was Miranda's. Their hair had the same black lustre, falling into the same soft curls around their shoulders.

Despite the likeness of eyes, nose, chin, hair, and proportions of the body, though, Despo slowly became more unlike Miranda to Vesuvio the longer he lay on the divan and stared in stunned silence at her. He fleetingly remembered that Miranda had told him that Menecrates had bought both her and her twin sister from their parents. But he had never imagined that the two sisters were so close in appearance.

Nevertheless, he was beginning to see the differences. He first noticed a hardness in Despo's eyes. A challenging smirk forming on her lips. She rested brazenly – overly assured in her nakedness – on the divan beside him, waiting to hear his reaction to her sudden announcement.

'Why did you allow me to go so far?' Vesuvio demanded, pulling back from her. 'Why didn't you say who you were sooner?'

'I considered it,' Despo said, flicking her long hair back from her face. 'But when I saw you in the courtyard, I thought, "Why not have a little game, Despo? If Fate had sent you such a handsome man, why not enjoy him before sending him away?" '

'But you spoke my name. You called me "Vesuvio". Do you also know my association with . . . your sister?'

She nodded, smiling.

'Where is Miranda?'

'I have no idea,' Despo said, shrugging her shoulders. 'Isn't she on your estate in Italy?'

'No,' Vesuvio said. 'She was sent for by Menecrates. Summoned back here to Athens.'

'That cannot be true. My husband is dead.'

Vesuvio gaped at her. 'Your husband?'

'Yes. Menecrates. We exchanged vows almost a year ago. He was much older than me, of course, but Menecrates was a generous and understanding spouse.'

'I do not care about your marital relationship,' Vesuvio impatiently blurted, becoming more repulsed by her careless manner. 'Where is Miranda?'

'Miranda!' she said impatiently. 'You keep talking about Miranda! Why do you think I know anything about her? Why do you keep asking me if she's here? She was your responsibility. You hired her as your . . . slave!'

'She was leased to me by Menecrates. But I told you, she was taken from my estate more than a week ago. A party of men came and said that Menecrates had instructed them to bring Miranda back to Athens. Now I come here. I find that Menecrates is dead. That he is married to you. And I learn that you enjoy impersonating your sister . . . in bed.'

Vesuvio was sitting on the side of the divan now. He demanded angrily, 'I want to know where Miranda is. And I want to know immediately.'

Despo dropped her thickly lashed eyes. Her lips set into a pout. She toyed with a strand of hair, shrugging her smoothly skinned shoulders again, saying, 'You must talk to Cleomenes about the slaves. He is the steward here. Perhaps he can help you. But I doubt it. Any decision my husband made before he died still holds until his last testament is read.'

'And where do I find Cleomenes?' Vesuvio pointed to the louvred door. 'Is he out there?'

She shook her head, saying with disconcern, 'Cleomenes is not here today.'

Vesuvio flared, 'Where is he? Selling more of his master's property to . . . Persians?'

Eyeing him with sudden suspicion, Despo asked, 'What do you mean . . . "selling more of his master's property to Persians"?'

Vesuvio saw that he had finally caught Despo's attention. He asked, 'Did this Cleomenes recall Miranda from my estate?'

'Miranda!' she shrilled, pounding her clenched fists against the divan. 'Why do you keep asking me about . . . Miranda?'

Glad to see her losing her veneer of annoying coolness, Vesuvio pushed, 'I do not understand how you could betray your sister?'

Again, she paused to study him. 'What do you mean, "betray my sister"?'

Although he knew that Despo would divulge no plot to him, even if she knew or were involved in one concerning Miranda, he nevertheless saw fear suddenly flicker in her eyes.

He explained, 'Betray your sister by letting someone make love to you who thought you were her.'

Sinking back onto the divan, Despo said, 'If you are going to make an ugly scene about that little incident, please leave.'

'Not until I see Cleomenes.'

'I told you, Cleomenes is not here today.'

'Then why did the porter allow me in when I asked for Cleomenes?'

'All these questions. How should I know what an oafish porter does? Did you give him money?'

Vesuvio nodded.

She sneered, 'Have you ever known a porter to refuse a tip? The ox would have probably left you sitting down in the garden all day waiting for Cleomenes.' She shook her head.

'Then why did you beckon me up here? How did you

recognise me? Why did you act as if our meeting might be . . . observed?'

'Oh, please, Roman, *please*! You are beginning to bore me. If you are still upset by what I meant to be a harmless game then I must demand you leave. Leave my house this moment.'

'Since when is masquerading as your sister in bed a harmless game?'

'You are becoming insulting now. You must leave or I shall have you thrown out.'

'I will not leave until I see Cleomenes. Or until you tell me when he is coming back.'

'I do not know when Cleomenes is returning home. He is a very busy man. Why don't you go to my husband's lawyer in Piraeus. His name is Coricles. Perhaps he can answer some of your persistent questions.'

Looking tauntingly at Vesuvio, she added, 'But do not expect to find out much of anything about your treasured Miranda from Coricles. Nor from anyone here in Athens either.'

'What do you mean?' Vesuvio asked. 'Your words always sound as if they might be hiding other meanings.'

She said firmly, 'I mean exactly what I say, Roman. That you will not learn anything about Miranda. Not in Piraeus. Not in Athens. Not in this house. So leave me now before I call the slaves to throw you out!'

'You speak so loftily of slaves . . . Despo. What are you yourself?'

'A slave? Me?' She threw back her head and laughed. 'I told you, Menecrates took me for his wife. You are a Roman citizen. You should know the legal procedure your Emperor sets down for all his subjects, foreigners or Romans. Or perhaps you have never fallen in love with a slave girl and wished to marry her . . . Vesuvio!'

Trying to control his anger, he said coldly, 'If you did not look so much like your sister, if you did not resemble her in so many physical ways, I could never believe that you both came from the same womb. I have known you for not even an hour but already I see you are a despicable, hateful, lying . . .'

Despo raised her hand and, screwing her red lips together, she slapped Vesuvio across the face.

His cheek still stinging from the blow, Vesuvio paused only momentarily before resuming his softly spoken diatribe.

'. . . disgusting, cheap, repulsive, profligate . . . bitch!'

Then, slowly rising from the divan, he pulled on his tunic and began lacing his sandals. Despo remained lying on her side, looking at him with contempt.

9

Waiting until she heard the porter close the courtyard door behind Vesuvio, Despo rose from the divan and quickly dressed herself in the linen *chiton* but left the golden brooches unclasped over her shoulders.

'*Zena*!' she called for her body slave. '*Zena*!'

A girl in a simple white gown soon appeared in the door of the small room, her head bent reverently low in the presence of her mistress.

'Fetch me the sheep's bladder which has been drying in the sun, Zena. Bring me a cistern of fresh water. Then tell Demetrius the driver that I want him to go soon and deliver a parcel for me to the Cavern of the Idiot.'

The serving girl bowed, backing toward the louvred door.

'Wait!' Despo said impatiently. 'I am not finished.'

Then contemplating how she should rearrange her plans for the evening, Despo finally said, 'I will not be here in the house when Cleomenes returns. I want you to tell him that I can not attend tonight's ritual on the shore.'

The girl motioned behind her, saying, 'Master Cleomenes stands only outside this door, mistress.'

Staring in momentary horror at the slave girl, Despo quickly brushed past her and rushed toward the door when a tall man dressed in a white robe appeared in front of her. He had handsome features with silver flecking his black hair at the temples.

'Cleomenes!' Despo demanded. 'How long have you been standing there?'

The steward's voice was deep and his words softly spoken. He calmly answered, 'I've been outside this door only since the Roman left the house. Before that I've been in the adjoining room, Despo.'

'Then you heard . . .'

Nodding to the serving girl, Cleomenes said, 'Zena, obey your mistress's orders. Bring her the sheep skin and a basin of warm water. Tell the driver to prepare himself to drive to the Cavern of the Idiot.'

When the obedient girl departed, Cleomenes moved into the room and shut the louvred door behind him. He said in an expressionless voice as he surveyed the rumpled coverings on the divan, 'This is a very interesting turn in our plans, Despo, isn't it?'

'What are you talking about?'

'The . . . Roman coming here.'

'You are jealous!' she accused.

Slowly shaking his head, Cleomenes said, 'I am above physical jealousy, Despo. I was talking about . . . Vesuvio coming to Athens to find Miranda. About him already learning about the Persians. I heard that, too.'

She flared, 'I told you that you should have insisted on the Persians paying you the full amount for Miranda when you first agreed to sell her to them. That you should have never allowed them to return to Athens to pay you the second half of the payment before they dragged her off to the desert!'

'Calm yourself, Despo. You are becoming upset. You must keep yourself calm to face this Roman intruding in the matter now.'

'What trouble can that Roman meddler cause? We have the money.'

'That "Roman meddler" can follow the Persians,' Cleomenes said.

'To Alexandria? Leave Piraeus with the harbour closed? Cross the desert from Alexandria even if he were to get that far?' She laughed at the idea.

'Do not underestimate the power of love, Despo. Also do

not forget that I heard everything – everything – through the adjoining door. I heard how angry he was with you for playing your little game.'

'You *are* jealous.'

'Would you like me to be?'

Throwing herself onto his chest, Despo pleaded, 'Oh, don't let us quarrel, Cleomenes. We have so many hopes. We are so close to achieving our ambitions now. Menecrates is dead. Dead! Finally dead! And his death was accepted as being from natural causes! We only have to wait a few more days until his testament is taken from the temple and made public before we . . .'

A knock on the door disturbed Despo's rush of words. Cleomenes coldly removed her hands from around his neck, saying, 'Zena has returned. Wash the Roman's seed from inside yourself, Despo. Send the sheep's bladder to the prophet as you had planned.'

She gestured awkwardly. 'What else of the Roman's do I have to send? What other personal possession for the prophet to read?'

Nodding knowingly, Cleomenes assured her, 'I understand you better than you think I do, Despo. I know that you, too, want to learn what you can about the Roman's involvement in our future. I know how you feared Miranda might have inherited both her freedom and riches from Menecrates's testament. And I approve of you sending the bladder full of the Roman's seed to your favourite prophet. I trust you'll go see him this very evening to hear his words on the subject.'

'Then you do not mind that I will go visit the prophet tonight in his cave?' Despo asked, staring up at Cleomenes. 'That I will not be by your side as I promised.'

'I know you too well, Despo, for you to try and play these little games of mock sincerity with me. I know that you are only interested in accompanying me one place. To Rome. But rest assured. The time for that will soon come. For the moment, we can only hope that Menecrates's testament does not hold any surprises for either of us.'

Looking at the crumpled covering on the divan again, Cleomenes added, 'Let us also hope that the Roman does not try to follow your sister across the desert to the tomb of Cis-u-ba.'

He shook his head, saying, 'Everything is becoming intricate, Despo. Very intricate. I do not feel the ease I did at the outstart of our ambitious venture. Our plan to marry you to Menecrates. Then to eliminate him. The way we devised of protecting ourselves from Miranda inheriting the bulk of Menecrates's estate by sending her to the Death Pits of Caldea. Our plan to . . .'

Cleomenes stopped, saying, 'We shall talk about all this later, Despo. Reassess our plans. Make any necessary changes. For the moment, I have my work to do. And you most certainly have yours.'

Turning away from Despo, Cleomenes opened the door and motioned for the slave girl to enter with the dried sheep's bladder, the intestines for tubes, and the basin of water with which Despo would wash Vesuvio's sperm from her vagina.

10

After leaving the house of Menecrates, Vesuvio took a small room in the first hostelry he found on the eastside of the *agora*. He sponged himself with cool water from a copper cistern, brooding about the bizarre meeting he had just experienced with Despo.

Neither Miranda nor he had talked much in their two years together about one another's family and background. They had both preferred to leave their pasts unmentioned. Their life together centred upon their present happiness, their son, the people and land of Villa Vesuvio.

Vesuvio sincerely doubted if Miranda would remember details about his own relatives, that he had a wastrel brother now working in Carthage as a *lanista* – a dealer in slaves trained to fight in the arena. He knew that Miranda was familiar with his Uncle Milo but, then, she had nursed the good old man in his dying days.

Drying himself with a felted towel, Vesuvio still could not recall Miranda ever telling him that her sister was an identical twin. He did recall her saying, though, that they were not close friends and, now having met Despo, he clearly understood the reason. He could not remember of ever before having met such an openly callous person.

He recalled again how there had been no reciprocation in the sexual act with Despo. That she had wanted nothing except pleasure for herself. He cursed himself for not realising sooner that she was not Miranda. How could he have been so stupid? So insensitive? So blind?

Vesuvio went down to the small garden of the inn and

ate a light supper of charcoal lamb amongst loudly talking young men also staying at the hostelry, exuberant young people whom he guessed were students.

He lingered over his last goblet of wine and weighed the facts which he had learned this afternoon, the news about Menecrates's death, the meeting with Despo, his growing suspicions that she and Cleomenes were somehow involved in Miranda's disappearance.

Vesuvio's intuition told him that it would be unwise for him to return to the house of Menecrates tonight. He felt that it was too soon to confront Cleomenes. That he must first try to learn more facts about Menecrates's death and the state of his business affairs before approaching the Thracian steward.

Feeling physically tired but too vexed to sleep, Vesuvio decided that he needed to do something to quiet his brain. And remembering the name of the lawyer in Piraeus which Despo had mentioned to him, he decided to hire a horse from a stables here in Athens and ride to the harbour town. The business offices in Piraeus would be closed at this hour, he realised, but he thought of even trying to locate the lawyer's home. His brain was still addled as he struggled to see some pattern in this growing mystery.

* * *

The blazing orange disc of the sun was sinking below the coastline of Piraeus when Vesuvio left his horse at a stables in the harbour town and set out on foot to explore the activity along the waterfront fastly replacing the business ventures conducted there throughout the day.

Barbers were opening their shops along the docks at this sunset hour, beginning to clip hair with clanking leaden shears and shaving whiskers with sharpened knives. The aroma of grilling fish drifted through the night's warm air.

Taverns were spreading their tables down to the commercial wharves and serving-girls carried earthen jugs of wine to sailors coming to perch on wooden kegs and three-legged stools for a night of drinking. Female prostitutes strutted through the tables, arching their backs of exhibit the fullness of their breasts; male whores minced back-and-forth, their tunics tucked-up into their belts to give ample views of their buttocks.

Despite the bad omens still hanging over Piraeus which stopped all ships from sailing from the harbour, a holiday feeling filled the dock area tonight. Small girls sold garlands of ivy to passersby. Bakers hawked sesame cakes. A troup of acrobats performed on a brightly coloured carpet in front of the Harbour's Master's office. A crowd of urchins encircled a minstrel playing a flute to his company of trained vipers. And as the lights from the bulky military triremes twinkled across the harbour, the songs of slaves drifted from the oar-holes in the galleys.

Walking through the congestion of public entertainers, vendors, and sailors haggling over prices with prostitutes, Vesuvio listened to the slaves' plaintive voices singing ballads from their homelands. Eerie songs from the Orient cut through the heavy dirges of German tribes. The slaves' songs, the thought that hundreds of men were chained in their hammocks only a short distance from him, began to depress Vesuvio. He was wondering where Miranda was at this very hour when he heard someone shout his name.

He turned and saw a tall black-skinned man stalking down the wharf towards him with long scarlet robes fluttering behind him in the cool evening breeze. The black man wore a richly embroidered cap on his closely cropped hair and he was waving at Vesuvio.

Vesuvio's face suddenly beamed. He now recognised the brawny black giant dressed in the costly garbs. He shouted, 'Balthazar!'

Locking one arm around Vesuvio's shoulder, the black

man named Balthazar warmly hugged him and boomed, 'You should have written to me that you were coming to Piraeus, my friend. Yiannoula will never forgive me for not bringing her here!'

'How is Yiannoula?' Vesuvio asked, remembering Balthazar's chubby Cypriot wife with great affection.

'She wanted to come to Piraeus with me on this trip. I told her that nothing here would interest her. But, ah! When I go home and tell her I saw her "Golden Eagle" – oh!' he said, shaking his head and reaching forward to tousle Vesuvio's blond curls, 'oh, how she is going to beat me for leaving her at home!'

Standing back to survey Balthazar's fine clothes, Vesuvio said, 'You look even more prosperous than the last time I saw you! The very picture of a rich merchant!'

'And how about the first time we met?' Balthazar asked. 'You also have changed from the "slave" I first knew in that dark citadel in Carthage called Byrsa!'

'Byrsa!' Vesuvio repeated with mock horror. 'Fortune has been kind to both of us since those vile days, Balthazar. I wonder if everyone at that slave auction fared as well as we did.'

'Fortune depends not only on luck, Golden Eagle. It depends on a man's ambition. You were driven by the goal of returning to your family, of protecting your young brother . . .'

Stopping, Balthazar asked cheerfully, 'But what good does it do to recall the old days? We have corresponded to keep ourselves abreast with one another's fortunes and misfortunes since we were slaves together. Let us enjoy one another's company like good neighbours. We live miles apart but perhaps the Gods are going to keep throwing us into each other's path!'

Laughing, the two friends warmly embraced once again and turned to walk together along the wharf.

'You are a father now,' Bathazar said to Vesuvio as they

passed tables of sailors drinking wine from wooden cups. 'I envy you. We still have no children. Yiannoula received the letter your Miranda wrote to her. She intends to answer before you and Miranda marry, sending her . . .'

Balthazar stopped. He looked closely at Vesuvio. He asked, 'Why do you suddenly look so downcast? I wanted us to be light-hearted. But I have obviously said something that's troubled you.'

Walking slower, staring out at the lights piercing from the rows of oar-holes in the tall triremes, Vesuvio said, 'It is because of Miranda that I am here, Balthazar. She's . . . disappeared.'

'Disappeared? How do you mean, my friend?'

Shaking his head, Vesuvio said, 'It is a puzzling story, Balthazar. I still haven't begun to fathom all the details myself.' He then began to explain how Miranda had mysteriously been taken away from Villa Vesuvio by men who supposedly were acting on behalf of her rightful owner and that he himself had only arrived here this morning to learn that Miranda's master was dead and that the old man had married Miranda's sister shortly before he died. Vesuvio concluded his account, explaining the strange way in which he had met Despo, sparing no details of the method by which she had led him into making love with her.

Letting Vesuvio complete his tale, Balthazar again expressed his sorrow about Miranda's disappearance before cautiously asking, 'This physician, Menecrates? Did he have a steward by the name of Cleomenes? A Thracian with a manner which many men would consider to be a trifle too . . . polished?'

Vesuvio looked quickly at Balthazar. 'Why do you mention Cleomenes? What do you know of him?'

'Am I to understand from your question that, yes, we speak about the same man? The Cleomenes who is a Thracian?'

Vesuvio answered guardedly, 'Yes, a Thracian named

Cleomenes acts as steward for Menecrates. But I have yet to meet him.'

Balthazar explained as they continued to walk again, 'Being a frequent visitor to Athens and Piraeus, I have heard of the wealthy Menecrates. I did not know that he had died. But I have heard talk only this morning about his steward. I heard men speaking of Cleomenes in regards to an ancient Thracian cult called Bendis.'

'Bendis?' Vesuvio repeated, wondering what new turn this mystery was taking.

Balthazar nodded. 'As I say, Bendis is an ancient cult. Like so many old religions, though, the worship of Bendis has greatly changed in recent years to supply the demands of modern Rome. It is now little more than a cult of voluptuaries.'

'And this Cleomenes is a follower of Bendis?'

'More than a follower, my friend! Cleomenes is the high priest!'

'A steward also acting as a . . . high priest?'

'The cult has no proper temple. No shrine in the *agora* or within the walls of the Acropolis. It is, by all the accounts, I hear, little more than an excuse for licentious activities in secluded spots.'

Vesuvio murmured, 'The more I discover here in Greece about Menecrates and his steward, the more I fear for Miranda's safety.'

'I do not mean to alarm you, friend,' Balthazar kindly said. 'I only tell you what I've heard about this Cleomenes for you to understand the man with whom you might find yourself dealing.'

Vesuvio stopped. He lay his hand on Balthazar's broad shoulder and said, 'There is one point I forgot to tell you. When I arrived in Athens this afternoon, I found directions to Menecrates's house from a physician in the *agora*. He was the one who told me about Menecrates's death. He also warned me about Cleomenes selling his late master's property. He said that a small group of Persians had passed through Athens, bragging that they had already made a purchase from Cleomenes.'

Balthazar asked, 'Did he say what Cleomenes sold to the Persians?'

Vesuvio shook his head. 'No. The physician only warned me because I was foreign. He said that the Roman consul here is looking for men trying to escape the seller's tax.'

Locking his arm around Vesuvio's elbow, Balthazar continued to stroll down the wharf, saying, 'I am going to make a suggestion which might at first sound odd to you. But hear me out.'

Balthazar began, 'First, I live nearby in apartments over one of my warehouses. A lamb is being roasted there for my supper. Why don't you join me? We can enjoy a visit and then take a ride later into the countryside. To a strip of beach a few miles to the north of here.'

Thanking Balthazar for the offer of supper, Vesuvio said, 'I ate at the inn where I'm staying in Athens. But I gladly accept your offer of companionship and wine. As for a ride into the countryside . . .'

Vesuvio shook his head, explaining, 'I think my time might be better spent if I look around the shops and taverns here in Piraeus, questioning people, trying to find out what I can about the lawyer who acted for Menecrates.'

Balthazar smiled, his line of white teeth gleaming as he said, 'I warned you, Golden Eagle, that you'd consider my suggestion odd. But I am not inviting you to accompany me on any idle ride. I told you about the cult of Bendis. Remember? I also explained how it concentrates on sexuality. My sailors talk about nothing but sex and I know that the worshippers of Bendis are meeting tonight for one of their infamous ceremonies in a secret spot.'

'With Cleomenes acting as high priest?'

Balthazar shrugged. 'Who knows what we will find? This will be my first visit, too!'

'Do they allow outsiders to witness these rituals?'

Balthazar laughed. 'I would say they will welcome us with open arms *and* purses! I also know from my sailors that, if there is one thing which the followers of Bendis hold more sacred than sexuality, it is their collection of alms. They *insist* on money!'

'People . . . pay to attend these rituals?'

'So I am told, Golden Eagle. So I am told. The only fact I know for certain about this Bendis cult is that it comes from Thrace. And that it had originally centred on equestrian worship and fire. Men supposedly race horseback, carrying flaming torches as they ride.'

'A torchlit race . . .' Vesuvio paused then said, 'I'll go!'

'Excellent!' Balthazar said. 'Now I beg you to remember that not too long ago you and I had to roast scorpions for our supper. On the ledge of a cell! Remember that? So why should we waste a juicy lamb being turned on a spit at this very hour in my home nearby. Who knows when our fortunes will turn again?'

The two friends laughed and disappeared through the holiday mood along the wharf, discussing the official Imperial auguries which forbade sailing from Piraeus, exchanging opinions not only about the official Imperial priests who made the morning offerings to Poseidon but also discussing the more esoteric prophets and soothsayers becoming increasingly popular.

11

Vesuvio finished his second supper this evening on the rooftop of Balthazar's warehouse apartments overlooking the harbour of Piraeus. When the moon was high in the sky, he and Balthazar rose from the heap of silk cushions and dressed themselves in hooded robes to attend the nocturnal celebration to the Thracian horse god, Bendis.

Galloping along a country road which passed through the barren landscape north of Piraeus, the two men came to a rocky ridge above the white-capped sea and saw a bonfire blazing on a long sandy shore below them.

They began to hear the hum of voices and, soon, they found themselves amongst a crowd of people abandoning their carts and donkeys to move on foot down to the beach.

Balthazar suggested to Vesuvio that they themselves remain on horseback. He then pointed toward the fire and said, 'Look. The riders are already preparing for the race.'

Vesuvio rose higher in his saddle and saw eight young men seated upon a collection of variously coloured horses around the fire. All the men were naked and the fire's leaping flames lit the muscular definitions of their bodies. He saw that the young men had the rugged bodies of soldiers and sailors, men who were proud of their physical strength achieved from strenuous work. They sat solemn-faced on their horses, oblivious to the crowd collecting along the edge of the sandy beach.

'We arrived at the right moment,' Balthazar said as he gently urged his animal down the incline, the horse's hooves sinking into the sand.

Vesuvio followed on his own mount as he kept his eyes trained on the fire and watched a man dressed in white robes beginning to light pine torches in the flames.

Balthazar called softly, 'The man in white is Cleomenes. He has been pointed out to me in Piraeus by my sailors.'

Vesuvio rode slowly alongside Balthazar across the flat of the beach, trying to obtain a better look at the Thracian. He saw eight young women dressed in pale *chitons* beginning to gather on either side of Cleomenes. He saw that Cleomenes was a handsome man but remembered Balthazar's saying earlier that the Thracian was a man whom many men would consider to be too polished.

Balthazar now leaned toward Vesuvio on his horse, saying, 'I don't yet see what are the duties of the high priest.'

Vesuvio remained silent, watching Cleomenes complete the torch lighting and turn to distribute reed baskets amongst the young women.

'I told you about the alms-begging,' Balthazar said as he reached into the folds of his robe. 'I suggest we both contribute a coin or two. I would understand your feelings about hesitating to give money which might find its way to Cleomenes. But votaries such as these have been known to scream at men who refuse to add to their collections. That is their way to embarrass you into giving them money. I do not think we should chance attracting that kind of attention.'

Appreciating the wisdom of Balthazar's words, Vesuvio dug begrudgingly into the money pouch hanging from his leather belt. He withdrew a coin and dropped it into the basket of the passing votary.

The bonfire soared higher into the dark sky. The eight naked riders sat motionless in a line across the beach and held their torches in their hands.

Balthazar whispered, 'Do you see any religious symbol? An altar or some representation of the god Bendis?'

Vesuvio shook his head and watched closely as Cleomenes

stepped toward the horses. He stood holding a silver staff in the air as he addressed the naked riders.

'Is the high priest no more than a man who conducts races?' Balthazar asked.

Before Vesuvio could reply, Cleomenes brought the silver staff down against the sand, signalling the race to begin.

The rush of horse hooves suddenly thundered against the sandy beach. The eight riders charged away from the fire, gripping onto the horses's manes with one hand and holding their torches aloft with the other.

Vesuvio and Balthazar danced their own horses to secure a better view of the race, seeing the torches disappearing in the distance and leaving trails of sparks behind them like sputtering ribbons.

The bareback riders reached the far end of the beach and, reining their horses to turn in a rush of hooves, they began galloping back down the beach in the direction of the fire.

Balthazar marvelled as the torches drew nearer, 'It is one thing to ride carrying a torch but quite another to race without reins or bridles.'

The riders did not slow their pace as they approached the fire. They galloped past the onlookers gathered into groups around the blaze and sped toward the opposite end of the sandy beach.

Balthazar raised himself on his stirrups, watching the naked equestrians disappear toward their second goal. He said, 'My bollocks hurt when I just *think* of the bumps they're taking!'

Vesuvio's eyes followed the eight smudges of the riders' torches disappearing in the distance and then he turned to study the activity developing around the fire. He had not yet seen Despo amongst the group. Where was she tonight? Did she not take part in these rituals? Vesuvio had suspected that she might be Cleomenes's lover but, if so, why was she not here with him tonight? Did she not believe in the Thracian god?'

The horses had turned at the far end of the beach. As the echo of their thundering hooves drew nearer, Balthazar excitedly said, 'The youth on the bay has already won! He's out-distanced the man on the chestnut stallion!'

Vesuvio and Balthazar both watched as the rider of the bay stallion reined his strong animal to a halt near the fire, sending a spray of sand over the ebbing tide. The youthful rider hopped off his animal and, flinging his torch into the flames, he threw himself onto the sand in front of Cleomenes.

The other riders halted their animals at the bonfire in an explosion of hooves. They also hurled their torches into the fire's soaring flames. But unlike the winner, the seven other naked equestrians remained mounted on their horses.

Also, at this time, the female votaries were beginning to shed their *chitons* and surround the winner's bay stallion. They reached to steady the heavily breathing animal, patting his hard-muscled flanks and smoothing his golden mane.

Cleomenes approached the maidens. He scanned their faces and, finally selecting a girl with a quick nod of his head, he motioned for the young man who had won the race to arise from the ground.

The youth obeyed; he mounted the stallion; the chosen maiden stepped toward him and raised her arms. The rider lifted the naked girl up from the ground and placed her to face him astride the horse.

Balthazar whispered to Vesuvio, 'I do not understand.'

'Nor I,' Vesuvio quietly answered, watching the young rider fondle the girl's bare breasts with one hand and beginning to work the other hand between his own legs.

The young girl soon leaned back against the horse's mane, protruding her feminine mound toward the rider who pushed his now erect penis into her. Once the rider and the young girl were coupled, she wrapped her slim arms around him. The rider then began to canter the horse, his stiff penis firmly placed inside the votary maiden's vagina. The steady motion of the stallion's slow gallop drove the young man's penis deeper, deeper, deeper into the Bendis votary. The ecstatic feeling of this sexual act performed on the back of a trotting horse soon showed on the young girl's face. She wrapped her arms tighter – more desperately – around the muscular young equestrian's neck, lifting herself higher onto his stiff phallus as the horse galloped faster and faster around the soaring fire.

*   *   *

The sexuality of the naked couple mounted astride the bay stallion soon spread to the people on the beach watching them. Some men reached toward the breasts of women standing alongside them. Eager women took men's hands and put them between their legs. Men grabbed one another's manhood and began to masturbate, squeezing their neighbours into hardness. Or many men stood alone, masturbating as the winning equestrian and the chosen maiden began to shout – to cry – in passion as they rode coupled upon the horse encircling the fire in a faster gait.

Balthazar said, 'If we stay one moment longer I might be joining them. I do not want that.'

Vesuvio was not listening. He was staring again at Cleomenes. Women and young girls had emerged from the crowd to kneel in front of him. They were reaching their hands for his groin. They were adoring him.

'Look now,' Vesuvio urged.

Balthazar remained silent as he watched the next woman kneel in front of Cleomenes. She took his maleness in her mouth as her hands held the front of his robes above her head. Balthazar whispered to Vesuvio, 'I do not understand how a man can reach satisfaction with so many people watching.'

'I have seen such men before,' Vesuvio said disapprovingly. 'They can only be pleasured when they *do* have an audience.'

'But would a man go to such extremes as this? To organise his own religious cult merely to be sexually satisfied in this strange way?'

'I suspect the gratification he receives is more than sexual. Cleomenes obviously has great power over his followers. Many Oriental cults include sex in their worship of gods. Nothing this base, this decadent, but . . .'

'I am sure he could find many followers in Rome!' Balthazar said, adding soberly, 'and more money than he can collect from an isolated beach north of Piraeus!'

He reached for his horse's reins, saying, 'Let us go, Golden Eagle. I do not want to allow myself to become aroused, too. I would rather remain faithful to my wife than fall prey to fever spread by a religious charlatan.'

'And it shows no signs of ending,' Vesuvio said. 'If anything, this is only the start.'

The sexual frenzy spread amongst the people on the beach. Men knelt on the ground and, spreading open women's legs, they began to drive into them like satyrs. Some young men knelt on their knees whilst other men drove themselves into their buttocks. Women were taking men in their mouths or licking the furry patches between other women's legs.

The remaining equestrians still mounted on their horses now also reached to lift female votaries from the ground. Each rider settled a naked girl in front of him on a horse, placing the girl to face towards him as the winning youth had done.

Once the riders and maidens were coupled in the established manner, they also began to canter in circles around the fire. One, two, three . . . soon all the naked riders were galloping their horses in the night, forming circles of orgiastic Bendis worship, their phalluses driving into the votaries, the movement of the animals' gait inching the riders' phalluses deeper and deeper into vaginal wetness, the horses's hooves pounding a rhythm like drumbeats in the night.

The horses gained speed as they encircled the fire lapping into the sky, encompassing the men and women losing themselves in sexual depravities whilst Cleomenes remained standing proudly alongside the fire. He pushed one woman away from her adoring position in front of him, making room for the next woman to pay homage to him as high priest of Bendis.

The sound of Vesuvio and Balthazar galloping away in the moonlight went unnoticed by the nocturnal idolators meeting on this isolated stretch of beach north of Piraeus.

* * *

The stark light from the same moon lit the jagged rocks surrounding the entrance to a cave which set at the foot of the Elevesian Mountains – the Cavern of the Idiot – where Despo visited tonight instead of accompanying Cleomenes to the celebration of the Thracian horse god.

The mountain prophet sat cross-legged in the entrance to the craggy cave, the glow of the moon illuminating his pale white skin and the tangles of pure white hair which spread over the bony shoulders of his naked body.

The prophet was a hermaphrodite: he had pendulous white breasts budded with dark red nipples and a tapering white penis with a long foreskin which covered its pointed crown.

The night's air was chilly but the prophet wore nothing on his man-woman's body except a leather thong dangling over his feminine breasts, a necklace to which were tied fingernail parings, locks of hair, pieces of egg shell, all small objects tied by bits of coloured silk to the leather cord.

The hermaphrodite's pale green eyes stared blankly at Despo as she knelt on the dirt in front of the cave. She wore a wine-red cloak pulled around her head and shoulders.

In a flat but shrill voice, the hermaphrodite said, 'I am a fool to think that you are visiting me tonight instead of paying homage to a horse god!'

Despo was impressed that the hermaphrodite knew without her telling him that she was meant to be with Cleomenes on the beach.

She murmured, 'The god is Bendis . . .'

Toying with the ragged foreskin of his limp penis, the hermaphrodite whined, 'I would be a bigger fool to say that you have been successful in betraying your own blood. That you have sold your sister to a tomb which soon will be a pit of skeletons.'

Despo quickly raised her eyes, protesting, 'But I acted on your advice concerning Miranda!'

'A fool does not give advice!' the hermaphrodite shrilled. 'And you are a bigger fool to believe I do!'

Despo sank back down on her haunches in front of the cave, knowing that this was the prophet's manner of advising her, that he constantly denied his prophetic powers.

The pale white hermophrodite fingered the leather cord encircling his neck and said, 'I am nothing but a fool! An idiot! A simpleton! Who but an idiot would treasure such worthless things as these? Fingernails? Hair? Broken shells from which mortals have eaten eggs? Who but a maniac would believe that he could foresee the future in such worthless trash?'

Despo said, 'Have you read the offering I sent to you this afternoon, Learned Prophet?'

'The dried bladder of a sheep?' The hermaphrodite's laughter was cruel and mocking. He said scornfully, 'Nobody but a lunatic would . . . *talk* to the bladder of a lamb! Nobody but a crackscull would *drink* a woman's bath water syphoned from her vagina by a sheep's dried intestine! *Savour* the polluted water! Say that it was laced with a Roman's seed washed from your womanhood!'

Despo said, 'I cleansed myself after a Roman lay with me this afternoon, Learned Seer. I cleansed myself with the syringe made from a sheep's bladder and intestine. I sent the bladder of water to you because the seed was the most personal possession I had of his.'

Leaning closer toward the hermaphrodite, she asked eagerly, 'Have you foreseen a way by which I can protect myself from the man from whom it came? Will he be a threat to me? Will this meddling Roman prevent me from inheriting my late husband's estate?'

'Gold!' the hermaphrodite shrieked, tweaking the dark red nipples on his pendulous white breasts. 'Gold!'

'I brought gold for you,' Despo quickly assured him, digging for the pouch inside her cloak.

'*Gold*!' the prophet shrilled louder, his voice spreading over the face of the mountain. 'I am a fool and a moron because only such a worthless ninny would say that gold is where the parchment lies! That gold grows when it is planted upon the waves. That there is to be gold upon the River Styx!'

Despo paused at the mention of these three points – gold . . . parchment . . . the River Styx.

'You say "parchment", Wise One,' she whispered anxiously. 'Does "parchment" represent the last testament of my late husband? The document which lies in the Temple of Diana in the Acropolis?'

The hermaphrodite sneered, 'Every fool knows where testaments are kept! It does not take a wise man to say that gold from the same temple also gives revenge! Why ask me, stupid woman!'

'What "gold", Mountain Prophet? What "place"? Temple coins? The gold coins which are minted in the Temple of Diana?'

The Hermaphrodite said smugly, 'Gold is planted upon water.'

'Does "water" refer to the River Styx? You mentioned

the River Styx, Prophet? Does that mean . . . death?'

'Gold is for the living!' he shrieked impatiently at her. 'The River Styx is water! Gold is planted upon water. Have you never heard of boats, artless slut? How do you think you are going to reach the centre of the world?'

'Me?' Despo asked. 'What do I have to do with boats?'

'You come here asking about a Roman. He is going one way but you are destined to go the other. He is gold. You are purple. The dye of a shellfish!'

'Murex?' Despo gasped, knowing that the murex dye of shellfish provided the purple colouring for the Imperial robes of Rome.

'Do you know of a horse named "Murex"?' the Hermaphrodite asked. 'Never! Do not treat me like a bigger fool than I am already!'

Despo eagerly pressed, 'Then I shall go to Rome as I've hoped? And the horse god, Bendis, will be accepted as a god in . . . the Imperial city of Rome? Cleomenes and I will travel there?'

'Travel? The travelling is done first by gold. The gold is planted on the River Styx. The River Styx leads to the pit of skeletons!'

Shaking his head in disgust at Despo, the hermaphrodite began to laugh. His pale green eyes widened as his laugh grew louder and more shrill. And, soon his pale eyeballs rolled back into their sockets.

But, suddenly, the Hermaphrodite stopped his unexpected seizure. He pursed his lips as he sat cross-legged in front of his cave. He reached to tweak the dark red nipples on his sagging breasts and again began to laugh.

The laugh grew louder and, soon, urine began to stream from his penis and form a yellow puddle between his legs.

Knowing that her audience with the Divine Idiot had ended, Despo tossed a gold coin onto the dirt in front of her. She rose to her feet and pulled the mantle farther around her face.

Walking down the rocky path which led to the road where the driver waited for her in a cart, Despo listened to the hermaphrodite's laughter following her down the face of the moonlit mountain. She was still trying to formulate the information she had gleaned from him. Temple Gold. The River Styx. A cave of skeletons. And the purple of Imperial Rome.

12

Vesuvio was awakened the next morning by a loud banging on the door of his inn room. He staggered from the bed, pulling a tunic over his head, shouting for the caller to be more patient. He was tired after spending the night tossing restlessly on his bed, unable to sleep as he became more and more certain that Despo and Cleomenes were not only lovers but responsible for Miranda's abduction from Villa Vesuvio.

Opening the door of his room, Vesuvio saw Balthazar standing in the hallway. The black man was dressed in a gleaming yellow robe embroidered around the neck and his eyes sparkled with excitement. He said, 'I've awakened you! Forgive me, my friend, but I have just learned news in Piraeus which cannot wait.'

Assuring Balthazar that he was always welcome, Vesuvio gave him the choice of coming into the room or going downstairs to wait for him in the garden whilst he dressed himself. Balthazar answered that he would go to the garden and order Vesuvio some breakfast which he could eat whilst he listened to the news.

Vesuvio joined Balthazar a few moments later at a round table placed under a grape arbour in the flagged garden of the inn. The morning sun shone softly through the ceiling of green leaves and the innkeeper's wife hummed a song as she carried fruit and honey-cakes from the kitchen for Vesuvio's breakfast.

Balthazar began, 'You mentioned to me last night something about Persians buying goods from the steward, Cleomenes.'

Vesuvio nodded as he selected a plum from a collection of fruit floating in a bowl of water. 'The physician I met yesterday in the *agora* told me about the Persians. He said that the news was only gossip but he obviously considered it to be plausible enough to warn me about Cleomenes.'

'I had the good luck this morning to talk to the captain of a vessel carrying lumber from Carthage. He stopped in Crete before he sailed here. He met another Carthaginian ship in Crete. A vessel sailing from Carthage to Alexandria, having made an intermediary stop in Piraeus nearly a week ago. A day or two before the port was closed because of the auguries. There was a small party of Persians aboard this other Carthaginian vessel. They were escorting a Greek slave.'

Vesuvio looked up from the plate of cakes. 'A female slave?'

Balthazar nodded, 'Now, I realise that there are many Persians in the world. And twice as many Greek slave girls. But the Captain said that these Persians guarded their slave girl with great care. Also, he reported that there was an illness in Crete last week. An epidemic of a fever. The captain told me that he took notice of the Greek girl because she was arguing with the Persians to be allowed to attend the sick on the shore. You see, she was a physician's slave.'

Vesuvio said, 'It is like Miranda to risk her own health to aid the sick.' He considered the idea more thoroughly, adding, 'Also, Persians are often confused for being Greeks. If Persians told my housekeeper and bailiff that they were Greek and acting on behalf of Menecrates, my people would believe them.'

Balthazar said guardedly, 'The girl could possibly be your Miranda.'

Looking soberly at Balthazar, Vesuvio asked, 'This Carthaginian vessel which stopped in Crete? Does it sail directly south to Alexandria?'

'I knew you would be interested so I put that very

question to the captain. He told me that the ship would stop in Cyprus before heading down for Alexandria.' Balthazar shrugged. 'As the Piraeus harbour is closed again this morning and the gods only know for how long, I cannot get word to my offices in Cyprus or I would . . .'

'No. Of course not. But to go to Alexandria . . .'

'I know what you are thinking, Golden Vesuvio. That you will follow the ship to Alexandria. But you cannot travel to Cyprus – let alone all the way to Egypt – if the omens do not change in the harbour here.'

Vesuvio's mind suddenly churned with facts and possibilities. He said, 'I could always leave Piraeus in a private ship. A small boat manned by oarsmen.'

Balthazar grinned at him, saying, 'That is exactly what I thought my good friend would say. But listen. I have a better plan. The trip in a smaller boat from here to Alexandria would be very dangerous. I suggest you go in such a boat . . . but only as far as Cyprus! From there you can sail to Alexandria on a freighter I have leaving from home in ten days' time.'

Narrowing his eyes, Vesuvio asked, 'Do you think I even have a slim chance of reaching Cyprus in time to catch your freighter?'

'With good weather, yes. Easily.' Balthazar assured him as he grabbed for a grape bunch in the bowl of water. 'But first you must find a crew to take you from Piraeus to Cyprus. A boat is no problem. There are always fishermen or sponge divers willing to sell a *kayiki*. I can arrange that easily.'

Popping a grape into his mouth, Balthazar explained, 'What you need, my friend, are men to row you when the winds drop. Unfortunately, sailors are all a superstitious lot. They will not budge from a port if the omens are bad. And unfortunately, I have no men to offer you or I would *order* them to row you!'

'No, you are doing enough, Balthazar. I do not look to you for manpower.'

Balthazar popped another grape into his mouth and, arching one eyebrow, he asked, 'Would you consider buying slaves?'

Vesuvio held Balthazar's stare. He knew that they shared the same opinion about slavery, about the system which treated men like mere chattel, a life of slavery which they had both escaped.

Taking a deep breath, Vesuvio asked soberly, 'Is there a reputable slave-house here?' He saw the merit in the suggestion.

'In Athens, the slaves are mostly sold in the *agora*,' Balthazar explained. 'The ones I have seen there would be of no service to you. The same holds true in Piraeus. That is, except for one slaveyard in Piraeus owned by a man called Delos.'

'Delos? A man from the historic slave island of Delos?'

Balthazar nodded. 'His family were slave-masters there when Delos was the prime slaveport in the Mediterranean. You might find something worthwhile at his place. I have never been there but I heard . . .' He shrugged.

Vesuvio admitted. 'There are no other choices open to me, Balthazar.'

'You do realise that you are taking a great chance by pursuing this course, Vesuvio. That the slave girl whom the captain saw might *not* be Miranda. That the odds are overwhelmingly against you.'

Vesuvio ignored Balthazar's cautionary words and said, 'Let us return a moment to the conversation you had this morning with the captain from Carthage who saw this other Carthaginian vessel docked in Crete. Did he say where the vessel had stopped after sailing from Carthage? One of its first stops? Before it even reached Piraeus?'

Balthazar lowered his eyes, answering, 'The island of Melita . . . to take on the Persians and their Greek slave girl.'

'Melita,' Vesuvio repeated gravely. 'Melita lies to the

south of Sicily. The vessel I sailed on stopped at Melita, too. And if Miranda's ship had only reached here a week ago, then that matches the time almost to the day that she was taken away from home.'

Balthazar leaned forward and put his hand on Vesuvio's shoulder, cautioning, 'Before you decide what you are going to do, let me also tell you this. I sent out inquiries this morning about the man called Coricles, the lawyer who acts for Menecrates. This . . . Coricles left Piraeus yesterday. Shortly after your arrival. He will be away for an indefinite length of time.'

Studying his hands folded in the lap of his tunic, Vesuvio said, 'Cleomenes is behind this. I know it. Cleomenes and Despo. But why?'

'They certainly are not going to tell you if they are. You will only be wasting your time if you try to learn the reason from them. And, quite possible, be risking your life with them if what you say about Menecrates holds true.'

Vesuvio raised his head and said, 'I accept your offer of finding me a small open boat, Balthazar. I will ride back to Piraeus with you now and visit this slave-dealer, Delos, to see if I can buy eight oarsmen.'

Balthazar said, 'Golden Eagle, eight slaves can be dangerous. Especially if you are all alone with them at sea. Especially when the eight slaves you will need are strong . . . strong enough to row a boat and . . . the gods know do what other feats!'

Holding Vesuvio's blue eyes in his stare, Balthazar's sculpted face broke into a sudden grin and he beckoned Vesuvio to lean closer towards him across the table. He said, 'But, listen. I have had another thought about that, too. You and your slaves. If you were to *free* the slaves before you sail from Greece. Free them. Let them see their manumission papers and then send the papers to Cyprus with me. The slaves can be free once you arrive safely in Cyprus! Is that too generous?'

'Generous?' Vesuvio said, rising quickly from his chair. 'The only generous thing is you, Balthazar! Would that every man had a friend as generous as you.'

Also rising to his feet, Balthazar said, 'The only thing I have to fear now is that you arrive safely in Cyprus to catch my freighter. If anything were to happen to you between here and Cyprus, my Yiannoula would never forgive me!'

'Let me find eight strong men first before we start worrying about my safety!' Vesuvio said, moving toward the arbour which led to the inn's stables.

13

Riding the four miles from Athens to Piraeus with Balthazar as the morning sun was climbing higher in the cobalt blue sky, Vesuvio followed Balthazar's directions in the harbour town and found Delos the slave-dealer in a crumbling building located in a maze of winding streets beyond the dockyards.

A short, thickset man with a shaven head, Delos sat behind a wooden table and nodded without saying a word whilst Vesuvio announced that he wanted to purchase eight men strong enough to row an open boat.

Delos lifted a jangling ring of keys from the table and grunted for Vesuvio to follow him, first, to the slave pens located in the yard beyond the house. He grumbled that he had more slaves locked in a cellar which sank deep into the earth below the building.

Leading Vesuvio down a musty hallway in the slave house, Delos began to complain about the Romans seizing most of the worthwhile slaves which came onto the market. That the Roman government used the men for building public roads and aqueducts.

Stepping over bundles of rags spread across the dirty floor, Delos said, 'If there are any decent men for sale in this province, you came to the only place that has them. I belong to the old tradition of slave-dealers. I hail from a time when masters wanted *men* for slaves! Nowadays, people are just looking for pieces of fluff!'

Vesuvio knew that merchants often offered better prices when they were allowed to talk freely about favourite subject matters. He said, 'I was told that your family came from the island of Delos. Was it as prosperous as people say?'

'Delos? Prosperous?' the bald-headed man boomed as he now led Vesuvio down mossy steps which led to the yard behind his house. 'Every ship, every galley that sailed into the Delos harbour brimmed with hearty slaves. The island of Delos was the meat market of the Mediterranean! And not just for manly brawn! But for beauty as well. My father told me stories which his father had told him. Tales about the women brought to Delos that would set fire to your groin. Tribal harems captured from the east! Princesses wrapped in furs and carried from faraway tribes in Germany! Queens from Arabia sold with all their precious jewels! The most beautiful women of the world were auctioned at Delos and men fought with one another to pay enormous fortunes for them.'

Stopping at the foot of the steps, he faced Vesuvio and said gravely, 'But then the pirates came to Delos and began to use it for their base. That's when your Roman commander, Pompey, sacked Delos to make the Mediterranean safe for . . . Rome!'

He turned from Vesuvio and ambled across the garbage strewn yard to the first of the iron grilles which lined this back area of his slave house. He said as he walked, 'I sometimes wonder if it was better to have pirates as rulers rather than seeing slavery in the snivelling state it is today under Roman rule. The island of Delos was to manpower what Athens was to learning. But both were seized by Rome. Both destroyed in their own way.'

Stopping in front of the first pen, Delos pointed his ring of keys to two men crouched in opposite corners of their small prison. Dirt caked their faces. Open sores and bruises covered their sinewy bodies. Their clothes were little more than ragged shreds of peasant weave.

Delos's voice suddenly hardened as he pointed to his first

sample of slaves. 'These two men here. One is Spartan. The other Athenian. Both born into slavery. Both conceived with the ancient hatred between those rival cities. The Spartan and Athenian never stop quarrelling with one another. If the Spartan says it's day, the Athenian will argue that it's night. If the Spartan ever tries to escape, you can be certain that the Athenian will do everything to stop him. Hatred is the tool I use between these two. I hope to sell them as a pair.'

Vesuvio studied the two dark-haired men squatting in their separate corners and glowering at one another. He asked, 'What are their names?'

The slave dealer grunted. 'Names? Names are a luxury in this world! I told you – I call one the Spartan. The other is the Athenian.' Thumbing his barrel chest, he said, 'I am Delos.'

'And I am called after a volcano in southern Italy . . Vesuvio.'

Delos jerked his head, a half-smile suddenly playing on his thick lips. He nodded his bald head at Vesuvio as if a bond had suddenly been struck between them.

'This man here,' he said, continuing down the filthy yard to the next pen and pointed at a sallow-faced young male slave with thin black hair hanging to his shoulders. 'I cannot understand this cur. He is docile enough in appearance but look closely at him. Study those marks on his body. They're bruises and scars from fighting. But he didn't get them here. Nor does he look like a man who'd fight. He obviously has strength to defend himself, though, or he wouldn't be alive. Not with marks like those on his body. He's from Palestine. I call him the Jew.'

Kicking a few bones aside with his sandal, Delos stopped in front of the next grille. 'See how this man sits looking up at the branches of that scrub tree hanging over his cage. You can see from that far-off glint in his eyes that he's sitting there longing for freedom. Those eyes mark him as a potential runaway. Make no mistake about this rascal. He would try to escape as soon as you turned your back on him.'

'Where is he from?' Vesuvio asked, studying the flat-faced man with a broken nose and a chestful of wiry black hair.

Delos shrugged. 'Who knows? He looks too dark to be from the north but I don't have a Gaul here so that's what I call him. The Gaul. It saves confusion.'

Stepping across a puddle of rancid water, Delos paused by a pen with five women crushed into it, females with withered faces, snaggle-teeth, and breasts sagging inside their ragged, filthy smocks. He said, 'Too bad you don't need women. I could give you a good price on these five. Females with barren wombs are hard to sell. I bought these in a lot of ten other slaves. But they eat more than I paid for the whole lot and, if I don't sell them soon, I'll have to kill them. That's the cheapest thing for me to do. Drown them in the sea and leave their bodies to be washed out with the tide.'

Stopping at the pen located at the far end of the yard, Delos stood to one side and made room for Vesuvio to stand alongside him. He gestured at a male slave lying at the rear of the pen on a makeshift bed of rags and leaves. The man was healthy in appearance but his eyes were closed, his head resting on his folded hands.

Delos shook his head in bewilderment as he studied the sleeping man. 'This one here looks strong but the fool is always sleeping. A lash might keep him awake but what kind of price would I get for him then? I'd be giving him the whip ten, twelve times a day to keep him awake. Then I'd ruin his back. He does nothing but sleep, this one. I call him the Dacian.'

Vesuvio looked at the sleeping man. Delos had not whipped this slave only because it would detract from his selling price. The world of slave-dealing sickened Vesuvio. He remembered such attitudes from the days when he himself had been a slave. He hoped that he would never think so coldly now that he again was a master.

*   *   *

Beckoning Vesuvio to follow him down a steep and winding stairway which led to the underground crypts where he kept more slaves, Delos lifted a smouldering torch from an iron wall-bracket at the foot of the steps and asked, 'So what is the nature of your business?'

'I am sailing for a friend.'

'For pleasure or is your friend in trade?'

Not wanting to divulge too many facts, Vesuvio mumbled, 'My friend is a . . . sponge merchant.'

'You must only be delivering a shipment of sponges for your friend, not diving for them, or you would have asked me for swimmers.'

'Most men swim.'

Delos proceeded along the first musty corridor lying beneath the earth, saying, 'If my customers want to tell me their business, fine. If they don't, that is fine, too – as long as you don't mind if I bite your gold when you pay me!'

They now walked single-file along a damp corridor. Vesuvio caught the sound of water slowly dripping in the distance and heard the scamper of rats in the straw which covered the stone floor.

Delos continued walking deeper into the dark cavern, passing cells where Vesuvio saw children's small hands gripping at the iron bars, their grimy faces peering out at the two men passing with the smoking torch.

Delos called over his shoulder, 'Will you be sailing directly?'

'As soon as I know my slaves.'

'If the harbour here stays closed, I'll wager you'll get to know them soon enough!' Delos's laughter echoed in the musty cavern.

Stopping in front of a lewen cut into a stone wall thick with mould growing up from its base, Delos held the sputtering torch forward and said, 'This slave here is not bad. He's young and has an artful way with languages. If you plan to visit distant shores, he could be very useful to you. He speaks Latin, Greek, Persian, Egyptian, as well as all the island dialects. Plus a few desert tribal tongues I've never heard spoken before.'

'What do you call him?' Vesuvio asked.

'Babel. After the old Hebrew tale about the tower where men spoke many languages.'

Vesuvio leaned forward as Delos held the torch alongside the lewen. He saw a boy with a handsome face squatting on a bed of straw, a youth who was obviously not twenty-years-old and smiled when he saw Vesuvio peering in at him.

'Why do you keep such a healthy lad locked down here beneath the earth?' Vesuvio asked.

'He's too pretty,' Delos muttered. 'It's always wise to show a little punishment to pretty boys like this one. If you don't, they start thinking they're special and try to take advantage of you.'

Delos moved away from the mould-encrusted lewen, saying, 'You can make the rounds again to look at any slave who catches your eye on this trip. I'm just giving you thc first look, a sample of what I've got for sale before you examine any of them more closely.'

The burly slave-dealer pointed his torch at a small pen built into the wall like an oven. He said off-handedly, 'There's nothing for you here in these cages. I keep the lame and wounded here. Like that old man there.'

Vesuvio leaned forward and stared inside the oven-like cage. He saw a hunch-shouldered old man with two large patches of festering scabs where once had been his eyes.

Delos explained disinterestedly, 'This unlucky wretch walked in on his mistress being mounted by her lover one afternoon. She blinded him with a burning poker so that he could not describe the lover to her husband. I keep all the scum like him down here. Men who have tried to run away from their masters and have had their legs cut-off. Slaves with their hands severed for stealing. Any man who's mutilated or crippled.'

'Do you really hope to sell such miserable creatures?' Vesuvio asked.

'Sell them?' Delos laughed and assured Vesuvio, 'Of course I expect to sell them! I *know* I'll sell them! I'll sell them to the poor! Even the poorest of free men gets pride from knowing that he owns another man!'

Tapping Vesuvio on the chest, Delos said, 'And I'll tell you another thing. I'll sell these blinded, mutilated crippled bastards before I'll sell those barren women I showed you crammed into the pen in the backyard. And why? Because a free man will save and scrimp his money to buy a . . . male slave! When you buy a male slave, you're buying a cock, aren't you? A prick! And what does a prick mean?'

Continuing down the seeping hallway, Delos called over his shoulder, 'A prick means power! That's why! A cunt is just another hole! But a prick –' He nodded in the torch's glow. '– a prick means power. And the more mighty the prick is, the greater the price. Now take a man like yourself . . .'

Vesuvio quickly interrupted, 'I'm here to buy.'

Delos laughed. 'No man in the Roman Empire is always the buyer. That's the first Imperial rule! We all run the risk of becoming a slave to someone! You! Me! Anyone!'

Knowing that the words which the slave-dealer was saying were unfortunately true, Vesuvio thought not of himself being enslaved but again he thought of Miranda. He shuddered to think of her being discussed, bought, sold, pawed over by prospective buyers. Would people never come to understand that slaves were people? Would the day never come to pass when intellect, soul, the right to freedom would not be equally respected amongst all men and women, those lucky enough to be born free, those unfortunate enough to be born as slaves, as well as those who were captured and cast into slavery?

14

Despo and Cleomenes sat this evening in the *triclinium* in the house of Menecrates. Two nights had passed since Cleomenes had officiated at the nocturnal celebration to the horse god, Bendis, on the coastline north of Piraeus and Despo had visited the prophetic hermaphrodite in the Elevasion mountain range. They had been discussing the activity of Vesuvio since that time, weighing the information which had been brought to them throughout the day by paid informants.

They had learned that Vesuvio had purchased eight strong male slaves this afternoon from Delos the slave-dealer in Piraeus. Also, a black merchant by the name of Balthazar today had purchased a small boat to carry Vesuvio and his eight oarsmen from Greece to Cyprus. Vesuvio was planning to leave Greece this very evening.

Excited by the news that Vesuvio planned to sail a route that would take him through a group of islands commonly referred to as the 'River Styx', Despo repeated to Cleomenes what else she had done this afternoon.

She said, 'The prophet told me about the River Styx. I at first thought he meant the mythical river which leads to the netherworld. But when I heard from our industrious spies that the Roman plans to sail to Cyprus, I thought of that dangerous coastline off Lycia. He will have to pass through the channel islands called the "River Styx". I then remembered the rest of the prophecy. The words about gold!'

Small yellow flames flickered in clay lamps set in niches around the *triclinium* as Cleomenes lay upon his divan and lifted a chased silver goblet from a small citrus wood table which set in front of him. He dryly remarked, 'There is no denying your artfulness, Despo. Nor your tenacious memory. I compliment you on deciphering your prophet's words. Of not only translating the hermaphrodite's mutterings about "planting gold upon the water of the River Styx" but also having the courage to send a man to steal coins from the Temple of Diana.'

'Yes!' Despo said excitedly, sitting to the edge of her curule chair placed near Cleomenes's divan. She practised the Greek custom of a female not lying upon a couch to dine like a male, but, instead, remaining upright with a small dining table placed by her knees. 'I followed the prophecy to a letter! To obtain gold where parchment lies! Menecrates's testament is written upon parchment. It lies within the Temple of Diana. And golden coins are also minted in the same temple. What could be more clear than to stash stolen temple coins amongst the food supplies being loaded aboard the Roman's boat?' She sat back in her chair, gloating over her work – and the work of her faithful slaves.

Cleomenes's face was nevertheless traced with worry. He spoke uneasily. 'It seems ironic to me that it was so simple for a mere slave to steal coins from the Temple of Diana and hide them aboard the boat which the Cypriot merchant bought for Vesuvio. But yet we cannot get our hands on Menecrates's last testament and see who fares better in his will. You or Miranda.'

The mention of her sister's name brought a sudden rush of anger to Despo's cheeks. She said, 'Menecrates could not possibly leave his estate to Miranda. He was intent on freeing her before he died, true. And the old man was certainly pleased when he heard that the Roman was planning to marry her. But I cannot – I will not – believe that the silly old fool would name her as his beneficiary. Not Miranda. Not over me! His wife!'

Taking a sip of wine, Cleomenes wiped his lips on a linen cloth, saying, 'No, I have been thinking of another possibility. I have been weighing the fact that he might have known we were lovers all along.'

'Impossible,' she said firmly.

'Perhaps. But just consider my supposition. What if he did? Now, you know what he thought of adultery. The ways he prescribed of dealing with adulterous partners within a marriage.'

'But that use of a cane and public humiliation of adulterers was only to protect the families! I never bore him children!'

'No,' Cleomenes softly but persistently argued. 'But the old man had his pride. And he would not like to leave rumours behind him that he had been unsuspectingly cuckolded. Consider that, Despo.'

'What do you possibly think he would do? Have us caned?'

'No' Cleomenes laughed, looking into his silver goblet. 'He would have guessed that you'd enjoy that too much!'

Lying his head back on the cushions of the divan, Cleomenes said, 'I only wish your prophet in the cave could foresee what is written in the old man's will.'

Despo watched Cleomenes as he closed his eyes. She remembered how handsome she had thought he was when she had first seen him. She remembered the passion of their original love-making. The sight of him still kindled a lust in her but she was now beginning to see even more clearly how he could be useful to her ambitions.

She began in a soothing voice, 'Menecrates served our purpose, my love. Now we must forget entirely about him. I had fifteen gruelling years as a slave to that simpering old man. Learning about his stupid possets and cures. Listening to him advise useless people in their problems and worries. Trying to show my concern for the men and women who flocked to him. But worst of all for me was his constant praise for Miranda. Being told day-after-day how wonderful, how humane, how considerate she was.'

Laughing to herself, Despo said in a reflective voice, 'You

say I enjoy punishment in . . . love-making. I think my aged husband enjoyed his share of pain, too. He married me but, without a doubt, I was a replacement to him for Miranda. He adored reading her letters to me. When he heard that Miranda was going to marry the Roman he could talk of nothing else. Is that not self-inflicted pain? To dwell on the happiness of someone whom you wish to possess yourself?'

Despo shook her head. She said, 'It is all over now. Menecrates's body is cold. Burned to ashes. Miranda . . .'

Cleomenes held his eyes closed as he interrupted, asking, 'And your prophet saw Miranda in the deathpits?'

'Yes. The prophet distinctly said a "pit of skeletons".'

'Incredible,' Cleomenes murmured. 'Uncanny that the hermaphrodite should foresee that Miranda be entombed in the royal sepulchre of Cis-u-ba.'

* * *

Despo sat momentarily motionless in the chair facing Cleomenes lying upon his divan. She was thinking of her sister. She also thought of the Oriental queen called Cis-u-ba. The land, Caldea, where Miranda was being taken by the Persians who acted as agents for the Chamberlain of Caldea and had bought Miranda's deed from Cleomenes.

The situation was even bizarre to Despo's convoluted mind. She did not pretend to understand the workings of Oriental courtliness. She only grasped the basic beliefs held sacred in that land beyond Arabia.

The King of Caldea had died. His body was already embalmed and encased in the ivory sarcophagus. But the royal tomb could only be sealed when his wife was prepared to join him in the netherworld.

The queen of Caldea was called Cis-u-ba. The court law held that she was to be buried alive in her husband's tomb. But Cis-u-ba could not be interred until a retinue of attendants had been assembled to serve her in death as she had been attended in her life on earth. And the Queen's retinue must be composed entirely of female slaves.

Hand-maidens. Seamstresses. Hairdressers. Entertainers. All the necessary female slaves had been assembled to enter the Caldean tomb and be sealed shut with Queen Cis-u-ba. That is, all the attendants except for one.

A woman had yet to be found to be the medical attendant to Queen Cis-u-ba in the netherworld. As there were no female physicians or nurses in Caldea, the Chamberlain had commissioned a delegation of Persians to bring them a woman who was refined enough to be entombed with their queen.

Despo had heard the story about Cis-u-ba and the entombments of live female slaves when the Persians came to Athens and conversed with Cleomenes shortly after Menecrates's death. Despo herself had proposed Miranda. She explained how Miranda was contracted to a Roman living in Campania. She learned through a party of herbalists sent to Italy about the day-to-day schedules at Villa Vesuvio. She paid the herbalists to gather more than the kelp from the Bay of Naples known for its curing powers, and black volcanic mud from Herculaneum used for dropsy. Despo learned that Vesuvio planned a trip to Rome to secure Miranda's manumission. She corroborated this fact with his correspondence to her late husband. She told the Persians when to arrive at Villa Vesuvio to seize Miranda as a medical slave to serve Queen Cis-u-ba in the Netherworld.

* * *

'What are you scheming now?'

Cleomenes's voice jolted Despo from her thoughts about Miranda, the Persians, and Cis-u-ba. She saw him standing in front of her before she felt his fingers beginning to pinch her nipples through the linen *chiton.*

Sex. She knew that Cleomenes was always in the mood for sex as soon as he rested after his evening meal. She also knew that he wanted his spirits to be bolstered at the same time. Cleomenes was a confident man in appearance but Despo knew how insecure he was under that handsome, self-assured façade.

Her mind quickly searched for a bit of praise to pay him. She raised her head and, gazing mistily at him as she felt him increasing the pressure on her nipples, she said, 'I was just thinking what the prophet said about you, Cleomenes. About your religion being received with such acclaim in Rome. The colour of the purple murex dye he foresaw. How you shall probably have Imperial patronage.'

'And you shall be by my side in Rome,' he said, staring down at her through heavily lidded eyes.

'By your side, Cleomenes, and . . . at your feet.' She knew that he wanted to hear words of devotion.

Still working his hands on her breasts, he said, 'The Romans will welcome us as their newest religion. Nothing from Eygpt or Mesopotamia or even India can compare with the horse god I'll exhibit on each of Rome's seven hills. The priestesses of Isis cannot equal what I am bringing to Rome! The temples of Cybele cannot compare with the sexuality the Romans will find at the shrine to Bendis!'

'Nor its high-priest.' Despo remained seated in the chair as she reached to feel the hardness of Cleomenes's thighs beneath his linen robe. She said, 'I wonder if I will be the one to become jealous. I shudder to think of the beautiful Roman ladies who will be fighting to . . . serve you.'

'But surely that appeals to you, Despo. To know that other women want to be subjected by the man who loves only you.'

Despo fleetingly thought how naïve he was. That he sincerely believed the stories that his attractiveness to other women excited her. She could not believe that a man could be so sophisticated yet so innocent when it came to recognising her guile. The less she loved him, thc more she praised him. Could he not see through that ploy?

Cleomenes momentarily stopped working Despo's breasts. He said, 'I only hope nothing in Menecrates's testament will prevent us from following our plan. Will keep me from taking you as my wife or leaving this provincial city for Rome.'

'Shhh,' she said brushing her cheek against the front of his robe. 'Do not spoil our evening by talking about him.' She was thinking of Rome herself. She was wondering what lovers she would find there. She hoped that Cleomenes was indeed taken-up by Roman society. He clung too desperately to her lately. His insecurity was nearly suffocating her. He could be a service to her but only so far as taking her from Athens to Rome. From there she could organise her own future. She would let him promote his cult of Bendis. She secretly believed that even with moderate popularity, he would not last longer than a few months in the Imperial City. She knew how fickle the Romans were with their religious fads. She hoped to have found another patron when that time arrived.

The rustle of linen garments made Despo suddenly lift her head. She stared at Cleomenes's manhood hanging half-erect in front of her face. She leaned forward and brushed her lips against the soft skin.

Cleomenes ordered with effected authority, 'Take me in your mouth ...'

Despo's voice was sober. 'Before proper adoration ... my high-priest?'

'Adore me.'

She did not feel like falling to her knees. She did not want to feign another game to bolster Cleomenes's ego and make his phallus erect.

She whispered, 'I adore you.'

'Let me see you adore me.'

'I am afraid.'

'Why?'

'I am afraid that I will lose this when you go to Rome . . .'

The words were a lie but she saw that they had an erotic effect on Cleomenes. The idea that she was jealous of him made his phallus gain in length and width.

Leaning forward to kiss his phallus again, Despo decided to embark on her own fantasy. She whispered, 'I want you. I don't want . . . her to have you.'

'Her?' Cleomenes asked. 'Who do you mean?'

'Her,' Despo repeated, adding to make her words plausible to Cleomenes. 'Any woman in Rome.' She then closed her eyes and thought about the woman whom she truly meant. She thought about her sister, Miranda. She imagined how Miranda must have often licked Vesuvio's strong manhood. She fell quickly to her knees and imagined that she was taking Vesuvio in her mouth as Miranda would take him. She stretched her mouth around Cleomenes's phallus imagining it to be Vesuvio's. She still could not eradicate Vesuvio from her mind since she had tricked him into having sex with her on his arrival in Athens.

'I don't want you to go,' she begged to the phallus, brushing her cheek lovingly against it. 'I will never see you again. I will never see you again.'

The sincerity in her voice stiffened Cleomenes like iron. He grabbed Despo by the head and drove himself into her throat. He believed she was talking to him.

Despo opened her mouth wider to take the phallus farther into her throat, parting her lips as she pressed her eyes tightly shut, imagining that she was in subservience to Vesuvio.

Cleomenes pulled himself from her mouth, suddenly demanding, 'Who is your god?'

'You are,' she said, staring at the phallus moistened with her saliva.

'Who is your master?'

'You are . . .' She stopped herself from saying the name 'Vesuvio'.

'Who will all the women in Rome flock to see? Bring their gold to? Make a place for in their pantheon of gods?'

Closing her eyes, she assured the phallus, 'You are already Roman.'

Clasping both arms around Despo's shoulders, Cleomenes pulled her toward his groin, saying, 'I will never forsake you, my beloved. When I am sought after in Rome as high-priest to Bendis, I will have you constantly by my side.'

Despo tried not to listen to his words, to let them obliterate the excitement she was building about Vesuvio. She knew that her mind was strong enough to eke sexual pleasure from almost any situation. She had been the one who first devised the sexual facets of the Thracian religion for Cleomenes. She had told him to order young riders to copulate with maidens on horseback. Had promised him that people would throw coins at his feet if he gave them dramatic and different ways to indulge licentiousness. She had guided Cleomenes into turning Bendis into a cult of voluptuaries but now she cursed him under her breath for being so selfish. Did he truly think that she wanted nothing but to please him? What about her own fantasies? Did he truly believe that a woman with such a fertile imagination would not make-up fantasies for herself?

Rubbing her tongue around the base of the crown on his phallus, Despo kept thinking, Vesuvio . . . This is Vesuvio. I am Miranda. This is how Miranda makes love to Vesuvio. They are in love and, now that I am Miranda . . .'

She started to whisper to the phallus, 'I love you. I love you . . . I will never see you again but I still love you.'

BOOK THREE

THE RIVER STYX

15

The waters of the northern Mediterranean stretching between Piraeus and Asia Minor were abundant with small islands, the first and most populated group being called The Cyclades.

Many of these islands were no larger than dots of barren rock protruding like stepping stones across the Aegean whilst others were large and fertile, their sloping hillsides rich with vineyards enclosed by an intricate network of low fieldstone walls which zig-zagged down to the blue-green sea.

The boat which Balthazar had purchased for Vesuvio was freshly painted blue-red-and-yellow and had a short mast with a lateen sail made from bull hides. It was called the *Rhea* and enjoyed favourable weather for the first night and day out of Piraeus, the winds billowing the sail and saving exertion for the eight oarsmen who sat upon the boat's four wooden benches.

The *Rhea*'s first stop was at the small island of Spiros on the second morning following its departure from the Greek mainland. Vesuvio purchased bread, olives, cheese, and wine in the harbour marketplace to supplement the rations which Balthazar had ordered his men to stow in the aft-pit of the open boat.

The clement weather held as the *Rhea* sailed eastward, the winds filling the hide sail, swiftly moving the small blue-red-and-yellow boat past the larger islands of Paros and Naxos.

Anxious to reach the port of Paphos on Cyprus to meet Balthazar's freighter scheduled to sail south to Alexandria, Vesuvio travelled both day and night. He navigated by the stars and also utilised the warm hours of night to teach his men how to add to their food supply.

He showed the slaves, when they held a burning torch over the side of the boat in the darkness, small octopus were attracted to the light and could easily be speared as they remained transfixed by the torch's fiery glow above the water.

The sun climbed to a burning zenith at midday hours, a time at which the *Rhea* sought refuge from the heat and Vesuvio allowed his men to make forays ashore to dig upon the rocks for limpets or dive into the clear waters of the Aegean to scour the seabed for other edibles. The slaves emerged from their swims carrying prickly black sea-urchins. They carefully brought them ashore in the palms of their hands and split them open on the underside to suck out the nourishing orange roe.

In this quest for food from the sea – diving for sea-urchins, angling for mullet, discovering the brown marine delicacies called 'sea dates' – Vesuvio was momentarily able to control his anxiety for Miranda's safety. He tried to suppress his driving obsession of reaching Cyprus in time to board Balthazar's southerly bound ship.

Knowing that he could not control the winds, Vesuvio also recognised to what limits he could push his oarsmen. He had purchased eight slaves from Delos the slave-dealer in Piraeus and, following Balthazar's idea of freeing the slaves before setting out on the voyage, he had told the men that they could collect their manumission papers when they – and he – arrived safely at the port town of Paphos on Cyprus.

* * *

The Athenian. The Spartan. The Jew. The Gaul. The Egyptian. The Dacian. The Syrian. And Babel, the personable young man who spoke many languages and island dialects.

Although still calling the men by these titles, Vesuvio had asked them for their proper names and places of birth when he had taken them from Delos's slave house in Piraeus and composed their deeds of manumission in the offices of Balthazar's warehouse. He had learned that all eight men had been born into slavery and, as it was commonplace for masters to call infant slaves by adjectives which they hoped would apply to them in maturity, the eight men's names were no more personal than the geographical tags which Delos had given them – the Spartan had originally been dubbed 'Loyal'. The Egyptian, 'Strong'. The Dacian, 'Swift'.

Once at sea, Vesuvio sat above the food supplies in the aft-pit of the *Rhea* to keep surveillance on the eight oarsmen seated in front of him. His only protection against them was a short damascene dagger . . . and hope that the eight men recognised the fact that they had nothing to lose by serving him loyally until the *Rhea* reached Cyprus. That a mutiny would do them more harm than if they obediently served him.

As if by some plan privately organised amongst themselves, the eight slaves began to call over the tedium of the ebbing sea at the end of their second day out of Piraeus. They broke the brooding silence which had been hanging over the *Rhea* by shouting questions to Vesuvio about himself and his homeland.

'Is the city of Rome as crowded as Athens?' called the Athenian.

'Rome is larger than Athens now. But I do not live in the city of Rome. My home is in the south, in country much like the land in northern Achaea.'

'Why do the Romans import so much wheat from the rest of the world if the land in Italy is as fertile as people say?' asked the dark wiry man called the Egyptian.

'The Italian peninsula does not even supply enough wheat for its army,' Vesuvio answered, studying which men asked questions and which ones remained silent. He had been noticing all day that the Gaul still had a faraway look in his lifeless grey eyes. He wondered if he might be the first man to try to make a break for freedom.

The Egyptian spoke again. 'I've heard that the Emperor gives free wheat to the citizens. Is that true, *domine?*'

'Very true,' Vesuvio shouted over the crash of the water. 'It's called the *Annona*, the god which supplies the yearly food. But many citizens feel that free bread keeps men from working. That men don't work hard enough if they know they'll receive a weekly ration of food.'

'What a lucky lot the Romans are!' shouted the Dacian. 'Free wheat and circuses to attend! Is the Circus Maximus the biggest arena in the world?'

'The Romans would like to think so,' Vesuvio said. 'But many men say that the amphitheatre in Antioch is larger. And the games there much more cruel.'

The Syrian called from the front of the boat, 'So tell us about your loved-one!'

Vesuvio suddenly sobered. He detected a false note of frivolity in the Syrian's question. He studied the dark skin of the slave's back which was well muscled but mottled by years of toiling in the sun. He answered dryly, 'You tell me what you've heard, friend.'

The Syrian did not reply.

Vesuvio kept his eyes trained on him as a silence spread over the other men. The wind whipped the edges of the leather sail. The prow continued cutting through the white-capped waves. But no one spoke.

Why should one of these men suddenly be questioning me about a loved one? Vesuvio wondered. Had it merely been an idle question? But, then, it's not the custom of even the most careless slave to ask such an impertinent question from a new master. Especially not a master who controls the deeds to their freedom and promises to liberate them in literally a matter of days.

Vesuvio then considered the possibility that information

about Miranda had been given to the eight slaves in secrecy. Someone could have told the oarsmen why he had originally embarked on this voyage from Italy and had been so anxious to sail from Piraeus before the auguries presaged safe sailing.

Suspecting who the informant might have been, Vesuvio smiled. It was characteristic of Balthazar to give slaves such a piece of information. He and Vesuvio had been slaves together in Carthage. They both knew from personal experience that misfortune often casts men into slavery but that slaves retained the same curiosity as free men.

Balthazar had been kidnapped from his homeland as a child. Vesuvio had been abducted in young manhood from his parents' estate. They both had seen the indignities of slavery and had learned to trust masters who showed compassion for slaves.

Balthazar could have told these oarsmen about Miranda to make them trust me, Vesuvio thought. Trust would keep them from rebelling against me.

Vesuvio had never doubted the black man's friendship but he now understood beyond doubt that they shared the same beliefs about slavery. Men did not surrender all human qualities once they became enslaved. They still retained self-respect, desire for advancement, curiosity, all the natural traits of free men.

Vesuvio sat soberly in the aft-pit of the *Rhea*. He considered the irony of his voyage. He had left Italy to bring Miranda home to be his wife but here he was in these far-away islands called The Cyclades, following the same philosophy he struggled to promulgate at home. He was still trying to prove to slaves that some day men might all be equal. This realisation pleased him. He was warmed by the dignity which it added to this journey.

* * *

Vesuvio and the eight oarsmen sat around the smouldering coals of a bonfire on their third night out of Piraeus. They were finishing their supper of mullet skewered in chunks upon the fire built in a cove of an uncharted island. An inky darkness was spreading across the sky. The night's blackness was fastly obliterating the pastel hues which had only moments ago painted the sea's unbroken horizon.

Vesuvio hoped to reach the island of Rhodes tomorrow. The men's conversation during this evening meal had been about the ancient statue which had been built there in the harbour.

The men passed a dried sheep's belly around the fire, finishing the resinous white wine from Piros which the belly contained and had been allotted to them for their meal.

Young Babel was proving to be the most loquacious of the group. He now was cautioning the other oarsmen not to expect to see much of the statue – the Colossus of Rhodes – still standing in the harbour. He explained to them that more than two-hundred-and-fifty years ago an earthquake had toppled the bronze plated monolith.

Vesuvio listened half-interestedly to the young man's account of how the people of Rhodes had built the statue in gratitude to the god, Hera, for delivering them from a long siege by the Macedonians.

Babel was engaging as a storyteller but he was beginning to trouble Vesuvio. He could not fault Babel as a strong and disciplined oarsmen. The young man pulled more than his weight aboard the *Rhea*. But during the last two days Vesuvio had begun to see Babel as a possible threat to the peace aboard the small blue-red-and-yellow painted boat.

Vesuvio sat on the stony ground nearby the fire. He remembered that Delos the slave dealer had kept Babel locked in the cellar of the slave house in Piraeus, that Delos had said that Babel was too physically attractive to be allowed in the outside pens, and that pretty boys often took advantage of their physical desirability.

Babel had not tried to obtain special favours from Vesuvio since they had sailed from Greece but Vesuvio still could not forget the slave-dealer's words. Babel was comely and this troubled Vesuvio. The seven other oarsmen were surly and overtly masculine, and like most robust males, they were sex-starved. They probably had little concern over the gender of the person with whom they could satisfy themselves.

Vesuvio sat by the fireside, listening to Babel's softly spoken words and studied the other men watching the pretty young boy.

Babel spoke in dulcet tones about how the citizens of Rhodes had built the tall Colossus on their island. 'The Rhodians first erected a scaffolding on the ground. They built a framework to represent a pair of feet and ankles. When the craftsmen finished hammering brass plating around the feet and ankles, workmen filled the scaffolding in with dirt and then built another scaffolding on top of that. They proceeded in such a manner, building scaffolding, hammering brass upon the framework, filling in the scaffolding with more dirt until, at last, they had heaped a mountain over their entire creation.'

Vesuvio watch the Athenian and the Spartan appraise Babel's olive-coloured skin. He remembered these two men's history of hatred for one another. He recognised a sexual desire in their wine-dulled eyes and wondered if they would fight over Babel.

He looked around the fire at the faces of the other men. He saw the Gaul staring at Babel's muscular legs. He watched the Egyptian scrutinise his thick thighs. He kept his eyes on the Syrian as he leaned back to see Babel's fleshy buttocks. Each and every oarsmen was undressing Babel with their eyes and raping him in their imagination.

But Babel was oblivious to the desires he was arousing in the other men. He continued, 'Historians have written that a ship at sea could see the bronze statue standing above the harbour of Rhodes. The Colossus faced east, shading his eyes against the rising sun.'

The Jew marvelled, 'The Colossus of Rhodes must certainly have been one of the great wonders of the world.'

Babel nodded. 'It was counted as one of the world's seven wonders by ancient historians.'

'What are the other six?' asked the Eygptian. His smile lingered on Babel.

Babel held up one hand. He began counting on his large fingers. 'The Pyramids of Egypt are one. The Hanging Gardens built in Babylon are another. The third was the Mausoleum in Halicarnassus. Two more are located near Athens, one being the Temple of Artemis and the other is the statue of Zeus at Delphi. The Colossus of Rhodes makes six. But the seventh wonder of the world . . .'

Babel paused, shaking his head.

The Syrian winked at him, saying, 'Certainly it must be the Grove of Daphne in Antioch. Where a good man can get any girl or . . . boy!' He grabbed his crotch in a lewd gesture and again winked at Babel.

'No.' Babel shook his head, showing no response to the Syrian's sexual overtures. He innocently explained, 'The Grove of Daphne in Antioch is very famous. Especially for the orgies which are practised there day and night. But it is certainly not counted as one of the seven wonders of the world.'

He looked towards Vesuvio, asking, '*Domine*, what is the seventh wonder of the world?'

The question jolted Vesuvio from his thoughts about what he must do if trouble should arise amongst the men over Babel.

He answered, 'The lighthouse in Alexandria.'

'Ah!' the Spartan blurted. 'We might all see the Colossus of Rhodes. But after *domine* leaves us in Cyprus and sails to Alexandria to find his slave girl, he . . .'

The Spartan suddenly stopped. But it was too late. The

other men glowered at him from their places around the fire. He had divulged the fact that they knew that Vesuvio was sailing on to Alexandria.

Vesuvio tried to keep all expression from creeping over his face. He knew now for certain that the men had been told about Miranda.

Breaking the silence, Vesuvio told the men to dismantle the camp and pack the provisions aboard the *Rhea*. It was still too early to take the eight men into his confidence. He did not want to allow them familiarities which he did not yet know they might disabuse. He also knew that many men, slave or free, liked to speak lightly of females, seeing them only as objects of sexual pleasure.

*   *   *

The oarsmen began storing the equipment aboard the *Rhea*, rinsing out the wineskin with salt water for future use, dowsing the embers of the fire. Vesuvio motioned for Babel to sit alongside him by the damp ashes. He said, 'Tell me, friend, how you know so much about history?'

Babel sat down nervously, answering, 'I was fortunate enough to be owned once by a master who took great pride in teaching me, *domine*.'

'You do your previous master justice,' Vesuvio complimented. He noticed that the boy was not effeminate but that his manner was definitely passive.

'Lucius Agrippa was a great man,' Babel said with growing confidence. 'Agrippa served as a tribune in the Roman Army. But he loved to gamble. He lost both his military commission and estate by gambling. He took his own life to avoid dishonour. I was sold along with his other personal effects and . . .' Babel shrugged his broad shoulders.

Vesuvio asked, 'What are your plans when we reach Cyprus? When you receive your freedom?'

Babel again shrugged. 'I will probably look for a position in some man's household.'

Thinking that Balthazar and Yiannoula might be able to find employment for a multi-lingual young man with a gregarious personality, Vesuvio asked, 'Do you hope to find any particular job? Such as being a tutor?'

Babel hung his head. His voice was apologetic and low. He said, 'I am afraid I have no interest in children, *domine*. I would prefer to serve a . . . grown man.'

Vesuvio asked, 'Do you have hopes to marry?'

Babel answered meekly, 'I have never known a woman, *domine*.'

Vesuvio's questioning became even more personal. He asked, 'Do you feel the physical . . . desire?'

Babel slowly lifted his head. He turned to Vesuvio and looked him directly in the eye as he admitted, 'I have only the physical desire to serve a man, *domine*. A male master. To serve him and serve him . . . well.' His brown eyes lingered on Vesuvio. His sculpted lips gently parted as he searched Vesuvio's face for some reaction to this blatant admission.

Rising from the bank of dead coals, Vesuvio said, 'We will talk later about your future. The time has come for us to shrink the distance between us and Cyprus.'

Vesuvio walked alongside the sturdy young man to the *Rhea* and now feared more than ever that Babel could be the spark for trouble amongst the other men. The youth had certainly displayed sexual hunger in his eyes. And if such a smouldering look were to be directed toward any of the other men aboard the *Rhea*, Vesuvio could foresee . . .

He then remembered the words which Tia had told him on the night that he had left Villa Vesuvio. Part of the old crone's words had already proven true. She had curiously foreseen that Vesuvio's search for Miranda would take him past Athens. Tia had mentioned that Vesuvio would visit many countries.

Remembering how Tia had also warned him about 'trouble building upon trouble', Vesuvio now wondered if Babel might be the instrument for Tia's predictions.

He climbed aboard the *Rhea* and, taking his usual place over the aft-pit, he decided that he must lose a few hours from travelling tomorrow. He must stop on the island of Rhodes and find an establishment where the men could ease their sexual frustrations. Two or three hours in a brothel would be an investment towards everyone's well-being.

16

The *Rhea* entered the the small harbour at Rhodes late the next morning, finding little activity in the stone-paved cove except for a few fishing boats bobbing along the wharf.

Vesuvio directed the men to row the *Rhea* in the direction of a weathered shed standing on a quay where fishermen were mending their nets. The eight men pulled their oars in unison as they stared to the left of the open boat at two bronze plinths rising from a sand jetty which separated the harbour from the open sea – the remains of what once had been the Colossus of Rhodes.

The Athenian muttered, 'I thought the statue stood above the harbour entrance.'

The Spartan scorned the Athenian. 'What did you expect, numbskull? That we'd sail between the giant's legs and let him piss on us?'

The Athenian doubled his fist and spun around on his bench. He shouted, 'I'll piss on you, pig of Sparta!'

Vesuvio immediately rose from his seat above the aft-pit. He moved between the men, firmly announcing. 'We are going to stop here for a while. I think it's time to share some wine together . . . as friends. How does that sound to you squabbling lot? Perhaps I will even be able to find a house which has a few snaggle-toothed crones willing to spread their legs for you ugly bunch!'

Vesuvio dropped the anchor into the clear blue water with a splash. He turned and saw a boatful of smiling faces. The Athenian, the Spartan, the Dacian, the Gaul, the Egyptian – everyone welcomed Vesuvio's suggestion of finding wine and women. Every oarsmen except for one grinned at him.

Babel stared soberly at Vesuvio, looking as if he had been betrayed.

* * *

Vesuvio led the unkempt oarsmen up a narrow incline of white-washed houses which rose behind the harbour. All the men – except for Babel – looked eagerly for a red wooden dolphin which a fisherman had told them marked a brothel called 'Elena's'.

The Jew was the first to spot the weathered sign. The men crowded anxiously around the brothel's flame-red door as Vesuvio banged its tarnished brass knocker.

A small wooden slat opened in the door. An eye painted with green and black grease peered out at them.

Vesuvio jangled a leather pouch of coins in front of the open slat and announced, 'I sail from Campania, mistress. I have eight men in need of wine, food, and companionship!'

The garishly painted eye continued to study Vesuvio through the slat.

Vesuvio leaned closer to the door and explained, 'We look unclean and wily, I know. But be considerate, mistress. I am willing to pay in advance for eight of your best women.'

A coarse voice answered, 'No slaves allowed here.'

'Slaves?' Vesuvio laughed and jangled the pouch again. He asked, 'Would slaves have enough money to spend in Rhode's most splendid establishment, mistress? These men are sailors! Lonely and thirsty sailors! Good men in need of a soft shoulder to lay their weary heads upon. And we have good money to pay for the best women you can offer. Listen!' He jangled the pouch again.

The painted eye disappeared from view. The slat slammed shut. The bolts rattled on the other side of the flame-red door. The door opened. And Vesuvio stood facing an obese woman wearing a yellow wig which towered over her brightly painted face. She wore a brilliant green *stola* and held her fleshy pink arms folded across her enormous breasts. She stood solidly in the threshold and surveyed the men.

Vesuvio addressed the fat woman as if he were speaking to the grandest matriarch in Rome. He asked, 'Are we honoured by meeting Mistress Elena herself?'

The painted fat lady twitched her pug nose.

'My name is Macrinus,' Vesuvio announced in a flourish of courtliness. 'It is a great surprise for me to meet a lady of such apparent breeding in a remote spot like this.'

The fat woman narrowed her painted eyes. She grunted in a deep voice, 'I am Elena.'

'Greetings, *domina*,' Vesuvio said, bowing to the fat bordello-keeper.

Elena did not budge from the threshold. She asked suspiciously, 'You say you come from Campania? From where did you sail, Roman? From Ostia?'

'Brundisium, *domina*. Our last stop was in Piraeus.'

Elena puckered her carmined lips. She dryly announced, 'But the harbour of Piraeus is closed. No ship has stopped here from Piraeus for well over a week!' Her eyes rounded like large eggs centred with brown yolks.

Vesuvio said, 'But we did not sail from the Piraeus harbour *domina*. We left Greece from a spot farther down the coast.' He winked at her, adding, 'We also think of business.'

Elena glanced at Vesuvio's money pouch, saying, 'Your manner is too refined for you to be that scoundrel thief called . . . Charon.'

'Charon?' Vesuvio asked.

Elena suddenly erupted. 'Charon and the Priests at Piraeus! They'll be the ruination of me! The priests prevent ships from sailing out of Piraeus. And that thief, Charon, keeps Eastern travellers from sailing through the River Styx!'

Vesuvio knew the area which she meant by the 'River

Styx'. The *Rhea* would be entering those waters tomorrow. But he had not heard of a thief plaguing that region. He asked, 'There is a thief called "Charon" in the River Styx? A man named after the mythical ferryman which carries men's souls to the netherworld?'

'There indeed is a man called Charon on the River Styx! But he is no ferryman! The Charon we all fear is a robber and a thief! Between him and the Imperial priests in Piraeus we are near ruin here on Rhodes. Men have gone to hunt that scoundrel, Charon. But to no avail. A council has even sent a *pharmakos* there. They tied the *pharmakos* to a wooden raft and cast him off into the River Styx. But still we are plagued by this Charon and his desperate band of outlaws!'

Vesuvio did not understand. He asked, 'A "*pharmakos*"?'

'A scapegoat!' Elena explained. 'If you are a stranger here, you would not know our customs. Greeks send a person from a city or a town to be a scapegoat for their misfortunes. But as we Greeks are all very generous people, the scapegoat is always the most ugly, the least intelligent person in a community!'

Elena stood aside. She beckoned Vesuvio and the men into the courtyard, saying, 'Enter! I believe you are foreigners. Also, why should I starve? Charon has already cost me enough money. Why should I be suspicious of every unshaven stranger who arrives at my door with a stiff rod poking out between his legs?'

She locked and barred the flame-red door behind the last man to enter and suddenly grunted, 'I count nine men, Roman. You told me you wanted *eight* women. Who's not having pleasure? I'll tell you now, I keep no boys here.'

'We do not wish boys!' Vesuvio quickly assured her.

'Two men sharing the same woman will cost you no less,' Elena argued, wiggling her pudgy pink fingers towards Vesuvio's money pouch.

Vesuvio emptied the coins into her hands whilst he looked

over her shoulder to study a group of prostitutes lying on divans placed around a shallow blue pool. He saw a diverse collection of women of various nationalities and ages. Some women had light skin like Macedonians. Others were dark like Cretans. Also, many women were lowering their *stolae* to show themselves to the male customers.

Elena clapped her hands for a slave to bring wine to her customers. She next shouted for the reclining prostitutes to move themselves from the divans.

Vesuvio seized Babel by the arm and whispered, 'Stay close to me. Wait until the others choose their women.'

Babel looked down at his sandals and nervously confessed, 'I do not know, *domine*, if I will be able . . .'

'Have no fear,' Vesuvio interrupted. He lifted two tin goblets of wine from a tray being offered to them by a slave. He held one goblet to Babel, saying, 'Drink this and trust me.'

The sound of a lyre now drifted across the courtyard. Elena was beginning to command the women to parade themselves in front of the men. Some prostitutes started combing their fingers back through their manes of glistening black hair. Young girls lifted their *chitons* to exhibit the smoothness of their torsos to the men. Older women cupped their breasts in their hands and proudly exhibited them like cheese loaves at a fair. The oarsmen shouted their approval.

* * *

Vesuvio chose a prostitute called Asiatica. She had an Oriental's honey-coloured skin but her eyes were round and blue. Her breasts were pendulous like a Sicilian woman and her hips youthfully rounded like a Greek girl. She wore her black hair in a multitude of plaits with yellow ribbons braided into each twist.

Asiatica closed the door to a small room above the courtyard and slowly began to untie the sashes on her filmy gown of Cosian weave as she studied Vesuvio and Babel standing side-by-side inside the plank door.

Dropping the garment to the floor, Asiatica stepped from it and said with a smile, 'I knew when I woke this morning that today would bring me riches!'

She reached to feel Vesuvio's yellow hair, saying, 'Gold-' She gently tousled Babel's black curls, praising, '-and onyx.'

Vesuvio knew that he had made a fine choice. He had looked for a woman in the collection of prostitutes who might be willing to lay with two men. But many women would be too brazen. Would dampen a man's sexual desires.

He had felt no burning urge to make love but the sight of Asiatica's rosy nipples spreading up her rich brown breasts made his penis harden inside his cincture. He had not lain with a woman since Despo in Athens but now the blood surged to the crown of his manhood as he gazed at the flatness of Asiatica's stomach descending to a furry clump between her legs.

He quickly lifted his tunic over his head and tossed it onto a wooden stool. He politely warned, 'We have bathed only in sea water for the last three days.'

'I love the sea!' Asiatica assured him as she fell to the floor to untie his sandal thongs. She leaned her face forward to sniff the soft yellow down growing on his thighs. She whispered as she rubbed her ribboned hair against him, 'I especially love the *smell* of the sea!'

Babel remained alongside the closed door. He nervously observed Asiatica deftly unwrapping the cincture from Vesuvio's groin. His eyes widened when he saw Vesuvio's manhood spring from the cloth.

Vesuvio reached down and lifted Asiatica from her kneeling position. He began to fondle her breasts and groaned with satisfaction as she pressed her furry mid-section up and down his leg.

Asiatica next rose to the tips of her toes and, nibbling at

Vesuvio's ear, she whispered, 'Your pretty young friend? Is he bashful?'

'This is his first time to be with a woman,' Vesuvio quietly answered. 'Ignore him for the moment.'

Asiatica understood. She wrapped her smooth arms around Vesuvio's neck and promised, 'We shall show him how a man and woman make love.'

Vesuvio fell onto the linen-covered pallet with Asiatica in his arms. He pressed his mouth to hers and tasted a minted sweetness. She wrapped her legs around his thighs and wriggled her patch against his phallus which now jutted up between their naked bodies.

Asiatica rolled playfully across the pallet with Vesuvio, soon rising to drag her breasts across his face. She brushed her furry patch on the caps of his muscled shoulders. She tousled his tangle of yellow curls and – suddenly – she dived down between Vesuvio's thighs and gobbled at his scrotum. She stretched her lips to encase both testicles in her mouth.

Still ignoring Babel standing in the corner of the room, Vesuvio groaned as he felt Asiatica's warm mouth soon encircle his hardened phallus.

Asiatica now lay with her head pointing toward Vesuvio's feet, her legs in front of his face. He pulled her legs closer toward his shoulders. He locked his arms around her knees and clamped his mouth over her pubic hairs, darting his tongue to lick her perfumed vagina.

Without warning, Asiatica turned herself again on the pallet. She kissed Vesuvio, exchanging the taste of his penis clinging to her tongue for the sweetness of her vagina flavouring his mouth.

They lay embracing tightly in a clench, rubbing their tongues against one another's lips, probing the crevices of their mouths. Vesuvio finally began to push his penis into her female slit.

Asiatica pulled back from Vesuvio and grabbed the middle of his phallus with her clenched fist. She squatted over it and teased her moist vaginal lips on his swollen crown. She gyrated as Vesuvio inserted the first inches of its thickness into her. She closed her eyes, smiling, beginning to gasp and roll her shoulders in ecstasy.

Vesuvio suspected that the prostitute's groans and provocative movements were the stock responses of her profession. But he lay back on the pallet with his arms clasped behind his neck and watched her sinking his manhood deeper into her wiry-haired lips.

Asiatica's warmth continued to envelop him. Her vagina moved to grip him like a silken glove. Vesuvio looked from the corner of his eye. He saw Babel shedding his tunic. The young man was moving from his place by the door to come closer to the pallet.

Asiatica worked herself faster on Vesuvio's reclining body. She fondled her own pink nipples now as she twisted herself on his standing manhood. She tossed back her head, groaning, then noticed Babel standing alongside her.

Babel's penis now jutted from his groin, a phallus almost equal in size to Vesuvio's. Asiatica greedly grabbed for it. She first wet it with her tongue. She licked the definition of its purple crown. She finally enclosed her mouth around the entire head of the phallus whilst she still squatted on Vesuvio and continued to pump herself.

Vesuvio watched with amusement as Babel moved his large hands to fondle Asiatica's breasts. The boy was beginning to drive his hips in more rapid movements into her mouth. He was at last enjoying himself.

But fearing that Babel might explode his excitement down the woman's throat, Vesuvio raised himself from the pallet. He moved to lay Asiatica on her side whilst he continued to drive into her.

The gifted prostitute again understood. She beckoned for Babel to lay on the pallet behind her. She whispered, 'Lie back of me, beauty. Pretend that you are going to make love to a boy. But enter me where your friend now has lodged himself. Let me see if I can accommodate both of you. You are friends. Why not?'

Asiatica lay on her side facing Vesuvio whilst Babel obediently positioned himself on the pallet behind her. She winked playfully at Vesuvio as Babel clumsily jabbed the crown of his penis toward the roots of Vesuvio's manhood visible from the glistening slit.

Asiatica moved to assist Babel, firmly grabbing onto his hard penis and pushing it toward Vesuvio's. She next clasped Babel's large hands and pressed them over her breasts. She coaxed, 'Now ease yourself alongside your golden friend . . . Yes, like that . . . Yes, let me feel you inch inside me with your friend . . . Yes, I can now feel both of you . . . Stop! For a moment! Please! Stop! Do not move! Not for a moment . . .'

The three remained motionless on the pallet. Asiatica lay on her side facing Vesuvio. He held her legs spread akimbo.

Slowly, she again began to expand and squeeze her muscles. She gently ordered, 'Do not move, Roman. Let your young friend plumb his tool deeper into me. Let him reach the same depth as you . . .'

Babel quickly assumed faster drives. His slim hips increased their rhythm. A smile spread across his face as determination built in his dark brown eyes.

Finally, Vesuvio moved again, plunging his manhood into Asiatica's wetness alongside Babel, the two phalluses pressed tightly against one another in the moist grip of the prostitute's warm womanhood.

Vesuvio push, push, pushed his penis alongside that of Babel's. He felt as if the two phalluses were one, as if Asiatica were cohesing their veins, their skin cresting their excitement into one organ of pleasure.

He next saw a smile spread across Babel's face. The dark-haired boy was beginning to enjoy his first female.

Vesuvio nodded to the prostitute and pulled himself from her warm grip.

Babel stopped his movements. He stared quizzically at Vesuvio.

But Asiatica had understood the signal. She continued working herself on Babel's penis, raising one leg to pull him into the place where Vesuvio had been lying upon the pallet. She reached for the copper-coloured paps on the boy's smooth chest and gently pinched them. She wrapped her legs around his curved buttocks to pull him even closer towards her.

Vesuvio stood alongside the pallet until he finally saw that Babel was once again enjoying his first female conquest. He silently gathered his tunic from the wooden stool and picked up his cincture and sandals from the floor. He dressed himself and, looking one last time toward the pallet, he saw Asiatica wink at him over Babel's shoulder. He gently shut the plank door.

* * *

Vesuvio walked down the stone steps to the courtyard feeling assured that Babel no longer posed a threat aboard the *Rhea*. He hoped that he had averted one problem and decided that his time now might be well spent learning what facts he could about the next section of his journey.

Vesuvio had enjoyed the sexual respite with artful Asiatica but he asked himself what was sexual gratification compared to love? Nothing. He had a mission to complete, a son waiting at home in Italy, an estate busy with slaves and tenant farmers, a life to re-establish as a father, husband, and *padrone*.

His manhood now relaxed inside his cincture as he decided to have a conversation with the bordello's mistress. He remembered Elena talking about a thief called Charon who plagued the stretch of Greek islands through which the *Rhea* soon had to pass. He had to eke out all the information he could from everybody he met. The words of a brothel-keeper might insure him going one step closer to . . . *Miranda, you know now that I would go to the end of the world for you.*

17

Vesuvio departed from Rhodes before the island's fishermen climbed into their boats to begin their night of casting nets. The oarsmen jubilantly sang bawdy songs as they rowed across a sea lit by a sun slowly turning from gold to orange. They disregarded the fact that the winds were fading.

Everyone's mood had lightened. But the most visible change was in Babel. He told and retold his stories about lusty Asiatica, bragging about her prodigious appetite until the other oarsmen finally grew bored with the stories of his sexual conquest – and prowess – and they told him to shut his mouth.

The men ate supper aboard the *Rhea*. The winds still did not rise as they resumed pulling upon the oars. Night soon enshrouded the sea. The moon formed a luminescent globe in the blue-black sky and clouds began to spread across the sky twinkling with stars.

The clouds soon became fog. Vesuvio called a second recess for the men to doze inside the gently rocking boat. He himself remained awake and wondered when the winds would lift and the fog would disappear. But the fog grew thicker and Vesuvio awoke his men when he gauged that morning was nearing.

The oarsmen sleepily began to dip the wooden blades into the water, cutting the wrinkled sea like slowly descending knives. They propelled the *Rhea* deeper and deeper into the density of what Vesuvio hoped was no more than a morning mist peculiar to this area.

A stillness hung over the sea as the *Rhea* inched its way through the thick white haze which drifted down from the rocky boulders of what Vesuvio guessed must now be the Lycian shoreline. The winds still had not risen. Vesuvio gave the men orders to row gently. He feared for rocky shoals or hidden sandbars.

A strange bellow suddenly cut through the enshrouding mist. The Jew lowered his oar and whispered, 'Listen!'

Momentarily, the eight men remained frozen on their benches. They held the oars motionless in the locks and listened closely to hear the sound. They only heard the tide gently washing against the *Rhea*'s wooden hull.

'I heard a horn,' the Jew whispered.

'I heard it, too,' murmured the Spartan. 'But it was more like a . . . shout.'

The Athenian grumbled, 'A horn? A shout? Who would be shouting out in this fog?' He reached to regrip his oar and said, 'You're both crazy.'

'Shhh,' Vesuvio cautioned, gesturing for the men to fall silent. He had spotted a light through the blanket of fog.

Babel gasped, 'I see a torch!'

Vesuvio studied a smudge of yellow brightness in the haze. He saw that it was an open flame blazing in the foggy darkness. He said, 'The flare is stronger and higher than a torch.'

The tide carried the *Rhea* closer to the flickering light. The Jew whispered, 'It's a pot of burning oil.'

Babel gasped, 'No! It's the . . . *pharmakos*!'

The *Rhea* was now almost side-by-side with a small wooden raft bobbing in the sea. Vesuvio and all the men now clearly saw a large fire soaring from an iron cresset attached to the wooden raft.

Babel said in a guarded voice, 'That must be a flame to attract attention to the . . . scapegoat! The bordello mistress told us about him. How he's sent here to absorb all bad luck.'

Vesuvio and the oarsmen sat silently as they drifted

alongside the *pharmakos*. They stared soberly at the body of a man chained to the wooden raft. He was not an old man but the soiled rags which covered his frail body made it impossible to tell his age.

The scapegoat's hair was grey and tied with shreds of wool. His face was encrusted with warts and sores. His spindly legs were bound together with ropes which were pegged to the wooden raft.

The scapegoat lay on his side, giggling to himself, his mirth interspersed with songs which he trilled like a field bird. He slobbered glistening webs of saliva down his chin and ignored the *Rhea* drifting past him.

'He's a . . . simpleton,' murmured Babel.

Vesuvio's attention was diverted from the pathetic sight of the scapegoat when he again heard a sound cutting through the fog. He now definitely recognised the sound as the nearby blast from a conch trumpet.

* * *

'A scapegoat is supposed to attract all evilness,' Babel whispered as the *Rhea* drifted with the current past the bobbing raft.

'Let's hope he keeps the evilness,' the Gaul said flippantly, looking at the murky greyness lying ahead of them.

The Jew began, 'What was the name of the thief who . . .'

'Shhh,' Vesuvio again cautioned. He had seen another shape rising out of the water a short distance ahead of them. He could not yet tell if the shape was a towering cliff or a rocky monolith jutting from the ebbing sea.

The current carried the *Rhea* farther away from the scape-goat's raft. Vesuvio was beginning to wonder if he was actually seeing the outline of a long ship. Was the shape a double-masted galley equipped with a single bank of oars which protruded from its narrow hull?

The blast came louder.

Vesuvio again recognised the sound as the blast of a conch trumpet. It had come from the precipitous shoreline.

He turned his head to look in the direction from which the noise had come and saw murky shapes of small boats emerging from the fog to surround the *Rhea*.

'Dive! Dive overboard!' he suddenly ordered as he fell backwards into the water and the hiss of arrows began surrounding the *Rhea*.

* * *

Vesuvio surfaced in the sea a few yards from the *Rhea* and, shaking the water from his eyes, he saw that not all of his men had heeded his warning quickly enough. He spotted three bodies lying half-in, half-out of the open boat. Five arrows protruded from the Egyptian's back. Two arrows pierced the Dacian's throat. The Gaul lay bleeding with arrow shafts prickling from his head and chest and legs.

The small boats crept farther out of the fog and closed their circle around the *Rhea*. A man dressed in animal pelts jumped from his skiff to board the *Rhea*. He held a spear in one hand and a leather whip coiled from his thick black leather belt.

Vesuvio looked at the man and then glanced anxiously back at the long shape which he had earlier detected in the distance. He saw that it was indeed a low-built galley, a dark vessel designed in the Egyptian manner. A sober group of archers lined its deck with their arrows trained upon the *Rhea*.

The first oarsmen now began emerging from the sea around Vesuvio. The Jew bobbed to the surface. Babel appeared. Next the Spartan and the Athenian grabbed for support on the *Rhea's* oars.

'We are fishermen!' Vesuvio shouted as he moved to pull himself aboard the boat. 'You will find nothing of value . . .'

The man in the animal pelts drove his sandal into Vesuvio's face, sending him back into the water.

Vesuvio surfaced in the ebbing sea. His mouth tasted of blood. He saw more men jumping from the surrounding skiffs to board the *Rhea*. They began slashing long knives at the canvas bags stashed in the aft-pit.

'What booty's there?' a deep-chested voice shouted from the distant galley.

Vesuvio suspected who the men were. What man shouted to them. He was Charon. These men in skiffs were his band of thieves. Vesuvio hovered in the water between the oar blades and watched the thieves slashing and ripping at the food bundles.

'By Mercury!' the distant voice boomed through the fog. 'What booty have you men found there?'

'They claim they are fishermen,' answered the thief in animal pelts. 'But I see no nets. No floats. No lines. No signs of . . . Ah! What's this?'

Falling to his knees in the *Rhea*'s aft-pit, the thief stabbed his blade at a hemp bag which Vesuvio had not yet opened for food.

Digging deeper into the bag, the thief began to laugh. He shouted through the fog, 'Gold, Charon! More gold than any fishermen could ever dream to own!'

'Damn you, Rugo!' Charon called back across the foggy water. 'What kind of gold? Is it coins? Goblets? Jewellery?'

The thief named Rugo rose to his knees in the tilting boat. He held a yellow disc between his thumb and forefinger, answering, 'Gold coins minted to the goddess . . . Diana!'

'Diana!' Charon echoed. 'That's temple gold! These men aren't fishermen! They're temple thieves!'

Babel, the Athenian, the Spartan, the Jew, and the Syrian clung to the oar blades on both sides of Vesuvio and looked quizzically at him.

Vesuvio began to shake his head. He called, 'No! You must be wrong! We have no . . . gold! No gold from temples! Not any kind of gold!'

The thief named Rugo pulled the leather whip from his

belt and flailed it toward Vesuvio. The tip sharply cracked as he shouted, 'Silence, pig!'

He turned to his fellow thieves in the other skiffs and ordered, 'Drag in what's left of this sorry-looking lot. Take them aboard the *Cerberus*. Set fire to this boat. If the pigs try to escape, stab them with your lances.'

'Bring me the gold,' Charon demanded from his galley. 'Bring me the temple gold!'

18

Charon's galley was called the *Cerberus;* the cabin was built in the pointed prow. The air inside the low-ceilinged cabin stank from oil smoking in clay lamps. Musty animal skins covered both the floor and the walls. The furnishings were brass-plated chests and stools made from iron rods and tooled leather.

Vesuvio raised himself from a goatskin rug inside the galley's cabin and saw a bearded man leering at him. He struggled to raise himself higher from the floor, demanding, 'My oarsmen? What have you done with them?'

The bearded man leered at Vesuvio, saying, 'So you are the leader. I thought so. But now you speak Latin!'

Vesuvio studied the greasy-haired man, his broken nose, his bloodshot eyes, lips coated with grease, and animal hide clothing crudely sewn with leather cords. He blurted, 'You are Charon!'

The thief threw back his head and laughed. His hirsute chest expanded and Vesuvio recoiled from the foul stench of his breath.

Charon roared, 'And you must be a Roman! Have you heard of "Charon" all the way to Rome?'

'Every child knows of Charon,' Vesuvio said contemptuously. 'But the mythical ferryman we know does not kill innocent men.' He remembered the bodies of the Egyptian, the Gaul, and the Dacian lying over the side of the *Rhea* with arrows shot into them.

Charon pulled back his hand to strike Vesuvio and said, 'You talk proud, Roman. Too proud for a thief who steals gold from Roman Temples!'

Vesuvio protested, 'I know nothing about temple gold!'

Charon turned away from him and snatched up a gold coin from a leather stool. He said, 'These coins were minted in Athens. In the Temple of Diana. Is that the only temple you robbed? Come? Do not be afraid to confess to me? The Romans have a price on my head, too.'

Vesuvio insisted, 'This is the first time I have ever seen those coins.'

Charon examined the yellow disc, saying, 'You must be very brave or very, very stupid. This thievery can condemn you for a life in slavery, Roman.'

'Listen to me,' Vesuvio insisted, trying to lift himself again from the goatskin. 'Listen to my story.'

Charon glared at him. 'Story? What do I care for stories? I am only interested in what suits me! One is gold. And the other is . . . you.' He dropped the coin back onto the leather stool and studied the wet clothing clinging to Vesuvio's body. His greasy lips spread into a smirk.

Vesuvio began, 'You'll get no ransom for me . . .'

'Ransom? Who's talking about ransom, Roman? I'll collect money for you if I decide to sell you! But I'll only sell you when I'm ready.'

Charon continued to study Vesuvio's recumbent body, explaining with the smirk still on his face, 'I could not have found you at a better time, blond Roman. It is as if the gods had sent you to me when I needed you. You see, three of my wives are pregnant. And three or four women in my camp are suffering from their bleeding periods. I have heated passions but who wants to touch unclean women? Not me! By the gods, not me! And all the other whores in my camp are riddled with the pox or their holes are stretched so wide that your Emperor Trajan could march his accursed army through their legs!'

The words at first bewildered Vesuvio. He had forgotten how many uneducated Greek and Roman men believed that women brought bad luck during their menstrual periods, and that pregnant females were always avoided.

Still studying Vesuvio's body, Charon continued, 'Many of the men in my camp are as useless as the whores. Their holes are stretched as wide as craters. So you see, golden-haired Roman, what I need is a new . . . filly! And I shall enjoy turning a brawny stallion like you into my slut.'

Vesuvio stared up at the fur-covered giant. He clenched his fist to defend himself as he now clearly understood what Charon intended to do with him.

Throwing back his head, Charon bellowed, 'Rugo! Leave your new boy and come in here! Bring me some leather cords!'

Vesuvio saw that he was trapped, that he would be overpowered to submit to this thief's perverse appetites. His mind began to turn with frantic plans of escape.

Charon looked at him, saying, 'My captain is called Rugo. He is pleased with the doxy boy with black curls you travel with, Roman. Rugo has him for his own whore and I have you . . .'

Withdrawing a dagger from a leather studded scabbard hanging from his belt, Charon leaned over Vesuvio and warned, 'You stay put on your furry bed, filly whore, and do not move.'

His bloodshot eyes continued staring at Vesuvio as he reached with his other hand to dig amongst the animal skins clumped over his bulging groin.

Vesuvio defiantly held Charon's stare; he did not know what he was going to do. He now clearly understood who had survived from the attack in the fog and who had been taken prisoner here aboard the *Cerberus*. All eight oarsmen had lost their freedom in one way or another – either killed or captured by the thieves. He was amongst them. Charon intended to treat him as a slave, too, to debase him in any way which pleased him.

Vesuvio's hopes for escape, an unformed plan by which he could survive these threats of enslavement and emasculation, were disrupted by the thud of footsteps coming into Charon's cabin.

*   *   *

Charon stood with his captain, Rugo, and two other thieves a short time later around Vesuvio's naked body pegged facedown into a spread-eagle position on the cabin floor.

Charon ordered, 'Bring me a whip. Not the Thracian whip. Bring me my quirt, Rugo. A good little quirt to redden the Roman's pretty buttocks with. To warm him up before . . .'

Rubbing his groin, Charon said, 'Seeing a light-haired man with his buttocks tensed like this puts iron in my pizzle. I'll drive into this Roman until I'll have him *begging* for my spunk!'

Rugo moved to obey his master's orders whilst Charon lowered the pelts knotted between his legs. He freed his genitals, pulling down a greasy penis which stuck with sweat to his pendulous scrotum.

Vesuvio lay with his face pressed against the floor. He kept turning his head in opposite directions when he heard Charon's clomping footsteps approaching his face.

'Indeed,' Charon said as he stood appraising Vesuvio's muscular shoulders, back, and thighs. 'A fine price I would get for a man set-up like this one. This temple thief is indeed a fine specimen of manhood. But he won't leave this ship a man. I'll turn this blond stallion into my filly. My Roman . . . bitch whore!'

Rugo returned to the cabin and handed Charon the short leather-braided quirt. Charon snatched it from his hand and immediately swung it against the smooth skin of Vesuvio's naked buttocks.

'Look!' he called as he stood back to see the first welts rising on Vesuvio's nakedness. 'See how the Roman flinches.

But no! He does not scream; He is a real man for me to enjoy!'

Charon next knelt behind Vesuvio's bare legs, cupping his fist around the dark foreskin of his thick penis whilst he began roughly prodding the butt of the leather quirt into Vesuvio's orifice. He said, 'I'll have to work open this stallion. His hole is too tight to take the size of me. He comes virgin to Charon. A real tight virgin filly.'

Vesuvio tried not to think. He tried not to listen to Charon's abusive words. He told himself that he would survive this humiliation. That it was only a disgusting nightmare. He thought of Miranda, his son, his responsibilities as a *padrone* and master to the oarsmen who had not yet been killed by these dissolute thieves.

A ruckus on deck suddenly attracted Charon's and the thieves' attention. They looked toward the leather curtain which separated the cabin from the deck. They heard the sound of scuffling.

Vesuvio raised his head to see Babel trying to push his way into the Charon's cabin. Two guards in leather skullcaps struggled to hold back the young boy.

Babel fought them, shouting, 'Leave me alone, you dirty scum! And leave my master alone!'

'Your master?' Charon roared. 'This Roman is my *slave*!' He turned to Rugo, ordering, 'Get your doxy boy out of here!'

Babel continued to fight the men holding his arms. He shouted, 'My master is more of a man than all of you. Leave him alone you ugly . . . pigs!'

'Rugo!' Charon boomed. 'Shut that whining whelp's mouth.'

'Scum of the sea!' Babel persisted.

Charon jumped from the floor and, jerking his knife from its scabbard, he thrust the rusty blade toward Babel's stomach. He pulled out the blade and rammed it into Babel's chest. He repeated the motion, stabbing Babel in the chest and stomach and ribs until the young boy collapsed into the arms of the men who held him. His intestines hung in red and yellow swags from his rended stomach.

Charon grabbed for the boy's head by the hair and, wiping the blood from his knife in Babel's mop of black curls, he snarled at Rugo, 'You bring one more brat like that aboard my ship and it's you who gets the blade.'

Rugo was not listening to Charon's warning. He gaped in disbelief at Babel's body hanging from the arms of the two guards. He whined in a childlike voice, 'You've killed my . . . whore.'

'Yes!' Charon said, nodding his head. 'I killed your stinking whore. And the next time it'll be *you*.'

Rugo kept shaking his head. 'But now I don't have my own . . . whore.'

'What do I care?' Charon asked, motioning for the guards to drag Babel's body from the cabin. 'Get him out of here. Wipe up that bloody mess. It stinks. It offends my nostrils!'

Rugo persisted, 'But you promised me I could have my own whore, Charon . . .'

'Silence, scum!'

Then, angrily mumbling to himself, Charon knelt down alongside Vesuvio's naked body, saying, 'You see how I treat fillies who don't obey me, Roman.'

Vesuvio held his eyes shut. He tried to obliterate the image of Babel's body spilling its intestines. His ears still rang with the sound of Charon's blade cutting through tissue, skin, and bone.

He thought how this had to be a nightmare. Babel could not be dead. He could not believe the irony that Babel died in an attempt to save his masculine honour. He remembered how he had been worried about peace aboard the *Rhea*. He had stopped in Rhodes to prevent his oarsmen from sodomising young Babel. He himself had chosen the comely woman, Asiatica, for Babel to enjoy but now Babel had died trying to save him from . . .

A sharp pain cutting into Vesuvio's anus suddenly obliterated all thoughts. He next felt Charon's fur covered body lie down on top of his naked back. The thief's hot breath filled his ears as he spoke profanties to him. The pain cut deeper between Vesuvio's legs. Charon grabbed him by the blond hair for support as he drove harder to deepen his phallus into Vesuvio's anus. Charon started laughing, talking more profanely to Vesuvio, and Vesuvio remembered no more.

19

Vesuvio lost count of the days. He did not know his whereabouts. He wondered who hc was, the gender to which he had been born; he retained no memory of his home, nor the purpose for which he had left it.

The rare moments in which he did regain consciousness, he awoke in a dark world of squalor. He vaguely recognised the thieves' galley. He heard himself being called abusive names. He did not fight the numbness spreading over his brain.

Charon's voice taunted Vesuvio at the outstart of his feverish nightmare. He called him a 'filly', a 'cow', an 'ewe', and every description of a female prostitute. The chief next began deriding Vesuvio for losing the strength of his manhood and all muscular control.

Vesuvio's buttocks had been smote until they were as raw as fresh meat. His legs had been spread so wide apart until he felt as if his groin would crack. His paps were mutilated by Charon's rough fingers until he believed they were afire and fluid would soon begin dripping from them. His first relief from this torture came when he finally heard Charon say that he had grown tired of his Roman 'slut'.

Vesuvio was dragged naked from the cabin and tied onto the deck. He felt the chill of the biting sea air. A hideous pain again began to cut into his buttocks. His head was yanked back by his hair and a continuous succession of phalluses were pressed toward his mouth. He was often slapped for not taking the phalluses into his throat and then punished for not taking them properly.

Vesuvio did not know how many days – or nights – he

suffered these degradations. Gruff voices continued to call him crude names and he continued to drift farther away from the robust male he had once been, a man not even good enough for Charon.

*   *   *

The deck of the *Cerberus* stopped heaving. Vesuvio did not at first know if he was in fever and was imagining that the galley had anchored. He lost consciousness and awoke on what he believed to be a cold dirt floor. He felt hands prodding him. But they were not the large rough hands of men. He began to recognise the sound of new voices, too. They were the voices of women.

'Roman?' a woman's voice whispered into Vesuvio's ear. He heard the sound of feminine giggling encircle him. He felt cold slim fingers prodding the orifice between his buttocks.

'Look!' another woman's voice said. 'The Roman bleeds like us! He is unclean, too!'

'Oh, Charon must have tired of him,' said a third woman. 'The Roman stud is unclean. Like a woman with blood each month.'

'Woe the plight of females!'

The women's laughter spread at the idea of Vesuvio being one of them.

He eventually heard a soft voice say, 'He must have been a handsome man.'

'Do not get excited, Silia. Your belly is near bursting with a child. This stud will do you no good even if his pizzle could get hard. But look! See how limp he hangs.'

The women turned Vesuvio over onto his back onto the dirt floor of their hut. He felt their hands fondle his groin.

Another woman's voice said, 'He can't even get hard.'

'Why don't you suck him, Ulia?'

Vesuvio felt a wet mouth on his phallus. He wretched to vomit but his stomach contained no food to spill. His chest felt as if it threatened to collapse. His ribs cut into his sides.

The women's laughter grew louder in the circle they formed around him. A shrill voice said, 'This corpse is no good to any of us! Not to us pregnant women – or to you women having your bleeding periods. We are all useless to a good man. Even this . . . catamite with yellow hair!'

'Do you think this bleeding catamite will be sold in Antioch?'

'Fool? What price would Charon get for a worn-out man like this? The poor thing could not even get buggered in Antioch's Grove of Daphne!'

Another voice argued, 'But the smallest coin would be more than Charon is getting for him here. When Charon finishes with a man, he gives him to his sailors. Now that they have got what they wanted from this poor bugger . . .'

'The sailors finished him good, too, by the sight of him.'

Vesuvio did not know how long he listened to these scornful words. He eventually tried to speak but his tongue was thick with fever.

'You are in the women's hut,' one female explained. 'This is the camp of Charon the thief. The camp lies in the foothills of Lycia.'

'But the camp will not be here for long,' said another woman. 'Those of us women and girls who cannot be moved further inland will be taken to Antioch and sold to a slave house. Barren women. Battered women. Worthless girls and . . . broken-down sodomites like you!'

'Sold . . .' Vesuvio wanted to speak. To beg for information

'Try to suck him again, Ulia. His pizzle is big. You like to chew on a nice soft big pizzle . . .'

A woman interrupted in Greek, *'Ali psihomahovn, ge ali gavlomahovn.'*

Vesuvio understood the words. The woman had considerately said, 'Whilst some people are dying, others are still thinking about having sex.'

Vesuvio knew that the Greek woman meant that he was dying. He no longer cared. Not about sex, nor the women, nor himself.

20

Despo had gone again tonight to the Elevasian mountain range north of Piraeus to learn from the prophet in the cavern if the plan to divert Vesuvio in the River Styx had succeeded. Vesuvio had been gone from Piraeus for three weeks now and tonight Despo brought a pouchful of drachm *with her to the cave to learn from the prophet if Vesuvio had been prevented from following her sister, Miranda, across the deserts of Arabia to Caldea.*

The hermaphrodite sat cross-legged in the opening of the cavern as Despo fell to her knees in front of him. She eagerly began to explain the reason of her visit to him tonight. He suddenly interrupted her.

'We are all fools,' he shrilled, toying with the ragged foreskin of his penis. 'I am a fool! You are a fool! The moon is foolish not to be golden like the sun!'

Despo answered reverently, 'To be compared to a creature so wise as you, learned seer . . .'

'Wise?' the hermaphrodite's breasts shook as he laughed at her. 'Wise, you say, foolish woman? Look at me and see if we are wise!'

The prophet unbent his knees and leaned onto his back. He spread open his spindly legs and reached to feel his anus with the tips of his long pointed fingernails. He grunted to strain his muscles and, suddenly, a golden coin popped from the rosy pinkness of his anus.

He snatch the coin from the ground and held it in front of Despo's eyes. He said, 'You left a coin for me at your last visit, woman. You left a possession of . . . yours! I tasted it.

Savoured it in my body. And now listen to what I learned. . . .'

Bending forward, the hermophrodite idly played with his necklace of fingernail parings, locks of hair, and bits of egg shell. He guardedly whispered to Despo, 'You keep asking me about a testament. Your husband's last testament which sets in a temple within the Acropolis. A testament not yet read by you!'

Despo anxiously studied him. The moment at last had come to learn the truth about what was written in Menecrates's will.

'You have been begging me for details about travelling to the city of Rome with a horse god. I foresee you going to Rome, Woman. But the horse god will not carry you to the Imperial City. Your husband's testament will be your transportation.'

Despo began to shake her head, saying, 'No, this cannot be true. My husband did not know that Cleomenes and I planned to go to Rome. How can his testament send us there if he had no idea . . .'

'Fool! The plans of fools are often bettered by the wisdom of dead men!'

'What does the testament say?' Despo impatiently demanded. 'I will pay you much gold if you tell me that now!'

'Much gold?' the hermaphrodite repeated with amusement. 'It is better if you forget gold and take a knife . . . a lance . . . a gladiator's blade . . . or even a spade to the Rome which you will see, foolish wife.'

'But you mentioned murex dye? The purple colour of Imperial robes.'

'Be no fool to think that your Rome does not like a spectacle!'

'My Rome? What spectacle?'

The hermaphrodite recrossed his legs. His eyes began to roll back into their sockets. And, then as a stream of urine began to pass from his penis and form a puddle on the ground, Despo continued to stare at him. Was he warning her about some future danger? What spectacle did he mean? Why had he mentioned a knife? A gladiator's blade? Or a . . . spade?

The urine gushed faster from the hermaphrodite's penis, running toward Despo's knee, a sign which told her that her interview had finished at the Cavern of the Idiot.

BOOK FOUR

ANTIOCH – QUEEN OF THE EAST

21

The bright Syrian sun poured through the open doorway of a stable behind the Palace of the Dates in the eastern city of Antioch. A young girl knelt in the shaft of sunlight and looked at Vesuvio's unconscious body lying upon a bed of clean straw made upon the stable floor. An old man with long white hair stood behind the pretty girl. He was dressed in a wide-sleeved robe worn by the patriarchs of Jewish households in the province of Syria. His name was Nicodemus ben Seth, gem merchant and owner of the Palace of the Dates situated in Antioch's most princely district – the Way of the Orontes.

The kneeling girl anxiously studied Vesuvio's bruise-marked body and whispered, 'He moved, Father! I saw the slave's eyelids flutter!'

Nicodemus ben Seth raised his hands to hold back three long plaits which dangled from either side of his silver-embroidered cap and he peered farther over his daughter's shoulder. He said, 'I saw the movement, too, my Rachel.'

Rachel reached for a small earthen bowl which set beside her on the straw-covered floor. She lifted a wooden spoon from the bowl and slowly moved it toward Vesuvio's cracked lips.

She urged in a soft voice, 'Drink this . . . You have been lying here for three days . . . You *must* take nourishment.'

Nicodemus said, 'We do not know yet, Rachel, if the slave can understand our words.'

'They told you at the slave house that he is a Roman, Father. Speak to him in Latin.'

Ignoring his daughter's suggestion, Nicodemus whispered, 'Look! I saw the movement again! Only the faintest flutter of his eyelids but they moved.'

Rachel held the spoon under Vesuvio's nose for him to sniff the broth's aroma.

The lips moved; they slowly parted.

Reaching quickly but cautiously to cradle the back of his head with one hand, Rachel gently coaxed, 'Sip . . . sip slowly. This is nourishment for you.'

Vesuvio's head rested motionless in Rachel's hand. His eyelids remained shut. His face was pale and covered with an unkempt growth of beard. His hair, a tangled mess of greasy shanks and blood clots. Soiled rags clothed his filthy body. He showed no visible signs of life except – now – his lips parted and the muscles in his neck contracted as he strained to swallow the spoonful of golden broth.

'He drank it!' the old man marvelled. 'He drank it all!'

'Father, you said he would live,' Rachel excitedly whispered as she dipped the spoon into the earthen bowl again and returned it to Vesuvio's lips.

Nicodemus stood behind his daughter as he watched her feed the next and the next spoonful of broth to the man he had brought this morning from an Antioch slave house. Nicodemus opened his own lips – as if he were being spoon-fed himself – whilst he watched Vesuvio swallow the liquid.

He said, 'I knew there was life in the rascal. I knew it!'

'Shhh, Father!' Rachel cautioned. 'Your voice! Do not raise your voice!'

Chuckling pleasurably, Nicodemus said, 'I must give you your due, good Rachel. You acted wisely by not allowing our kitchen slaves to attend this new slave immediately. We have good and trustworthy people here at the Palace of the Dates. But no one could show your patience.'

Rachel was an obedient daughter but never refrained from giving her opinion about domestic matters. She said as she continued feeding Vesuvio, 'I worry about this heavy iron collar locked around his neck, Father. See how its roughness rubs his skin. Such burns fester.'

Nicodemus shook his head. 'No. We must leave the collar be, Rachel. If this Roman is to live, then he is to live as a slave. He must wear the collar of servitude put around his neck at the slave-house.'

'But, Father,' Rachel argued, 'certainly such a burdensome collar does not help a man . . .'

'No, Rachel. You must trust me. It was dangerous for me to buy a slave who is whispered to be a temple thief. We must observe all precautions. The Romans watch this house.'

Rachel sat back on the heels of her yellow satin slippers to give Vesuvio a short rest before he finished the bowl. She asked, 'Do you wonder about the history of a man like this, Father? Do you wonder whether he has a wife? Children? Brothers and sisters? Do you truly believe that a man with such a noble face could actually steal coins from his own people's . . . temple?'

Rachel held her head at a quizzical angle and narrowed her rich brown eyes, asking, 'Do you think that the man you bribed at the slave house told you the truth about this poor creature?'

'We will find out more about him in time, Rachel. For the moment we must remember that this slave could become dangerous when he begins regaining his strength. We must keep him here in the stable. We must chain him to this wall.'

'No, Father! Not chained like an . . . animal!'

Nicodemus nodded. 'But, yes, Rachel. He might run away. Or cause trouble amongst our other slaves. Perhaps slit our throats whilst we're sleeping. I bought this slave on a premonition. But . . .' Nicodemus shook his head, saying, 'He might prove to be dangerous.'

'Father, you have taught me to look for character in

people's faces. This man is bruised and marked. But I do not truly believe that a man with a face so nobly structured could commit an unholy crime.'

'Faces, daughter! Faces! A face is not always the map to a man's soul! Men are often born with masks which hide their treachery. I did not buy this slave for his face. I bought him for his *muscle*! Yes, he is weak. He has been mistreated like a poor dog. But I studied his tendons. His sinews. His frame. That is the map which instructed me, Rachel. Not his . . . face!' Nicodemus looked at the ragged clothes covering Vesuvio's body and refrained from telling his daughter about the bruises and rends which he had seen on him at close inspection. How badly he had been sexually abused by men.

Rachel said, 'I wish you would tell me what you plan to do with him, Father.'

'My plans may never reach fruition, Rachel. My plans depend on the type of man he proves to be. On his fortitude and bravery.'

'You mean to say, Father, that you gambled? That you bought him totally on speculation?'

'Twenty *sesterces*!' the old man laughed. 'If twenty Roman *sesterces* were the biggest gamble I ever made and lost, Rachel, I would be five times as rich as I am today. Ten times! Even a hundredfold!'

'Ah! Perhaps you spent twenty *sesterces,* Father. But do not forget the bribe you paid to the custodian at the slave house to learn facts about this poor man which the slave dealer would not tell you.'

'Rachel, my little Rachel,' Nicodemus ben Seth said with kindness to his dark-haired daughter kneeling on the floor. 'If your good mother were alive today how she would praise the way in which you keep such a close account of coins.'

The girl was unmoved by her doting father's compliment. She studied Vesuvio's face and asked, 'Why did they sell him to you so cheaply?'

'Because the slave dealer thought this Roman was going to die. Every merchant in Antioch is waiting for an opportunity to make a fool of Nicodemus ben Seth. Especially the Roman traders. The slave dealer on the Street of the Moon would like nothing better than to sell me a man who would cost me the price of a Roman burial!'

'Do you truly think he's a Roman?' Rachel asked. 'Or was that only another ploy to fool you? And if he is indeed Roman, Father, do you think he is cruel like the other Romans who plague us?'

'Are all Jews human?' Nicodemus shook his head. 'No, Rachel. Our tribes have fought amongst themselves for generations of kings. The Roman's disagree amongst themselves as do our people.'

The gentle smile again spread over the old merchant's face as he looked at Vesuvio lying upon the straw. He said, 'Seeing this young slave, Rachel, reminds me of when I was a boy. When my father cobbled sandals on the Street of the Jews. When my mother stayed up all night to treat the skins. I found a pigeon with a broken wing when I was a small boy on the Street of the Jews, Rachel. Oh, how I looked after that pigeon. How I pleaded with my mother not to cook it for our meal. I watched and cared for that pigeon, Rachel. I waited anxiously for his wing to mend. I prayed for the poor creature to fly.'

Vesuvio had finished his broth. His head lay against the straw. Rachel rose from the floor with the empty bowl in her hands. She stood alongside her white-haired father and said, 'It is sad to think of a man as a pigeon but I know your meaning, Father. I have the same feeling.'

Resting his hand on his daughter's slim shoulder, Nicodemus said, 'All this talk of pigeons and childhood does us little good. The price I paid for him was negligible but it was still money spent. It will be as good as thrown away into the River Orontes if this slave does not live . . .'

Rachel interrupted, 'Or if he does not fulfil your hopes.'

She turned toward her father, saying, 'You still will not tell me your plan for him?'

'My plan? Plans change. If this Roman does not fit into my plan then I will devise another plan for him. No one stays for long in the Palace of the Dates who does not work. You can be certain that your father will find some work for this Roman – or may God strip the honour from me of being a son of Israel!'

Then the widower, Nicodemus ben Seth, and his daughter, Rachel, departed arm-in-arm from the stable, leaving Vesuvio lying on the bed of straw in the stable behind the Palace of the Dates.

22

The city of Antioch was connected to the north-eastern corner of the Mediterranean by the River Orontes, a fifteen-mile course conned by both merchant vessels and Roman patrol ships. Rome claimed Syria as one of her richest provinces. She counted Antioch – along with Alexandria to the south in Egypt – as one of her leading eastern capitals.

The original founders of this city were plainsmen called the Seulicids. They had brought Greeks and Macedonians to settle the rich valley to the south of the Orontes Mountains. Next, Aetolian and Eubeans immigrated to the rich plains of Antioch. A large Jewish community had lived and prospered on the banks of the Orontes River since the days of the original king, Seleucis I.

Rich from the sea trade and caravans travelling across the deserts of Syria and Mesopotamia. Vibrant with the tongues of many nations who people the tented bazaars and cobbled marketplaces. Aromatic with spices from the Orient. A farrago of architectural styles – columned Greek, arched Roman, domed Arabian, minaretted Persian – Antioch was lavish to eye, ear, and nose.

But many travellers came to Antioch not only to trade or see the spectacular buildings and muralled walls which lined the sun-baked street. They also came to Antioch to visit the famous Grove of Daphne which lay to the north-west of the sprawling city.

The Grove of Daphne had originally been built by King Seleucis I, a park dedicated to Apollo and other royal gods. Temples were constructed for sacrifices amongst its verdant hills. Towering cypresses surrounded marble theatres. Small altars stood at every turn and bend of the many winding paths. The ancient kings of Antioch had constructed a stadium within the parkland in which games were held in honour of favoured gods. Pompey enlarged the grounds of the Grove of Daphne when Syria first became a province of Rome. More deities were introduced to the wooded area by the Roman conquerors and, soon, when Oriental religions began to move eastward, the Grove of Daphne became known as the 'Gateway of All Gods to the Roman World'.

Exotic. Mysterious. Splendid. Antioch was praised by many people for its architectural beauty but was also becoming increasingly criticised by others for its decadence. The Grove of Daphne was beginning to win this eastern port the reputation of being a *cloaca* – the sewage system through which gushed depravity, perverse habits and wantonness practised in the name of religion.

* * *

Vesuvio first saw Antioch from the bed of straw where he lay chained to the stable wall of the Palace of the Dates. He possessed little curiosity about his whereabouts. He noticed when sunshine filled the stable. He lay in darkness and knew that it was night. He registered little more.

The first image he had of people was a girl with sparkling brown eyes who spoonfed him from an earthen bowl. A male slave next brought him trays of food. Vesuvio did not raise his eyes to study the man. He voraciously attacked the food, the first nourishment he had been given to chew for as long as he could remember.

Vesuvio tried not to dwell upon his injuries during these first days in Antioch. His brain was no more than a vacuum of ugly images. His body began to heal but he had been damaged in a far worse manner. He did not feel thankful he was alive. He did not wish for death. But neither did he grasp for life.

When Vesuvio thought of life and living, he thought of a journey. A voyage from Italy. He had been born in Italy. His home was there. But when he began to remember where he had been born, to picture his home, to recall why he had left it, he suddenly pulled an imaginary curtain across his mind.

Vesuvio lay without the protection of blankets in the chill of the night. The Syrian sun grew hot during the day but Vesuvio only understood the heat when he touched his forehead and felt wetness – beads of perspiration slowly dripping down his temple.

Through that manner, though, through touching beads of perspiration, recognising the different aromas wafting from the food trays which the male slave regularly brought to the stable, and noticing new straw lying around him when he awoke each morning, Vesuvio gradually began to reconstruct a basic system of values.

Cleanliness. He had escaped from a world of filth into cleanliness. He still had yet to learn what he was and who owned this stable. But the iron collar fastened around his neck made one fact clear to him – he was awakening not as a free man but as somebody's . . . slave.

* * *

The iron manacles were finally removed from Vesuvio's wrists. He was unchained from the wall. The iron collar still encircled his neck but the restricting irons had been unlocked and taken from his ankles.

Vesuvio sat for three days on the stable floor rubbing his wrists. Listening to the sounds outside the stable's white walls, he heard the voices of women arguing, the snorting of horses, the approaching footsteps of the man who brought him the food.

The man did not speak to Vesuvio for the first three days. But when he came to gather the empty tray on the morning of the fourth day, he nodded his head toward the stable door and said, 'You know you can go outside and walk in the sun, Roman.'

The man departed with the tray. Vesuvio remained sitting on the floor. He eventually arose to his feet. His head felt dizzy and his legs were weak.

But soon he stood in the stable door. He smelt the fresh air. The sky was painted in pastel hues. The fragrance of oleanders scented the neatly swept dirtyard.

Vesuvio began to walk slowly across the yard. He saw no one. The only sounds he now heard came beyond the high brick walls surrounding the stableyard.

He saw a wooden postern with an arched top. The door set ajar. Vesuvio approached the postern and looked beyond and saw horses eating oats inside an oval race track.

Horses. Stallions. Fillies. Colts. His mind became jumbled with images. He remembered men abusing him. His head echoed with derogatory names he had been called. He felt his stomach sickening.

Vesuvio nervously turned to move away from the postern. The sight of the horses frightened him. But then he stopped.

He glanced back at the animals grazing upon the grass inside the oval dirt track. He saw how unnoticing the animals were of him. That they were only . . . animals.

Horses. He looked at their healthiness. The colts nudged their mothers. The stallions were proud and strong.

Vesuvio stood appraising the horses' peacefulness. He nodded his head, smiled, and slowly walked back to the stable where he lay down upon his bed of straw to enjoy his first untroubled sleep in days, weeks – he again began to count time, to think about Miranda.

23

'*I am Nicodemus ben Seth!*'

Vesuvio reined the horse he was riding to look at the man who had emerged through the postern of the stable-yard and stood at the edge of the oval track. Vesuvio had been giving morning exercise to a white Arabian stallion. Eight days ago he had asked the male slave who brought him his food if he could ride the horses which he had seen on the course. The slave had assured him that he could ride any and all of the horses. After rising this morning, Vesuvio had not only trotted the horses but brushed their coats until they gleamed and joined in performing other stable chores.

Vesuvio had learned that the man who brought him food was named Isaac. That the stables belonged to a great house owned by a Jewish merchant. That this city was Antioch in the eastern province of Syria. But of all the events slowly beginning to give shape to his life, the most fulfilling to him was that his body was on the mend. He felt a vigour growing inside him and he attributed this to the daily stable work he had been doing: he was profiting more from these morning exercises than the animals.

Vesuvio now sat astride the Arabian stallion and looked down at the man whose long white hair was plaited over each ear and who wore a wide-sleeved robe stitched with golden threads. This was the first time for him to see Nicodemus ben Seth.

He asked, 'Are you the man I am to call "Master"?'

Nicodemus nodded. 'I bought you from a slave house. Although I do not even know your name, I am glad to see you are recovering.'

'I am called Vesuvio.'

'Vesuvio! Ah, then perhaps you are from southern Italy. Named for the fierce volcano there.'

Vesuvio nodded as he studied the kind-faced Jewish merchant. He had known Jews before and knew how they were divided into tribes and sects. A previous friend of his, Reuben ben Sahm, had belonged to a sect called the Essenes who did not believe in slavery. Vesuvio knew that this man, Nicodemus, could not be an Essene. Not a Jew who owned slaves.

Nicodemus shaded his eyes from the sun, saying, 'I would guess that you must be twenty-five or -six years old.'

'Twenty-six,' Vesuvio said soberly. 'I was born in the year that Mount Vesuvius erupted.'

'I am glad to see that colour has returned to your face, Vesuvio. You look healthier now than when you first came here. You also hold the reins of that spirited horse with strong hands. Yes, you have changed much since I first found you at the slave house.'

'May I ask what they told you about me at the slave house . . . Master?' Vesuvio asked, trying not to flinch as he said the word 'master'. He had thought long-ago that he would never again have to address another man in that way.

'They knew very little about you at the slave house. They didn't think you were going to live.' He chuckled.

'I hope you did not have to part with much money for me.'

Nicodemus shook his head. 'That is why you are here. You were even too sickly for a poor man to risk buying. Only the rich can afford to gamble with death.'

'Did they tell you I was a temple thief?' Vesuvio asked candidly.

Nicodemus answered, 'There is a rumour here in Antioch that the temple of Diana in Athens was recently robbed. But I never believe all the rumours I hear. I will speak honestly to you, Vesuvio. I examined you closely before I purchased you. I saw that you had been misused by men in a very despicable way . . .'

Vesuvio began to speak but he stopped. He would dwell only on practical matters. He asked, 'Is the governor looking for a temple thief?'

'The governor is always looking for thieves! A proconsul rules in Antioch. A man named Lutarius Pictor. He considers everyone a thief except the men who work for him. That is his mistake. But do not be worried about such matter. Let us talk instead about your recovery. Your wounds are healed What now about your mental disposition?'

'I still have nightmares,' Vesuvio shrugged, wondering how much Nicodemus knew about the injuries done to him by the thieves.

'There is a famous spot here in Antioch. A section of the city which purports to be a shrine. It is not an ordinary shrine but a place set aside for what modern men call "love".'

'I do not think any shrine will ease my phantoms.'

'I speak of the place not for its religious virtues. I am an Israelite. I hold the gods there as pagan. I tell you about the place only as a cure.'

'I have seen enough pagan ritual to last me a life-time,' Vesuvio said soberly. 'Religion in any guise cannot cure me.'

'Be patient, Roman,' Nicodemus firmly said, his eyes momentarily flaring at Vesuvio. 'Hear out my words!'

He then continued in a more conversational tone, 'The park is called the Grove of Daphne. You have met a slave here named Isaac. He has been bringing you your food. I have instructed Isaac to escort you soon to the park. When you go there you will understand my purpose of recommending it for your physical needs.'

'Why did you buy me?' Vesuvio asked. 'If you thought I was dying, why did you risk your money on me? And now why do you show such interest in my total recovery?'

'I am a man of business.'

'But what profit can you possibly obtain from buying a misused slave?'

'I am also a man of sport.'

'Sport?' Vesuvio shrugged and said, 'That is a master's prerogative.'

He then lowered his eyes and, staring at the leather reins in his hands, he asked, 'Were other men being sold with me?'

Nicodemus answered, 'I learned little about you at the slave house. Thieves from Lycia supposedly brought you to Antioch with a sad looking collection of female slaves. I do not know who else was included amongst your lot. I only know that you lay in my stable on the verge of death.'

'I remember lying upon straw. I remember gentle care. I thank you for that.' Raising his eyes, Vesuvio added, 'I also remember a young girl feeding me. A girl with long hair. Brown eyes. A kind manner.'

Nicodemus asked guardedly, 'Why do you mention the girl, Roman?'

Vesuvio hesitated. Then seeing no reason to withhold a small part of his story from this apparently considerate man, he calmly replied, 'I only wondered if I was demented in my fever, Master Nicodemus. I know that it is common for many slaves to brag to new masters that they were once princes or lords in their homeland. I will only say that I left an estate in Campania before the Ides of April of this year. That was two months ago. I was sailing through islands off Lycia when thieves attacked me and the eight oarsmen rowing my small vessel. I was on a quest to find someone very dear to me. A girl with dark hair, brown eyes, and a gentle manner. As there was a vague similarity between her and the girl whom I believed I saw nursing me in the stable, I wondered if my mind was playing tricks on me or . . .'

Nicodemus said, 'You will soon go with Isaac to the Grove of Daphne. You will purge your phantoms there. We will discuss all these matters in good time. These and other matters.' He turned toward an iron grille which separated the race track from the vineyard behind his house.

Vesuvio called, 'Will we also discuss the sport for which you purchased me, Master Nicodemus?'

Stopping, Nicodemus glanced over his shoulder at Vesuvio. He obliquely answered, 'I am pleased to see you are interested in horsemanship. Continue with these exercises and perhaps neither of us will be disappointed, Vesuvio. Like slaves often claim to be princes or lords kidnapped from their homelands so do many merchants brag about their keen sportsmanship. We both will have to prove ourselves.' He disappeared through the iron grille.

* * *

Vesuvio sat alone that night on his straw bed on the floor of the stable after he had finished his supper. He listened to the chorus of crickets chirrup outside in the otherwise stillness of the night. He felt tired from his days' work but the ache of his limbs was a refreshing fatigue.

Remembering the same feeling from working alongside his own slaves in Campania, Vesuvio thought of the words which Delos the slave dealer had said in Piraeus, that a man must always be prepared to be captured and thrown into slavery, that no Roman was ever safe from enslavement.

Vesuvio was only now beginning to gather enough strength to think how he could prove that he was a victim of a plot. He had not had enough confidence up to now to think about convincing his new master that he was Aurelius Macrinus, born a free man and the master of Villa Vesuvio in Italy.

But did it matter what he claimed to be? Would Nicodemus ben Seth even listen to him? The old man had bought him in a slave house and, to challenge a deed of sale, Vesuvio would have to prove that he was guiltless of the charges which might be made against him that he was a temple thief.

Sitting on the floor with his elbows resting on his knees, Vesuvio thought of the few people who knew his story to be true and would argue his innocence. Balthazar was the closest. But would Nicodemus ben Seth contact Balthazar if Vesuvio told him his story?

Is freedom the first thing I need? Vesuvio next asked himself. It is one thing being a free man but if I am not able to find Miranda, nor to make love to her . . .

Vesuvio soberly lowered his eyes between his legs to where his tunic stretched across his groin. He heard Charon's harsh voice calling him a 'filly' and a 'whore'. He remembered the women in the camp feeling his soft penis and saying that he would never again be useful to a female.

Slowly untying his cincture, Vesuvio lifted his tunic over his head and lay back upon the pallet with his back against the coolness of the stone wall. He looked down at his chest, his stomach, the softness of his masculinity lying over the spread of his scrotum.

He reached toward his groin. His hand stopped. He did not want to masturbate . . .

Again, his hand moved downwards and grasped his penis, the crown falling top-heavy over the clutch of his thick fingers. He closed his eyes as he debated what thoughts might help him become sexually aroused.

He thought of Miranda but quickly eliminated her as a possibility for a sexual fantasy. He did not want to profane their actual love.

Next, he remembered the prostitute, Asiatica, but the memory of her brought back the vision of Babel and his brutal death aboard the *Cerberus*.

His mind went over all the slave girls on Villa Vesuvio, remembering smiling faces, breasts rounded under the cleanly washed dresses, their curving hips and often flirtatious winks toward their master.

Vesuvio's hand began to move. His mind was filling with a whirl of attractive faces, eager eyes, parting lips, taut nipples . . .

He stopped. He opened his eyes. He had not made love to any of the slave girls when he had been at home. He had wanted no one then but Miranda and he could not use them now in his fantasies.

Closing his eyes again, he thought that perhaps he should think of Miranda. No one else truly existed for him.

As his hand began to work again to create a hardness on his masculinity, he wondered what he would do if he could *not* become erect, if the sodomy had left him impotent.

He dropped his hands to his side and stared blankly down at his penis lying useless across the top of his thigh. What had happened to him? What had the men on the River Styx truly done to him? Into what kind of useless creature had they transformed him?

24

'Antioch! Gem of the Orient! Queen of the East! Ancient capital of the Selucids!' The slave, Isaac, led Vesuvio along the Way of the Orontes, passing castellated walls behind which golden domes gleamed in the sunset. They walked beneath tall windows intricately latticed with brass shining like many-faceted jewels. They gazed at strong doors bossed with iron studs to keep out intruders. The Way of the Orontes was a street of palaces, most of the vast homes being built in terraces which rose like mountain ranges of honey-coloured stone.

Isaac explained to Vesuvio about the Romans trying to rebuild parts of Antioch, refurbishing old buildings and laying-out forums in the new section of the city which lay at the end of this wide avenue lined by drooping palm trees. Isaac ridiculed the fashionable style called 'Hellenistic' by the Romans – columned porches and low-pitched roofs. He complained, 'Why do the Romans want to tear down ancient beauty and replace it with buildings bastardised from another culture?'

Vesuvio said, 'You are proud of this city.'

'I was born in Antioch and raised in the Palace of the Dates. My mother was a hand-maiden to the wife of Nicodemus. Ah! There was a good woman. But she died giving birth to the one child of Nicodemus.'

'Nicodemus ben Seth has obviously been generous with your education.' Vesuvio was eager to talk about someone other than himself. He knew that no cure lay in brooding.

Isaac answered, 'Nicodemus is a shrewd man. He is generous yet often very selfish and stubborn. He gives but protects what is his. He asks for his slaves' opinions in certain matters. But . . .'

Isaac stopped. He shook his head, saying, 'I am a Jew like Nicodemus. That is why I understand him. But you and I are not out walking this evening to discuss our master. We are going to the Grove of Daphne to forget about worldly matters. Let me tell you about the Grove.'

The two men turned from the Way of the Orontes, leaving the sphinx-flanked portals and followed a winding street lined with high, stark white walls. They passed children playing with hoops in the cobbled streets of this more homely district. They nodded to old men sitting on their doorsteps fingering strings of amber beads. They saw women gathering laundry from shrubs on which it had been placed to dry in the sun.

Isaac talked as they leisurely strolled. 'There is only one key to the Grove of Daphne. That is "love". You enter with love. You find love within. You leave sated with love. It is the various interpretations of that word "love" which gives the park its infamous name.'

Walking with his hands folded behind his back, Isaac explained, 'There is a splendid race track within the Grove of Daphne. But Nicodemus refuses to visit it. As you have probably guessed, our master is a keen horseman. But he will not step foot into the ivy-covered walls of that park. He considers it to be too corrupt. And he is right. The old man is usually right. I suspect he only allows me to visit the Grove in order to prevent me . . .'

Stopping, Isaac said, 'Listen to me! I am again telling you my life story when I am supposed to be talking to you about the Grove of Daphne.'

The road now wound between a wood of thickly growing cypress trees. It was becoming congested with men, women, and children – people walking alone or in small groups. Some young men led bulls garlanded with fresh field flowers. Women carried kid goats in their arms for sacrificing on altars. Many young girls and boys held flower and sea shells in their hands. Others swung tinkling strings of copper bells.

Isaac pointed toward the people flocking to the park's main entrance which towered ahead of them and said, 'You began to see the spirit of Daphne. Carefree. Happy. Ethereal. Many people are saying that the new Roman proconsul has plans to change the park. The proconsul is simple-living compared to many Romans. He looks disapprovingly on loose ways. He does not even visit the horse-track here. In that way, he is like Nicodemus. The proconsul also prefers the city's stadium. Oh, the stadium in Antioch is far bigger than the arena here in the Grove. Antioch's circus is even bigger than Rome's. And the new proconsul is planning many new and diverse entertainments in the Circus. He is ambitious to increase his own reputation. Every Roman sent to govern a province thinks only of how he can improve his reputation in Trajan's court in Rome. They think much less about the people whom they are supposed to govern.'

Isaac lowered his voice, confessing, 'I should not speak so freely about Roman officials. The proconsul is very suspicious of Jews. He maintains that men like Nicodemus hold too much power in Syria. That Jews threaten Roman supremacy. And in that token, Nicodemus imperils the proconsul's reputation in Rome.'

The fear which Romans had of the Jews intrigued Vesuvio. He had always marvelled at how a power as mighty as Rome should be frightened by a people who were little more than a desert tribe in comparison to the Imperial forces.

He asked, 'Is Nicodemus worried about the new Roman proconsul?'

'Nicodemus is a puzzling man. Although he constantly expects the Romans to seize his holdings, he flaunts his independence in front them. I told you he does not race his horses in the Grove of Daphne. But try to keep him away from the Antioch arena. It is the centre of all Roman life in Syria. A veritable temple of Roman brawn and wealth. This obviously intrigues Nicodemus. Or kindles his competitive spirit. He lives in anticipation for the games held there.'

'Are there racing clubs in Antioch as there are in Rome?'

'No. The charioteers race here according to nationalities and tribes. The Syrians, the Egyptians, the Greeks, the Lycians, the Jews – all the people living in Antioch have a favourite driver in the arena, a chariot sponsored by some rich man or a club in their community.'

'Does Nicodemus sponsor a driver?'

Isaac did not hear Vesuvio's question. Or, at least, he did not answer.

They were approaching a large gate standing at the termination of the road, a gateway composed of a pair of twisting ebony columns decorated with gilded depictions of gods and goddesses, its archway topped with a cresset spouting fire.

Priests wearing acanthus leaves around their heads stood by this towering entrance to the Grove of Daphne. They tossed flower petals at the men and women entering the black-and-gold gates, calling good wishes to the pilgrims coming to see Apollo, Diana, and the multitude of other deities.

'How good are you at gauging time?' asked Isaac.

Vesuvio looked overhead at the lavender-tinted sky, saying, 'The sun is fastly disappearing. But I have lived long enough with water clocks to gauge the hours in a rough manner at night.'

'If you are familiar with water clocks we have no worry,' Isaac said as he stepped aside for an auruch festooned in clematis to lumber past him. 'Apart from being a vast woodland, the Grove is richly appointed. There are water clocks placed throughout the park. Meet me back here at the gate by the time which you Romans call "*hora quarta*".'

Isaac moved to enter the gate but stopped and beckoned

Vesuvio to come toward him. He said, 'One last thing. Do not be offended if some people turn their back to you. Although this is a grove of love you still wear a slave collar around your neck. But do not let that hinder you. I do not think a man of your good looks will have much trouble meeting a partner.'

Patting Vesuvio on the arm, Isaac quickly turned and disappeared into the crowd.

Vesuvio stood alone outside the gate. He wore only a length of homespun knotted over one shoulder. His skin was bronzed from the warm sun of the stableyard. A golden sheen had returned to his hair casually tossed back from his forehead. His body had regained its athletic suppleness. He felt in good health but, nevertheless, he could not forget his sexual impotence.

Deciding that he could at least enjoy the sylvan beauty of the parkland, Vesuvio joined the throng of people passing under the cresset which flamed over the entrance to the Grove of Daphne.

A priest tossed a handful of flower petals at Vesuvio as he entered the gate. He felt the softness of the flowers slide over his skin, ticklishly falling down the flatness of his stomach toward his cincture.

* * *

Vesuvio slowly trudged up the main path leading beyond the gates, seeing that the Grove rose in a series of hills to a verdant forest. Men and women rushed past him in the quickly fading daylight and disappeared across lawns which were bordered by thickly branched trees. He remembered that Isaac had told him that the park had originally been dedicated to Apollo. The frenzied attitude of the visitors made him think that they instead were under the influence of the wine-god, Bacchus.

Keeping to the main path, Vesuvio reflected on the facts

which Isaac had told him about Antioch's proconsul, details about his new master, and that there was an arena in the main section of the city.

His 'master'. Nicodemus ben Seth. Vesuvio decided that he must not worry about his sexual inabilities and concentrate instead on freeing himself from slavery. He tried not to think of the fact that he could still be arrested as a temple thief. He had talked this morning to Isaac, though, about having a friend named Balthazar on the island of Cyprus. He had mentioned Balthazar to Isaac as the first step of a safeguard against any false accusations made against him in the future.

Vesuvio had no doubts how the temple gold had found its way into the food sacks aboard the *Rhea*. He realised that Despo and Cleomenes had undoubtedly bribed a dockyard roustabout to put the gold there. They did not want him to find Miranda. But why? And could Balthazar help him prove this fact?

The evening's air was sweet. The path which Vesuvio now climbed was empty. Flowering shrubs lined the sides. The sound of a piping flute floated with the breeze. But despite the evening's pastoral serenity, Vesuvio found himself becoming despondent. He was thinking about the *Cerberus* and Charon and the hut of women in the thieves' putrid encampment on the hillside of Lycia.

He stopped at the crest of the knoll and glanced toward a vale from which came the sound of jangling bells. He saw three girls merrily skipping up a far slope toward him.

'Stranger!' one girl called, waving a garland of flowers. 'Let us crown your moongold head with honeysuckle!'

Vesuvio smiled at the three girls. They were dressed like mythical wood nymphs. Their happy voices momentarily obliterated his thoughts about the death of his oarsmen and his captivity in Charon's squalid encampment.

The girls suddenly stopped a few feet below Vesuvio on the slope. One girl touched her companion's arm. She whispered, 'Oh, he's a . . . slave!' They turned and scurried quickly across the face of the hillock.

Vesuvio resumed walking, telling himself that the snub was unimportant. He knew the boundaries of slavery and the restrictions which many slaves suffered. Why should he torture himself by feeling slighted?

He heard the sound of a tambourine from a copse of sycamores at the foot of the hill. Not wanting to risk being scorned a second time, he turned in the opposite direction. The evening was warm. He would merely try to enjoy the beauty of this rolling parkland.

'*Domine*?' a voice called from a copse.

Vesuvio glanced toward the trees and fleetingly considered answering that he was not a 'lord' but only a slave.

The soft voice asked, 'Are you a visitor to Antioch, *domine?*'

Vesuvio saw a slim figure crowned with a headful of curly black hair emerge from the darkness. He answered with forced honesty, 'This is my first visit to the Grove. I am a slave to a merchant of Antioch.'

'No man crowned with golden hair such as yours could ever be a slave in the Grove of Daphne!' The person moved closer toward Vesuvio.

Seeing that it was a boy, a curly-headed boy with large brown eyes, Vesuvio immediately thought of Babel.

The boy raised his hand to trace the bulging outlines of Vesuvio's upper arms and softly asked, 'Do you like what the moon lights for your eyes to see, *domine*?'

Vesuvio said, 'I looked closely at you because you reminded me of someone I once knew.'

'A lover?'

Vesuvio shook his head. He was thinking of Babel. Of Charon stabbing Babel with the sharp blade of his knife. Of the young man's intestines spilling to the floor.

He answered, 'I was thinking of a . . . friend. A true and dedicated friend.'

'Perhaps *domine* needs a new friend tonight.'

'No,' Vesuvio said, pulling away from the persistent youth. 'I was only wandering by myself.'

'May I join you?'

'Thank you. But I would rather be alone.'

Vesuvio turned and walked slowly away from the boy; he ignored the boy's boast that he had the best mouth in the Grove of Daphne to drain a man's seed, calling that Vesuvio looked as if he needed a good mouth to serve him.

* * *

As the sky grew darker and the shadows more richly shaded, Vesuvio's mood became more dispirited. He continued to walk deeper and deeper into the woodland. He climbed hills. He wandered across meadows. He glanced at the water clocks which Isaac had promised would be setting at intervals throughout the park – two transparent vessels containing water which were placed one on top of the other, the lower vessel marked with dark lines to denote the hour.

Passing marble replicas of satyrs and maenads, Vesuvio glanced at lovers embracing in makeshift beds pressed down amongst tall grasses.

He now clearly saw that the Grove of Daphne was a love spot, a nest created from the most luscious trees, plants, and flowers of nature which composed a bordello roofed by the twinkling stars, a meeting place for sexual practises where the only price was willingness and a mutual agreement.

Vesuvio stood on the edge of a lagoon. A willow tree gracefully tented its grassy bank a few yards away from a profusion of reeds and lily pads decorating the still water. Vesuvio sat down by the edge of the lagoon and gazed out over its shimmering flatness which reflected the moon.

It is wrong to be so morose in such a restful spot, he told himself as he crossed his arms over his bare knees. *I do not believe in dwelling upon trouble. Miranda would not approve of it either. And old Tia* – Vesuvio smiled when he thought of the crone – *Tia would deplore the idea that I am allowing sorrow to engulf me.*

Troubles build upon trouble, true. But out of all trouble grows some happiness, he told himself . . . *doesn't it?*

A splash in the water attracted his attention toward the willow tree. Was it a fish jumping?

He heard a second splash and, now seeing a shape in the water, he thought that he saw a bather standing under the willow tree – a girl with long hair hanging to her shoulders.

Soon, he saw a second shape standing alongside the first girl. It was another bather.

Vesuvio lay on his side on the sloping grass and studied the dark water under the willow tree. He counted one, two, three, four, five girls bathing in the lagoon. They were all naked. They all had long hair to their shoulders. Some girls wore flowers over their ears. Others wore their hair knotted back behind their heads. Their skin shone creamy white in the moonlight as they moved silently, slowly, languidly, in the dark water.

One girl soon saw Vesuvio observing them. Then they all turned to look at him. The five girls were not alarmed at his presence but neither did they call nor beckon him to join them. They stood in the water and benignly returned his gaze.

Vesuvio rose to his feet and, walking across the dewy grass toward the willow, he parted a few hanging branches with one hand to approach the bathers.

One girl moved through a collection of lily pads, wading closer to the bank. She lifted her arms toward Vesuvio.

Kneeling by the edge of the bank to grasp her hands, Vesuvio leaned his head forward to kiss her.

The girl reached toward his face; they embraced, softly brushing their lips against one another's.

Vesuvio lay upon his stomach to hold his arms around the girl as she still stood knee-deep in the water. Their kiss turned into a more passionate embrace. Her hands moved down from his face. She touched his iron slave collar. She ignored its black coldness and began to stroke his broad shoulders, his chest, his back.

Vesuvio continued kissing the girl – and hearing the others move from the water he felt the pressing of their cool bodies surround him.

He opened his eyes to the girl whom he was kissing. She opened her eyes to him. She had gentle and understanding green eyes and she continued to hold his gaze even as her companions began to wrap their arms around Vesuvio, kissing his shoulders, smoothing his yellow hair with their fingertips, unknotting the tunic from his shoulder and slowly beginning to undress him.

Vesuvio soon did not know which girl he held in his arms. They became interchangeable to him in touch and tenderness. They showed no jealousy amongst themselves for his kisses or masculine dominance. They wrapped themselves around him and, when he moved, he felt another girl pressing her naked breast against him, or another smoothing her mid-section against his thigh.

The succession of smooth bodies and sweet mouths was new for Vesuvio. His penis became more firm as his confidence was kindled by the girls' lavish attention. He was not aware of his firmness until he felt himself driving deep inside the vaginal warmth of one girl. Another girl lay alongside him holding her arms around him. He continued to feel the kisses of the other girls on his shoulders, neck, and back.

The five girls lavished their love upon Vesuvio as he cradled himself on their bodies, lay between their spread legs, enjoyed the warmth beneath the hair growing like tender brown moss between their thighs. They did not speak, the silence was only broken by sighs, gasps, the sound of moist kisses and the press of eager bodies.

Vesuvio was too excited by the newness of their attention

to concentrate on his actions until he finally felt himself reaching a sexual crest. He slowed his drives, trying to prolong a physical sensation which gave strength to his entire body.

Lying on his side on the grass as the girl gently pulled away from him, he looked down at his groin and saw two of the girls now holding his erect phallus between their faces. They kissed it from the roots to his fully expanded crown.

He strained to resist exploding as another girl moistened his phallus with her pressing mouth, enclosing him with her lips as she darted her tongue against his hardness. His testicles were beginning to ache for an explosion. He could no longer resist the urge to allow his excitement to erupt. He rolled over onto one girl and began driving himself between her legs at a quickening pace until he began to feel the excitement of his groin build into a gush of virility. He held the girl tighter in his arms and, as her friends pressed themselves around Vesuvio's jerking body, they kissed him, praised him, urged him with their touches to release himself as a man.

25

Vesuvio awoke refreshed and invigorated the next morning on his straw pallet in the stables behind the Palace of the Dates. He drew a bucket of cold water from the well in the dirt yard and tipped it over his head. His skin tingled as the water cascaded across his broad shoulders and rushed down his chest, waist and legs. He slicked his hair back from his forehead and, quickly knotting the tunic over his shoulder, he set about to feed the horses. He next swept the stalls. He was whistling happily as he led a pair of Arabian stallions across the stableyard for their morning exercises on the track when Isaac suddenly appeared in the postern.

'You asked me last evening about chariots?' Isaac called to Vesuvio. 'What do you know about harnessing a pair of horses?'

'A pair!' Vesuvio cheerily answered. 'Why not *four?*'

Isaac wrinkled his brow, asking suspiciously, 'Do you know about the team of four horses which Romans call a *quadrigae?*'

Vesuvio patted the flanks on one of the white Arabians and said, 'These two would make a good inside pair. They are both strong and obedient. I would attach that lively chestnut called Saba for the outside horse of a *quadrigae*. And probably use that lively big bay on the inside.'

Isaac momentarily stared at Vesuvio. He was surprised to hear him speak so authoritatively about racing teams. He moved to one side of the postern and pointed to a wooden vehicle setting alongside the oval track behind him. He said, 'See what you can do with that chariot there.'

Vesuvio pushed past Isaac to study the chariot. He saw

that its red paint was bleached by many years of sun. That its hubs were depleted of all decoration. The driver's stand was no more than a flap of wood and the yoke mended with rusty iron.

But to Vesuvio's eyes this shabby chariot was the most pleasing sight he had seen in a long time. He turned to Isaac and excitedly asked, 'Where have you been hiding this little beauty?'

Isaac patted Vesuvio on the shoulder and said, 'Make a good show of the chariot and horses, friend, and you'll see what other surprises await you at the Palace of the Dates.'

Vesuvio quickly grasped Isaac's forearm in appreciation and then turned to rush toward the chariot.

He suddenly stopped. He looked fleetingly at the white Arabians. He anxiously glanced over his shoulder at the stable where the chestnut and the bay still stood in their stalls.

Isaac laughed at his confusion, saying, 'You're acting like an overly excited child.'

Having decided to bring out the other two horses from the stable to complete the *quadriga*, as well as fetch harnessing for all four horses, Vesuvio called as he rushed across the yard, 'I feel like a child, Isaac. I feel just like a child given a toy!'

Isaac watched Vesuvio disappear into the stable. He shook his head in amazement at the sudden change which the visit to the Grove of Daphne had wrought in Vesuvio. Isaac had met him outside the main gate of the Grove last night at the appointed hour. He had not questioned Vesuvio about his experience but he had seen that he emerged from the parkland as a different, more self-assured man than he had entered it.

Whatever had happened to Vesuvio in the Grove of Daphne had definitely changed him. But now this sudden announcement that he could harness four horses to a broken-down chariot and race it on the track had somehow made Vesuvio even more complete.

Isaac admitted to himself that Nicodemus ben Seth was a wise man. Nicodemus evidently had planned this all. The visit to the Grove. The chariot. The horses. Isaac only wished that the old man would show more understanding toward him.

Unlike Vesuvio, Isaac had not enjoyed himself last night in the Grove of Daphne. He had sat alone under a tree and thought about the girl he loved. He envied Vesuvio being able to speak about his loved one. Isaac could tell no one about the girl whom he wanted to marry. The nearness of her to him only made matters worse for him and he had sat last night in the Grove thinking how Vesuvio was in fact luckier than himself. Vesuvio did not have to suffer the torture of being close to the one he loved.

Isaac was deep in these thoughts when he suddenly heard Vesuvio say from behind him, 'I have been so involved in my own problems I have not noticed yours.'

Turning, Isaac asked, 'What do you mean? I have no problems.' He saw that Vesuvio led two horses and that his arms were laden with leather harnessing.

'You do not want to talk about yourself, Isaac, so you do not have to. Let me only say that if I can solve my problems that you will certainly solve yours.'

Shaking his head, Isaac said, 'I do not think so.'

'We will see,' Vesuvio said, continuing toward the race track, not wanting to pry any further into Isaac's secret. He was beginning to suspect, though, that Isaac was also suffering from the strict boundaries imposed on men by a slave system.

* * *

Nicodemus ben Seth's favourite room within the Palace of the Dates was a cedar-lined chamber overlooking the gardens which enjoyed an extensive view of the stableyard and private race track.

This morning he sat in an armed chair in front of an opened window and watched Vesuvio harnessing the two white Arabians, and the bay and the chestnut stallions to the battered old chariot.

Nicodemus's eyes closely followed Vesuvio around the track, judging how he cornered the animals, grinning as Vesuvio stopped to change the white Arabians as the outside animals of the racing four. That act convinced the old man that Vesuvio knew what he was doing. That he was an accomplished charioteer.

The mornings passed and Nicodemus continued to sit beside the window in the cedar-lined room watching Vesuvio drive the chariot around and around the track. He became increasingly impressed with Vesuvio's knowledge of charioteering. He did not hug the inside railings. He gained speed on the long runs. He never over-worked the animals. He wore the reins around his waist like a professional horseman, driving the animals as if he were part of the chariot.

Rachel joined her father in the third week after Vesuvio's training upon the track. She had heard the gossip from the house slaves that the Roman had become an obsessive charioteer. She mentioned this fact to her father and he invited her to his cedar-lined chamber to judge Vesuvio's skills with her own eyes.

The dust rose again this morning from the track, sometimes clouding so thickly that Rachel and her father could see neither Vesuvio nor the four horses.

'Isn't it dangerous for a charioteer to race with the reins tied around his waist?' Rachel asked her father as she stood alongside his chair. 'If he fell the horses could drag him to death.'

'No, my daughter. Have no fear for that man's life. He knows what he's doing. He controls all four horses by the reins but only the inside pair are connected to the chariot.'

'Why do they not run away?'

'That is the mastery of the *agitator* – that's the Latin name for a man who drives the chariot. An *agitator* uses the two outside horses to guide the chariot whilst the middle two are his strength.'

'You mean only the middle two horses are attached to that little . . . cart?'

'Precisely.'

'But, Father, the cart looks so flimsy and light. See how it bounces.'

'It must be of a certain lightness, Rachel. Some chariots are heavy but those are mostly Roman. And they are mostly for display. A good eastern chariot is made of the lightest wood not like the chariots brought here from Rome.'

'Your Roman slave must be very brave, Father. He does not seem to be frightened of the outside horses breaking loose.'

'It is not the horses that a charioteer needs to worry about, dear child. It is the other charioteers. In Rome, there are drivers from four different teams. The teams are all known by their colours. The Reds. The Greens. The Blues. The Yellow. There is a Roman senator who is bringing a chariot to race soon here in Antioch at the Arena. If you choose to attend, you will see exactly what I mean by Roman chariots being cumbersome and bulky.'

'Is it one of the chariots which races under a colour?'

'Yes, but the driver will be racing in Antioch as a private entry of the Roman senator. He is a very famous charioteer. The Green faction's most prized driver.'

'It sounds like children's games to me, all this talk of colours and racing and factions.'

'Oh, the charioteers often behave like children, too,' Nicodemus said, chuckling. 'But more roughly. The charioteers themselves are often no more than bully boys. It is not much different here in Antioch. Sometimes even worse. I am sure it will be the same in the race soon to be held in our amphitheatre.'

'Father!' Rachel gasped. 'The truth has suddenly occurred

to me. That is why you bought the Roman! You knew about this race you now keep mentioning. You bought Vesuvio to be *your* charioteer!'

Nicodemus did not answer. He kept his eyes trained on Vesuvio.

'Father,' Rachel scolded. 'I am surprised at you. Pitting your slave against the Romans!'

Nicodemus kept staring out the window as he said dryly, 'Aurelius Macrinus is not a slave, Rachel.'

'Who?'

" Aurelius Macrinus. That is the given name of the man we call "Vesuvio".'

'How do you suddenly know this astounding fact?'

Nicodemus began to explain the story in a soft voice. 'The Roman talks. Not much. When he talks it is usually to Isaac. Vesuvio is not a braggart like his fellow countryman. But he mentioned a black man named Balthazar. A merchant in Cyprus. It was not difficult to check such a story. I wrote to this Balthazar at his warehouses in Paphos. His reply arrived only this morning.'

'And?'

'Vesuvio was not born a slave. He belongs to the Roman senatorial classes and is a master of a large estate on the Italian peninsula. But more importantly, Rachel, he is in love with a slave girl. She was taken from his villa in Italy and he was in pursuit of her when this merchant named Balthazar last heard of Vesuvio. He is most certainly not a temple thief.'

'Then you must free him, Father. Free him immediately. You must not keep a man who has been wrongly enslaved.'

'I will, Rachel. I will free him. But in time. Providence has sent me a strong Roman. I must use him against the other Romans.'

Rachel fell to the floor alongside the ivory-inlaid chair. She begged, 'Why, why must you continuously remind the

Romans that you are smarter and richer than they? What good does that do you?'

'It is not for me, Daughter. It is for our people. The Romans treat us with contempt. It is the obligation of every Jew to let our adversaries know we have our own strengths. This Roman named Aurelius Macrinus – the man we call Vesuvio – will help me and all Jews.'

'How will he help us, Father? You often speak for our people. They come to you. You helped Benjamin the weaver keep his shop. When the sewage flowed into old Sara's home, it was you who got the Romans to make the small house habitable again for her children. But will a Roman like Vesuvio help us in those ways, Father? Do you truly think that he will?'

'Vesuvio will help us, Rachel, by competing in the chariot race. By winning against the charioteer brought from Rome by a senator to humble us provincials. Every triumph a Jew enjoys, Rachel – however large, however small – is another glory for all Israelites.'

'When is this race?'

'Soon. Very soon, Daughter.'

'Have you told . . . Vesuvio about his freedom? That you have been in correspondence with this Cypriot merchant, Balthazar?'

Nicodemus shook his head. 'Not yet. But I will, Rachel. I will not disappoint Vesuvio as he has not disappointed me.'

26

The proconsul of Antioch, Lutarius Pictor, was a Republican, a politician with beliefs embedded in the days when Rome had been a simple-living, hard-working society. Julius Caesar had first challenged the Republicans one-hundred-and-fifty years ago, turning Rome into a dictatorship and laying groundwork for the mighty Empire which Rome was today.

The Republicans were small in number these days but they still counted powerful men as their members. This select band of political conservatives were mostly senators and one of the diehards was Gaius Sullus, the Roman who had come to Antioch to race his charioteer in the city's main arena.

Gaius Sullus was thirty years older than Antioch's proconsul but the two men talked like peers as they discussed racing as it had been in the days before blood, cruelty, and sexuality had come to play an important part in Roman games. Senator Sullus believed that the amphitheatre in Antioch was one of the last outposts of sportsmanship left in the Empire and this pleased young Lutarius Pictor. He only hoped the old senator would not change his mind when he entered his driver there.

Lutarius Pictor also despised the decadence of modern Rome. He approved of men being rugged and blood-thirsty but he frowned upon the effetism creeping into Roman manhood. He and Senator Sullus lay on couches late tonight in the *triclinium* of the proconsul's palace located high above the harbour of the River Orontes. The meal was finished and Pictor's wife, servants, and musicians had long ago retired to their bedchambers. Senator Sullus was beginning to slur his words from having consumed too much wine throughout the dinner. He continued to fill his goblet from a chased silver urn as he complained about public distribution of money to Rome's poor and railed about foreigners flooding into the capital city.

Suspecting that the aging senator was reaching senility – apart from being drunk – Pictor quietly listened but tried neither to agree or disagree with his opinions. He also suspected that Senator Sullus was a sly old fox and might be trying to draw out his opinions.

Senator Sullus had been visiting in Antioch now for five days. He planned to return to Rome in three days' time, the day after the races.

Lutarius Pictor had originally planned to ask the Senator's advice tonight about a problem causing him great trouble here in Antioch, the perplexing problem of the Jews. But Pictor now reconsidered his intentions as he listened to Sullus talk unguardedly about life in Rome and the Imperial palace.

Senator Sullus said, 'That young Hadrian has as much power as the Emperor himself. Which proves to me that the provinces will ultimately rule Rome. Hadrian is from Hispania like Trajan himself.' The old man's rheumy brown eyes focused on Pictor, waiting for an agreement.

Pictor shrugged. He recognised the political danger in the old man's words. Senator Sullus was drunk, true, but for some reason Pictor still did not trust him.

Leaning closer to Pictor's couch, Sullus asked, 'You do know Hadrian, don't you? What he is?'

Lutarius Pictor answered guardedly, 'I know that he is a fine soldier . . .' He paused, thinking that he should not confide in the Senator about his problem with a leader of the Jewish faction in this city. He had wanted to ask Sullus's advice on how to deal with a merchant named Nicodemus ben Seth, a Jew who often counselled his people to withhold their taxes from Imperial collectors and to make demands for more cleanliness or for aqueducts to be extended to their quarters.

'No! I mean what Hadrian *really* is!' Senator Sullus leaned farther toward him.

Pictor shook his head. 'I do not hear much gossip in the . . .'

'The Emperor's boy!' Senator Sullus boomed. 'That's what Hadrian is! He's still Trajan's lover!'

Pictor took a deep breath. He now definitely did not trust this old hawk-nosed politician. He knew that Sullus had close contacts to court and so why was he speaking so dangerously about Trajan?

He answered, 'I have only met the Empress Plotina who . . .'

'Plotina?' Senator Sullus frowned and continued, 'Plotina puts on the airs of a good Roman matron – the Mother of Rome – but she knows exactly what happens between Hadrian and Trajan and that fast-living group called the Palatine Set. Behind her veneer of matronly respect, the Empress Plotina has a mind as well-informed as any brothel-keeper in Subura. And I know that for a fact, boy! I know that for a fact!' The Senator jabbed a finger at Pictor's chest to emphasise his point.

Pictor had wondered in the last five days if Senator Sullus had truly come to Antioch only to race his chariot. He suspected now more than ever that Sullus might had travelled here as a spy. Senator Sullus served as a provincial advisor to Trajan. Pictor did not want Sullus to return to Rome and report that he was unfit to govern Syria.

Moving to rise from the couch, Pictor said, 'The hour is late, my good friend. I have business tomorrow in the . . . Jewish quarter. I must rise early. Those Jews are shrewd men and one must have an alert mind to deal with them.'

Senator Sullus praised, 'Only a Republican would admit that a Jew is as smart – or smarter – than a Roman. This young breed we're raising, they would never recognise them as their opponents.'

Leaning back on his couch, the Senator waved his goblet and complained, 'The false pride of young Romans today augurs disaster for us. They think about nothing but their pride and . . . the arts! Art! I thought we had seen enough of that rubbish in Nero's forsaken reign. See what a fool Nero made of himself with all that drama and music and poetry. Hadrian? Oh, he has the same taste. The Emperor himself is a tough man. But he is not tough enough to cast aside his appetite for male love now that he no longer is a soldier but the emperor!'

Closing his eyes, the Senator continued in a softer voice, 'Many young soldiers have a taste for this love amongst men. I never did myself. I always preferred the camp whores. Ah! So did my good friend, Milo Popiliano. Milo Popiliano was the stud to Empress Agrippina, you know. Popiliano's sister was married to old Aurelius Macrinus, a great republican from Campania. Milo himself never rose above the Equestrian order. He had the one-hundred-thousand *sesterces* to buy a senatorship for himself and he had all the court connections to secure it. But that was not his ambition. He died a natural death – how many years ago?'

Pictor seized this pause and said, 'Ah, to be in a military camp now, Senator. To be free of intrigue and mistrust. But at least we can keep a soldier's hours.'

The Senator nodded his head, agreeing, 'I must rise early, too. I want to watch my driver, Jurgo, train on the track. A good man, that Jurgo. A dedicated athlete and an asset to the Greens.'

He raised his eyes, saying, 'You still haven't told me what the competition will be like here in Antioch. Who are the other contestants?'

'My agents collect the entry taxes tomorrow. We will know better when we see who pays to race in the arena. I have only heard of one Syrian, a Dacian, and a Jew.'

'A Jew?' the Senator sneered. 'Racing?'

'He is a sponsor. I know that Jews are not allowed to sponsor drivers in Rome but here it is tradition. And the Jew whom I speak of has a keen eye for horseflesh as well as business.'

'Is this Jew's driver a slave?'

'They usually are.' Pictor's eyelids were heavy.

The Senator said, 'If the slave's good, I might buy him and take him back to Rome.'

Pictor shook his head. 'Nicodemus ben Seth is not the kind of man who would readily part with a good driver.'

The Senator belched. 'There are ways for Romans to take things they want, Pictor.'

'We must continue this conversation in the morning, Senator,' Lutarius Pictor said as he held out his hand to help the old man from the couch. 'You might have some other answers for me.'

Brushing aside Pictor's hand, Senator Sullus moved to rise from the couch but he fell back onto it. He belched again and waved Pictor away from him, motioning for him to leave him alone.

Pictor turned, leaving the Senator lying on the couch. As he walked across the tessellated floor of the *triclinium* he again asked himself, Why has he come to Antioch? Is he here only to race his chariot and reminisce about old cronies who had been Agrippina's lover? Pictor realised more than ever that he should not trust this old man who compared the Empress Plotina to a brothel-keeper.

27

The next morning – two days before the chariot race – a house slave from the Palace of the Dates came to Vesuvio in the stable and announced that Master Nicodemus wished to speak to him in the privacy of his library. Vesuvio followed the slave into the side portal, walking behind him down cool corridors arched in yellow stone, passing latticed windows through which daylight poured in intricate patterns onto the honey-coloured floor.

The slave stopped in front of two tall ivory-inlaid doors. He knocked lightly and, opening one door, he stood to one side for Vesuvio to enter the room panelled in cedarwood.

Vesuvio saw Nicodemus seated in a high-backed chair facing a window. He walked toward the chair and began to call his greetings.

Nicodemus raised his hand from the arm of the chair and said, 'The time has come for us to prove ourselves, Roman.'

Vesuvio paused. He detected a new graveness in Nicodemus's voice. He wondered why the old man had not come to see him in the stable or on the track as he usually did, why Nicodemus had summoned him to this chamber.

Nicodemus spoke as he sat facing the window, 'You once told me that slaves often brag about being princes or lords in their homeland. I answered you at that time that merchants often speak freely about being keen sportsmen. The time now has come for truth –' Nicodemus paused before adding, 'Aurelius Macrinus.'

Vesuvio's eyes widened with surprise. His heart quickened. He wondered if he had indeed heard the name correctly? 'Aurelius Macrinus'. Did Nicodemus know his true identity at last?

'It is also time for bargaining,' Nicodemus said soberly from his chair. 'I know what you want from me and you have probably guessed what I need from you . . .'

Vesuvio was still stunned by Nicodemus addressing him by his family's name. He blurted, 'How did you learn who I am?'

'You have a good friend in a man named Balthazar. His letters confirmed the suspicions which I have been forming about you in recent weeks. When I first found you in the slave house, I saw how I might make a fine charioteer out of you. I knew you were Roman born but I had no idea at first that you had . . . aristocratic blood in your veins. You will be allowed to leave Antioch as a free man, to go where you please with no fear of any charges made against you for thievery if you . . .'

Nicodemus clenched his fist on the arms of the chair as he said, 'You must win that race, Roman. You win the chariot race for me and your prize will be your freedom.'

Vesuvio tried to retain his excitement as he assured Nicodemus, 'I hope to do nothing less even without such a promise from you. But the fact that you know who I am, that you and my good friend, Balthazar, have been in correspondence, only makes me. . . . I could not hope for . . .'

'There is no need to speak or pay gratitude. Not at this point. You must only concentrate on winning that race. A Roman senator has brought a famous charioteer from the Circus Maximus in Rome to compete in our race.'

'I have raced a *quadrigae* in Rome myself.'

'I have watched you,' Nicodemus said. 'I have seen that you understand a chariot and horses. But I do not know if you possess the brutality which is needed to survive in Antioch. The Syrians do not follow the same rules here as they do in Rome. This is a race without civilised forms and proper rulings. This is truly a . . . blood spectacle.'

'For my freedom, I will do anything.'

Nicodemus forlornly shook his head, saying, 'You are fortunate. You can achieve freedom by breaking an iron collar from your neck. But there are people in the world who are burdened by something much stronger than iron.'

Vesuvio knew what the old man meant. He had heard enough about Nicodemus's work for the Jews to appreciate his concern. He answered, 'You are doing much for your people. I realise what a public victory represents to you. I shall serve you as I promise, to give you the best of my strength.'

'Answer me one question honestly, Roman.'

'Ask me the question.'

'Do you find me crazed and a slightly . . . obsessive old man?'

Vesuvio answered directly, 'I was once befriended by an Israelite who belonged to a sect called the Essenes. He had a passion, too. He did not believe in slavery. I understood the Essene better than you because he and I agreed on the question of slavery.'

'Slavery? But how can commerce, farming, any life succeed without slavery? Slaves are the work-power of the world. They build aqueducts. Pave roads. Hew forests and propel ships. I know there are arguments against slavery but how can a world without slavery be?'

'That is what I am trying to prove on my land in Italy. To explain to you in words would take too long. I would have to *show* you how I give people land to work as their own. And provide strength for them, a protection which men and women often need when they suddenly find themselves free – and alone – in the world. You as a Jew should understand a struggle against oppression.'

'Answer me this, Roman. Have you seen suffering here in the Palace of the Dates? We have slaves. Answer me honestly.'

'Yes, sire, I have seen suffering.'

Nicodemus was momentarily silent. He finally asked, 'Tell me what suffering you have seen.'

'I do not see physical suffering. Not scourging and cruelty and neglect. But there are people who suffer in this house from the sharp distinctions placed on them because some are free and others are enslaved.'

'How can that be? The only free people in this house are myself and my daughter. Unless it is you who . . .'

'No. I do not refer to myself.'

'And it is certainly not me!' He chuckled.

Vesuvio soberly reassured him. 'Nor is it you.'

Nicodemus asked, 'Well, it certainly cannot be my daughter.'

'Your daughter is a young woman. She is of a marriageable age.'

'But Rachel has no suitors! She chooses to receive no one at the Palace of the Dates. She sees no males except for slaves, and the only one who is young enough to . . .'

Nicodemus paused. His hands fell onto the arms of the chair.

Nicodemus's voice was barely above a whisper. He said, 'You mean Isaac, don't you?'

'Yes,' Vesuvio soberly replied. 'And I hope I have not done wrong in mentioning this fact. But . . .'

'You are a good man, young Macrinus. In three days' time you will call no man "master". Let us not speak until then. Nor speak to anyone else of my daughter, Rachel, and that . . . slave.' He waved his hand for Vesuvio to depart.

*   *   *

Nicodemus did not leave his cedar-lined room for the rest of the day. The proconsul's legates came to the Palace of the Dates at late-morning to collect the tax levied against the sponsors of racing chariots in Antioch's arena. Nicodemus received the Roman officials in the room, paid them the money from a brass-hinged box, and guardedly answered their questions about his holdings in the city. The Romans had never before been so direct in questioning him. Nicodemus brooded upon this fact after the Romans left the Palace of the Dates. He next called Isaac to the room. He spoke to him behind closed doors and, after the meeting with him, he sent for the head-priests from the temple. He next summoned a scribe and a trustworthy messenger. He did all these things throughout the afternoon and, when evening came, he finally called his daughter to him.

Rachel was surprised to find her father looking so downcast when she joined him. A flame sputtered in the neck of a hammered brass lamp, making the tall back of the chair cast an ominous shadow against the silk wallhangings. Rachel had heard horses arriving and departing throughout the day. She knew that Romans had come to the house. She had thought that this was due to the preparations for racing in the arena.

'Father,' she said moving quietly across the thickness of the delicately dyed carpets laid on top of one another. 'I expected to find you jubilant on the night before the races. Not so . . .'

She stopped and asked, 'Did the Romans somehow upset you today?'

Nicodemus did not answer.

'Have no fear, Father,' she said, sitting on a cushion in front of his chair and resting her head against his knee. 'You made a wise choice in choosing Vesuvio in the slave house. He is not only a good man with noble blood in his veins. But he is a fine horsemen. Your team will win tomorrow. You will see.'

Looking up at him, she asked brightly, 'Have you told him yet that you will free him if he wins?'

Nicodemus nodded. He said, 'But that is not why I called you here this evening. I have more important things to talk of now.'

'Father, what *is* troubling you?'

Nicodemus stared straight ahead as he asked, 'Why did you not tell me you loved a slave, Rachel?'

She stared at him in disbelief.

He said, 'Isaac. Why did you not tell me about your feelings for the slave Isaac?'

'Who has been whispering stories to you, Father?'

'Then you do not deny it.'

'Do you want me to?'

Nicodemus smiled. He said, 'You know how to wriggle out of questions, Rachel. Just like your father.' He shook his head.

Staring momentarily at him, Rachel flung her arms around his legs and her body began to convulse with sobs.

Remaining upright in his chair, Nicodemus said, 'I spoke to Isaac this afternoon. He gave me no reason to rebuke him. He assured me he has behaved properly with you. That he did not press you for encouragement nor hope to achieve anything above his station. But he also spoke honestly about . . .'

Nicodemus closed his eyes. 'I do not know when you meet. How long your love has been blossoming. I must admit that I did consider selling Isaac when I realised he did love you. But then I thought of the hurt I might cause my little Rachel and I knew I could not sell Isaac. Not sell him and hurt you, Rachel.'

Opening his eyes and rubbing a knuckle against the hollow of each socket, he said, 'Isaac is a good man. He has a sharp mind. He learns fast. I fear that his only failing is his birthright. Isaac was born a . . . slave.'

Rachel remained silent at her father's feet. She had dried the tears from her face. Her eyes showed no emotion.

Placing his hand on Rachel's shoulder, Nicodemus said, 'The Almighty has always had ways of disguising His blessings, Rachel. I suspect tyranny to be close at hand for me. The Romans hate the Jews. Especially those who speak out for their people. This is no time for a Jew to distrust one of his brothers. You know how I feel about the necessity of slavery, how I disagree with Essene doctrine, but a brother is a brother, Rachel, and . . .'

Sitting straight in the chair, Nicodemus soberly announced 'I have freed Isaac. I have told him to take you to Tarsus. You are to leave here immediately. You will stay with your mother's sister there. If I can join you, I will. If I cannot, then you must marry without me. But marry according to the laws of the Talmud, Rachel. Do not abandon the Talmud.'

She jerked up her head and stared at him in disbelief, asking, 'Why do you speak like this? Why should I leave the Palace of the Dates? What "tyranny" do you mean, Father. What are the Romans doing to you?'

'Do not question me about my decision, Rachel. I have always known the climate of evilness. I know now that treachery is growing in Antioch. The Roman's questions today alerted me. I want you out of this city. Tonight.'

'Not without you, Father,' she said, shaking her head. 'Never without you.'

'Do not argue with me, Daughter. I know your mother blesses you. Go. Please. Do not make things more difficult for your father than they already are.'

'What treachery do you suspect? What is happening here that you will not tell me about? What did the Romans say when they came here today to collect the taxes?'

Nicodemus spat out the words as if they were venom on his tongue. 'The Romans!'

'You *are* in grave danger. I cannot leave you!'

Nicodemus pulled himself back from her, ordering, 'Go. Now. Please, Daughter! For your love of me.'

Rachel grabbed his legs and began to sob onto his robe. She begged, 'And you, Father? What is *your* protection against the Romans?'

Nicodemus ben Seth's face remained immobile. His voice

was barely audible as he insisted, 'Go, Rachel. Isaac is a free man now. He awaits you in a cart outside the stable. Leave this house in peace. Build your own home. Prosper. Propagate in the name of your people.'

Closing his eyes, he clenched his gnarled fingers around the arms of his chair as Rachel obediently rose from the floor. She bent over him and, brushing her lips against his forehead, she said, 'I can at least pray that Vesuvio will remain by your side.' She turned, leaving the room through a heavy tapestry hanging over a door.

*   *   *

Nicodemus's announcement to Vesuvio that he had written to Balthazar, and that he would free him if he won tomorrow's race, had so excited Vesuvio that he had forgotten to ask the old man one very important question this morning at their meeting. He had seen the arrival of the Roman collectors later that day in the courtyard in the Palace of the Dates. He also knew that Nicodemus had called Isaac and, then, Rachel, to his chamber. Vesuvio did not want to disturb those meetings but the information he needed was vital; there was also not much time in which to receive it. He waited late in the evening until he saw a house slave in the stableyard and, telling the woman that she must somehow get a message to Nicodemus, he then impressed upon her how important it was for him to learn a certain fact about the charioteer whom the Senator had brought from Rome to Antioch. The house slave delivered the news to Vesuvio later that night in the stableyard. He listened closely to the small but urgent bit of information which Nicodemus had miraculously managed to discover in the last few hours from a groom in the proconsul's stable. The report pleased Vesuvio and he lay on his bed of straw after the slave woman had left, smiling to himself, weighing his plan for tomorrow's competition. Nicodemus had told him at their first meeting that the races in Antioch were a blood spectacle. Vesuvio knew that he would have to break many rules – even personal codes – to win not only the race but his freedom. He drifted off to sleep that night with his penis forming a hard rod which protruded over his belly as he dreamed about soon being reunited with Miranda.

28

Lutarius Pictor stood in the glare of the bright Syrian sun and received the salute of fourteen charioteers lined below him in the arena. The drivers held themselves tall and proud in their chariots, extending one arm to the Proconsul's marble podium as they dedicated themselves to race – even to die – in the arena as servants of Rome. The chariots ranged from heavily carved Roman conveyances, decorated with brass and ivory, to simply-constructed chariots designed to speed across Eastern deserts. Each chariot was attached to four horses and the fourteen entries stretched in a long line down one side of the eighteen-thousand-foot-long oval track. The sun caught the brass studs on the harnessing. The muscle in the drivers' arms strained to hold their horses in control during the ceremony. This was a representation of all nations and tribes which lived under Lutarius Pictor's rule in Antioch – sinewy Syrians, auburn-haired Greeks, dusky Arabs, flat-faced Mesopotamians, sober Egyptians.

Senator Sullus stood a few feet behind Pictor on the official podium. The white-haired old man wore the Roman senatorial toga bordered in purple, a cumbersome garment too heavy for the afternoon's heat. As a rumble rose from the arena when the chariots now began to move toward the stalls at the far end of the track, Sullus gladly sank to the cushions on his marble chair placed alongside the proconsul's throne.

Beckoning for a slave to begin dipping an indigo-dyed ostrich fan, Sullus said with sudden criticism, 'Fourteen seems to be an unruly amount of contestants, Pictor. We never race more than eight chariots in Rome.'

Pictor ignored the Senator's remark as he also sank to his chair. He and the Senator had arrived only minutes ago for the main event of the day. The arena was crammed with two-hundred-thousand eager, shouting spectators. The preliminary races had obviously been successful, Pictor guessed, and he did not want the Senator to dampen his spirits. He looked toward the crowd seated on a rising bank of stone benches and felt reassured by their enthusiastic shouting for the race to begin.

Senator Sullus pressed, 'You *did* warn Jurgo about the irregularities of the race? That he would not be competing under normal conditions?'

Pictor had personally reminded the Senator's driver yesterday and again this morning that he would be racing against thirteen other chariots. He had told Jurgo that he should expect anything to happen in the Antioch arena.

Sprawling out his bare legs in front of him, Pictor tried to hide the fact from Senator Sullus that he was finding him increasing senile and difficult to entertain as a guest. He answered, 'Yes, I spoke to Jurgo as well as warning you, Senator . . . I warned you even before you came to Antioch that Syrians are full of surprises.'

'I was under the impression, Pictor, that you were not in the habit of giving way to a crowd's demand for a vulgar show.' The Senator glanced disapprovingly at the clothing which Pictor had chosen to wear today on the official podium to represent Rome – a military breastplate of hammered brass, a short linen tunic, and brown leather sandals.

The blare of trumpets sounded at the far end of the arena; the charioteers had formed a line in the stalls, the *carceres*, waiting for the Games Magistrate to give the signal to start from his position atop the marble *spina* which ran down the centre of the track.

Pictor beckoned his tribune to hand him a wooden-framed tablet of pressed wax. He flipped open the tablet and quickly perused the wagers which had been placed on the drivers.

Handing the tablet to Senator Sullus, he said, 'Your driver is favoured by six to one.'

Snatching the tablet from Pictor's hand, Senator Sullus grunted as his eyes moved down the list. He suddenly stopped, asking, ' "Seth"? Is that the name of the Jew whose property you are confiscating?'

'Nicodemus ben Seth,' Pictor confirmed, knowing that the Senator could not at least object to that fact. They had politically agreed last night that a proconsul could seize a Jew's property in the name of the Emperor if the Jew could be proven to be a traitor. It was Senator Sullus himself who had suggested to Pictor – in the presence of reliable witnesses – that bribery could be used to gather evidence against Jews. Pictor had already collected written testaments from Roman merchants in Antioch that Nicodemus ben Seth was currently plotting to form a monopoly of Jewish traders to cause a financial panic amongst Roman economy. Pictor's officers would wait until after the races to arrest him, hoping to avoid a riot amongst the Jewish population.

Sullus now asked, 'How does a Jew come to have a Roman driver for his chariot?'

Pictor furrowed his brow. He had not noticed on the tablet that a Roman was the charioteer for Nicodemus ben Seth.

Sullus held the wooden-framed sheets forward and looked suspiciously at Pictor. He, also, had been having misgivings in the last few days.

Reading the name 'Macrinus' printed behind Seth's entry on the pressed wax, Pictor glibly said, 'Many provincials assume Roman names.'

' "Macrinus"?' the old senator slowly questioned. 'I know of only one Roman family who bears that name. Aurelius Macrinus the Elder was the Republican who married Milo Popiliano's sister. Remember me telling you about my good friend, Milo Popiliano? He was the knight who bedded the Empress Agrippina.'

Pictor snapped the tablet shut and handed it toward the tribune standing behind his chair as he crisply answered, 'I am certain no descendant of the noble Macrinus family is racing here today under the sponsorship of a . . . Jew.'

Senator Sullus rejoindered, 'A young Macrinus heir could have been captured from his homeland. Many free men are sold to wandering slave traders. Such a thing is not unusual. Even Julius Caesar was once sold into slavery.'

'But that was many years ago, Senator. I repeat that I sincerely doubt that your army friend's heir is enslaved to a Jewish merchant here in Antioch.' Pictor tried not to be snide, not to lose his patience with this old man. But Senator Sullus's words about Julius Caesar being enslaved during the Republic represented further proof to Pictor that the Senator dwelt too much in the past.

A fanfare of trumpets blasted from the far end of the stadium. Attendants rushed to remove the wooden slats from the *carceres* behind which the chariot teams waited to begin.

Pictor said, 'Look. Jurgo stands at Number Six. A fine position. A very fine position indeed.' Pictor had no way to arrange for the Senator's chariot to win this main race of the day but he had been able to manage for Jurgo to draw the number of the most desirable starting place, the place which gave him the best angle to make a rush toward the inside position on the sandy course.

A momentary hush filled the amphitheatre as the Games Magistrate raised his hand and, when he dropped a white cloth from his platform high on the *spina*, the fourteen charioteers shot forward in a thunder of hooves – accompanied by a cracking of whips – and the spectators' roar filled the air.

The Senator sat forward on his seat as he watched the teams flood in an unruly stream onto the course. 'It's havoc!'

Pictor looked approvingly at the charge of strong horses,

the determination of one driver to clamour past another for a good position on the track. This was the first moment of skill being matched against skill, of strength against strength.

Staring aghast at the charioteers no longer dressed in the fine raiment which they had worn in the dedication ceremony, Senator Sullus gasped, 'The drivers, Proconsul! They are almost . . . naked! None of the drivers except Jurgo are dressed as they were when they presented themselves to you! What's happened to their helmets? Their breast-plates? Their fine leggings?'

'The sun is hot here in Syria, Senator,' Pictor answered disinterestedly as he concentrated on seeing who was to take the lead positions in the first lap.

The Senator asked, 'But what about their safety? What about . . . form?'

The chariots raced down the far side of the arena. The official podium stood high enough above the arena for Pictor to see that – apart from four chariots already entangled near the starting stalls – three chariots were in a lead position, with two following closely behind them. He was relieved to see that Jurgo was in the first four.

Looking from the lead chariots, back to the dust clouding in their wake, Pictor strained his eyes to see how many chariots would make it through the congestion created by the pile-up in front of the *carceres*.

He said to the Senator, 'Think of today's show as the races must have been when Rome was young. When men raced in the arena as they did in open fields. Is that not what you and I have been discussing, Senator? And is that not the reason you brought Jurgo here in the first place?'

The Senator stared aghast at the confusion of the four drivers in front of the *carceres* as the other chariots were already half-way down the first side of the course. He said, 'It is nothing but pandemonium. How do you tell which driver is which?'

Pictor now held his eyes on the far end of the *spina* –

opposite to the starting point – to see which chariots would first corner the bend. He said, 'Antioch drivers are dressed by colours like Roman factions. But the team colours here are not sporting clubs. Here the colours represent nations. The Greeks are fond of blue. The Syrians mostly wear black. The Egyptians dress in a yellow-dyed cloth.' Pictor raised one hand toward the sloping seats of the vast stadium and urged, 'Look, Senator. Study the benches behind us. You will see blocks of colours. Look how the benches are divided into patches of blue, yellow, black, red . . . Those are Greeks. The Egyptians. The Syrians. The Mesopotamians. They know who to cheer for.'

The old Senator sputtered, 'But . . . but . . . but how do *our* people know?'

'All good Romans will cheer for your chariot,' he assured Senator Sullus. 'All good Romans will cheer for Jurgo.'

Senator Sullus sat to the edge of his seat as three chariots now led the race in front of the official podium. He saw that Jurgo was in the leading teams but his eyes focused next on one of the drivers of the two teams which followed. He asked, 'Who is that driver in the white tunic knotted over his shoulder?'

Pictor glanced from where the arena slaves had cleared the debris of the chariots which had become entangled at the outset of the race. He looked to where the old Senator pointed. Seeing a light Eastern chariot pulled by a pair of wheat-coloured stallions and two snow-white Arabians, he said soberly, 'That is the Jew's driver.'

'My eyesight is not too good, Pictor, but the driver does not appear to me – even from this distance – to have the dark colouring of a Israelite.'

Pictor was becoming increasingly aggravated by this old man's interruptions. But remembering the influence that he had in Rome, he beckoned for his tribune and hoped to gather enough details for the old man as he could – and keep him silent.

Jurgo's chariot, along with the Egyptian driver wearing yellow, and the Syrian in black, were still in the lead. Nicodemus ben Seth's chariot followed closely behind, racing abreast with the Thracian driver dressed in a green tunic.

The tribune returned to the podium; he whispered into Pictor's ear and then discreetly stepped behind the chair.

Pictor leaned his head toward the Senator and asked, 'Where did you say the Macrinus family had their estate in Italy?'

Senator Sullus looked at Pictor with blank, rheumy eyes and answered suspiciously, 'Campania.'

Pictor considered this fact. He crossed his arms and said, 'Campania is where the volcano Vesuvius erupted.' His words were a statement.

Senator Sullus slowly nodded.

Pictor explained, 'The Jew's driver is called "Macrinus" as it is written on the tablet. But I have just heard that his stable boys and grooms call him "Vesuvio".' He turned his eyes to the arena and saw that the third lap had not only begun but that the driver, Vesuvio, had gained on the Thracian and was gradually gaining on the three chariots in the lead. Was he in fact the nephew of the senator's old crony, Milo Popiliano?

* * *

Nicodemus ben Seth had come to today's race attended only by litter-bearers; he had dismissed them at the southerly gate to the amphitheatre and now sat on a stone bench amongst the Jews. He had seen on his arrival that Roman soldiers disguised in foreign robes sat amongst the Jewish people. He knew why they were there.

Nicodemus tried to concentrate on the race but even when he watched Vesuvio overtake the Syrian driver, and then thunder past the Roman charioteer, he did not feel a competitive excitement. Vesuvio gained on the Egyptian driver in the lead but Nicodemus knew that, even if Vesuvio won, he would not get his freedom.

Nicodemus realised by the conduct of the Jewish people seated around him that word had spread amongst them that Lutarius Pictor planned to seize him and place him under arrest.

When would it happen? What would the charge be? Subversion? Did it matter? He knew that Lutarius Pictor would invent any charges he wished. Pictor would bribe the necessary witnesses to give evidence that Nicodemus was a threat to Roman peace in Syria.

Nicodemus sat forlorn amongst the Jewish spectators now cheering Vesuvio's progress to the leading chariot. The Egyptian, Vesuvio and the Roman led the race, their teams now charging down the far side of the arena, the furrowed section of the course which passed in front of the proconsul's podium.

Although Nicodemus had many friends amongst the Jewish people present in the arena today, he did not encourage their signals of friendship. He knew that Roman officials were watching him and he did not want to involve any of his people in the false charges which Lutarius Pictor would soon make.

Glancing toward the brass dolphins on a pole which stood at the end of the *spina,* Nicodemus saw to his surprise that six of the dolphins were already turned down. This was a sign that six laps were completed. This quick passage of time proved to Nicodemus that he had been lost in his worries.

The disorder of Antioch's races usually excited Nicodemus On any other day, he would thrill at the chariots first rushing from the *carceres,* watching spellbound to see which drivers would become entangled in the frenzy of horses to gain a prime position on the course.

Today's race was raucous, true, but Nicodemus was preoccupied with more important matters. He was sad from losing Rachel. The uncertainty of his own future dejected him. He felt like a very old man approaching death.

The thunder of hooves drew closer as the leading three chariots bounded around the corner. The Eygptian came first. Vesuvio was close behind him. But the Roman driver, Jurgo, was not yet in view.

The Jewish spectators around Nicodemus rose to their feet as Vesuvio and the Egyptian drew closer in a billowing cloud of dust. Nicodemus also rose from his seat to achieve a clear vision of Vesuvio and saw that his chariot was now abreast with the Egyptian. His mood momentarily lightened with pride. He knew he had made a fine choice with Vesuvio.

At the moment when Nicodemus judged that Vesuvio was going to pass the Egyptian, he saw him instead beginning to edge the Egyptian's chariot toward the outside wall of the arena. He could not understand why he was doing it. He saw that Vesuvio had a clear passage to rush past him.

The Egyptian faction seated at the far end of the amphitheatre hissed at Vesuvio's sudden move sideways on the course. The shouts of disapproval spread around the amphitheatre as Vesuvio continued to crowd the Egyptian against the wall.

Nicodemus heard the first grating of the Egyptian's axle against the wall and, as the Egyptian spectators now screamed their rage, Vesuvio kept moving closer and closer to the chariot.

The Egyptian steadied the reins tied around his waist with one hand and began snapping his whip at Vesuvio with the other.

Bending over his chariot, Vesuvio held his own reins tightly as he continued to edge the right wheel of his chariot against the Egyptian's nearest axle, bumping him closer and closer toward the wall.

Sparks flew from the iron hub grating against the stone wall at racing speed. The Egyptian's horses were beginning to shy away from the wall in fright, sending the chariot closer toward the stone enclosure. The Egyptian pulled back his whip to lash again at Vesuvio when the inside wheel cracked and sent him flying from the chariot whilst the horses jerked in freedom in the opposite direction.

Vesuvio quickly tugged his reins to avoid racing into the veering horses and, pulling his own team into a sharp turn, he proceeded then to make a complete sweep on the track.

Nicodemus stood gaping at Vesuvio, unable to believe his eyes. Vesuvio had turned his team around on the track. He was now racing into the direction from which he had just come. Yes! He had turned his team around and was now driving headlong toward the Roman's chariot!

The Thracian and the Syrian chariots had not yet cornered the far end of the arena when Vesuvio had unexpectedly turned, rushing directly toward Jurgo's team.

As the Jewish spectators cheered at Vesuvio's daring act, and the Egyptian faction stopped their hissing, Nicodemus stood looking at Vesuvio bent over his galloping horses. He glanced quickly at Jurgo's team. The Roman was trying to swerve to the left to avoid a headlong collision with Vesuvio. But Vesuvio followed him to the left – then to the right – still aiming to hit in a direct collision.

It was then that Nicodemus remembered the question which Vesuvio had sent a house slave to ask him late last night. *Does the Roman charioteer, Jurgo, like horses or is racing merely a competitive passion for him?*

Nicodemus also recalled the answer he had learned from a slave working in the Proconsul's stables – that Jurgo treated his horses better than if they were people.

A roar from the two-hundred-thousand spectators in the arena drew Nicodemus's attention back to the course. Jurgo had swerved too far in an attempt to keep his team from racing into Vesuvio's horses. He misgauged his swerve and went crashing against the stone wall.

Nicodemus sank to his seat when the Thracian and Syrian chariots were cornering the far end of the arena. Vesuvio turned his team in a clatter of hooves to complete the seventh – and last – lap of the race. Nicodemus knew that he did not have to watch the conclusion to see if Vesuvio would be the victor. He had already done much more than win this racc. Vesuvio had jeopardised his horses, his own life, to make a Jew triumphant over the Romans.

* * *

'Preposterous!' Senator Sullus angrily shouted as he and Lutarius Pictor strode down the stone passageway which led from the podium to a subterranean room beneath the arena where Jurgo's mangled body lay waiting for the surgeon. Torches sputtered in iron brackets along the dark passageway; the crowd's roar still echoed behind them. The Senator continued, 'I have never seen such a public outrage in my life, Pictor! You do not conduct races here in Antioch. You give shows of wild men!'

'You are upset about Jurgo,' Pictor eagerly consoled as he hurried to keep in step with the Senator. 'But I assure you that Jurgo will be fine. The best physicians in Antioch are with him. He would not get better care even if he were in Rome. My tribune assures me that Jurgo can be . . .'

'Jurgo? What do I care for Jurgo? He is a coward! He was challenged by the Jew's driver and he turned away! Pictor, I never believed that I would see such a thing in an arena! A driver eliminating one charioteer by squeezing him against the wall and then turning around his chariot on the track to drive headlong into the driver behind him! What kind of vengeance races do you conduct here?'

'It was the Jew's plan, Senator, I assure you. It was the Jew's crafty plan to shame us Romans. Nicodemus ben Seth will pay for this, Senator, I promise you. Ben Seth shall pay!' Pictor's face twisted with anger as he not only thought about the Jew but also imagined the report which Senator Sullus would make in Rome about this visit to Antioch.

'What do I care about the Jew?' Sullus flared. 'He is your problem. I am thinking of Rome's reputation. You are wrong to allow such lawless competitions to take place in this arena under the aegis of Rome. You include too many drivers. Then there's the matter of protocol! The uniforms! You are supposed to be a representative of Rome, Pictor! You are supposed to impose an . . . Imperial decorum!'

Senator Sullus and Lutarius Pictor emerged in the small room at the end of the stone passageway and saw a group of sober-faced men standing around a wooden table on which Jurgo's mangled body lay. Pictor's tribune turned from the table and reported to Pictor in a sober voice, 'The surgeon will try to save him, Proconsul. The ribs are broken. Both legs badly crushed. He is still conscious but . . .' He shook his head.

Senator Sullus brushed past the tribune and stared down at Jurgo's blood-matted body. Jurgo's face twisted with pain as he reached to grip the Senator's hand.

Stepping back to avoid the touch, Senator Sullus shook his head with disdain.

A deep-chested voice spoke from the shadows beyond the table. 'Senator, your driver is a brave man.'

Senator Sullus quickly demanded, 'Who are you to speak?'

Vesuvio stepped forward into the flickering light of the torch. His face was covered with dirt, his tunic drenched with perspiration. He said with equanimity to the Senator, 'I am not proud of what I have done, Senator Sullus. I did not set out to take a man's life nor to injure his horses. I was told I must be prepared to race in a blood spectacle where no rules were held. I did what I had to do to win my freedom as a slave.'

Lutarius Pictor stepped alongside Senator Sullus and asked, 'Your "freedom as a slave"?'

Vesuvio nodded. He knew the identity of the barrel-chested Proconsul. He answered, 'My master, Nicodemus ben Seth, promised me my freedom if I won today's race.'

The Senator said, 'You would have won without driving the first chariot from the track. You had no reason to turn your chariot around and drive headlong into my driver.'

'A slave has many duties to his master, Senator,' Vesuvio solemnly answered. He turned to look at Lutarius Pictor as he continued, 'Especially to a man whose life is in far more danger than any charioteer in the arena.'

Pictor held Vesuvio's gaze, saying, 'You speak fine Latin but your insolent manner is one of the basest foreign to Rome.'

Senator Sullus raised his hand for Pictor to be silent and, stepping closer to Vesuvio, he said, 'You are listed as "Aurelius Macrinus". Do you claim blood ties to the Macrinus family in Campania? The *gens* related to a man called Milo Popiliano?'

Vesuvio answered soberly, 'Milo Popiliano was the brother of my mother, a good woman now dead who was called Cornelia Popiliana Macrinus.'

Senator Sullus studied Vesuvio's body, saying, 'Yes, I see a physical resemblance between you and the Popiliano family. They also had light colouring. Tell me, how did you come to be racing for a . . . Jew?'

'I was captured by thieves east of here in the strait referred to by some men as the "River Styx". They sold me to a slave house where I was bought by the good man named Nicodemus ben Seth whom you simply refer to as "the Jew".'

Pictor said, 'Senator, do not allow this slave to speak so insolently to you. He is obviously demented. He is wasting your time while Jurgo lies dying before us.'

Keeping his eyes on Vesuvio, Senator Sullus calmly said, 'Jurgo will die regardless of your efforts, Pictor. Any fool can see that. But try to save him if you wish. That is your affair. In the meantime, though, I am taking this man back to Rome with me. He wears a slave collar and I am seizing him in the name of Emperor Trajan. He will sail with me tomorrow on the *Silena* for the port of Ostia.'

Vesuvio demanded, 'You will take me back to Rome as a . . . slave?'

'Your wear a slave collar, don't you?' The Senator motioned for Pictor's soldier to take Vesuvio from the room.

*   *   *

A raw wind blew against Vesuvio's face two days later as he stood alongside Senator Sullus on the deck of the *Silena*, a Roman military trireme on its voyage back to the Italian port of Ostia.

No longer wearing the iron slave collar around his neck, Vesuvio clutched a woollen cape across his chest as he listened to Senator Sullus elaborate on the plans which he had for him as a slave in Rome.

'The house in which you will be confined is a pleasure villa, a house in the district of Tibur which is run for the pleasure of those citizens of Rome called "the Palatine Set".'

Vesuvio knew of the people to whom the Senator referred, a loose-moralled group of patricians who squandered their time and money in prurient pursuits. His mind was dulled by the harsh realisation that he would not gain his freedom, that he was unable to sail south to Alexandria in search of Miranda but was being taken back to his homeland.

The Senator continued, 'I cannot disclose the identity of the person who pays for the upkeep of this villa but you will be placed in the care of a man there named Polybius, the master of the male slaves. Polybius will not know, of course, that I am responsible for sending you. You will live there as any of the other pleasure slaves but, in due time, I shall re-establish you on your estate as a free man.'

Vesuvio could no longer argue with the Senator. Nor could he disagree. They had talked all yesterday and late into the night about the advantages of Vesuvio performing this service for Senator Sullus in a villa in Tibur. The Senator had carefully pointed out that, as Vesuvio had been bought in a slave house in a Roman province, a legal hearing to prove his innocence – or freedom – would take much longer than this mission to a pleasure villa.

'It will do you no good to worry about your slave girl, young Macrinus. She would not be in Alexandria even if you went there.'

Vesuvio jerked his head. He had been thinking about Miranda but had not suspected that the old senator was conscious of his wandering mind.

The Senator said, 'Your Uncle Milo is a man to set as your example in life. He loved empresses! Follow in his footsteps, young man. Do not torture yourself over . . . slave girls!'

Vesuvio took a deep breath as his fists tightened at his side. His mind flooded with an angry explanation of his late uncle's loneliness, how the old man had never known love in his lifetime. Deciding that he would only be wasting his time trying to argue again with stubborn Senator Sullus, Vesuvio shook his head, saying, 'I have no choice of which footsteps I take.'

'You have courage, young man. I saw that in the arena in Antioch. Also, you are loyal. I also saw an example of that there. You can at least console yourself now by knowing that Lutarius Pictor will *not* arrest Nicodemus ben Seth. I personally advised Pictor not to pursue troubling the old man. Nicodemus ben Seth and his family will live from now on in peace.'

Vesuvio thought about Nicodemus, about Isaac being freed from slavery and allowed to marry Rachel. He realised that he should at least feel elated about that. But standing on the deck of the *Silena* bound for Italy, he could only think about himself and Miranda. He did not even care if the Senator's promise did not come true. What good would it be to have freedom now without sharing his life with Miranda?

He soberly listened to the Senator explain to him about the villa in Tilbur, remembering when he had gone to the Grove of Daphne with Isaac and his worry had been potency. It now seemed so foolish, so senseless, so trivial.

BOOK FIVE

VILLA ORGIASTA

29

'Animals!' Polybius bellowed as he kicked at the nearest table, his sandal sending a chased-silver urn crashing onto the floor which spread a red pool of wine across the black-and-white chequered marble. 'Sicilian scum! Dogs of Germany! Jackals of Egypt!'

The collection of athletically built young men lay motionless on their dining-couches, momentarily stunned by the unexpected entrance of their master into the *triclinium* at Villa Orgiasta. The young men wore only loin-cloths or briefly cut tunics which pulled tightly across their muscular bodies as they lolled on the couches. Their skin ranged from the colour of alabaster to the blackest of obsidian. Their hair varied between the hue of ripe wheat to coarse black wool. Their eyes were like almonds with blue centres or darkly gleaming black pearls.

The short but muscular man named Polybius stood in front of this unique assembly of males whom he had unexpectedly disturbed during their midday meal. Polybius was older than these men. He had a shaved head and his mature features now contorted into a red mask of rage, the cords in his neck standing out in anger as he railed at them.

'How dare you whores continue talking to one another when I enter a room! How dare you keep sipping your wine. Gossiping like old women. You are supposed to be . . . men! The finest specimen of manhood in Rome! Disciplined. Respectful. Impeccably mannered. If you treat me like this, how will you conduct yourself tomorrow night at the banquet when I will be parading you to the richest, most powerful people in the Empire?'

A young man with curly black hair and thick eyelashes was the first to regain his voice. He calmly asked, 'I mean no offence by interrupting, Master Polybius. But do our visitors come to Villa Orgiasta to see how quickly and politely we rise from our couches? Or do they want to see how long we keep our *cocks* standing?'

A murmur of guarded amusement passed amongst the couches.

'Antoninus,' Polybius patiently said, planting his fists on the leather belt cinching his trim waist. He held out his bare chest and appraised the young man with the curly black hair. 'True, General Pila's wife has asked for you on each of her seven visits to this villa. But I could easily provide her with a burro. Lady Pilina would be equally satisfied by a burro's equipment. And she would probably have to spend less time paying compliments to *that* jackass to get a good performance!'

Loud laughter filled the *triclinium* as the other men turned on their couches to look at the blushing young Sicilian named Antoninus.

Polybius paced closer to the cluster of small dining-tables. He beckoned toward a line of rose-coloured marble columns which flanked the far end of the room. He said as he faced the young men, 'I am bringing a new comrade to join you. I want all you Apollos and Adonises to help our new arrival adjust to the life at Villa Orgiasta.'

Vesuvio entered the room between two guards and the young men stared at him from their couches placed on the dais. His face was ruddy from the sea voyage and a simple cloak thrown around his shoulders. He looked at the pampered men lying on the couches and thought, Did I regain my sexuality only to become one of . . . them?

Polybius announced to the group, 'The new slave's name is "Vesuvio". My agents tell me he's Italian born but is fresh off a boat from Antioch, Antioch! Home of the fabled Grove of Daphne!'

He turned to a flat-faced man whose black hair was cropped closely against his light skin. He asked, 'Do you know what that means, Lupus? The Grove of Daphne? Our new friend might have a few tricks for the ladies that even your artful tongue cannot perform!'

Polybius next turned to a broad-shouldered youth with a square chin and widely placed eyes. He said, 'You, Mnester! You have the endurance to pleasure a woman till dawn. In the Grove of Daphne, though, the record is counted not by hours but days!'

Pacing back and forth in front of the dais, Polybius held both hands behind his back, saying, 'I want you men to make Vesuvio feel comfortable here in Villa Orgiasta. I want you to explain the rules to him. It is good for a new man to learn from other . . . slaves. It is also good for you to *repeat* the rules. Repeating rules only helps you remember them better, doesn't it? Norax!' He stared at a black man resting a silver goblet on the cushions of the couch. 'Use your table!'

Polybius moved his eyes along the line of faces now staring at him. He continued, 'I want you to tell our new man about the mastiffs patrolling the walls at Villa Orgiasta. I want you to tell him about the armed guards. How those guards both envy and . . . despise you. How they wish that they also had the opportunity to pleasure the richest women in Rome. But how they secretly jeer you. You are the most sexually desirable men in the world but ordinary, red-blooded men laugh and sneer at all of you because, despite your beauty, your potency, all your famous endowments, you are all just as helpless as children in a nursery. Poor things! You live in splendour. This villa is less than an hour from Rome's Forum. The crossroads of the greatest city in the world. But you might as well be marooned on an island. You are imprisoned here as sexual objects. Prisoners. Ungrateful, spoilt, self-centred prisoners.' A smile slowly crept over Polybius's face as he stared at the men now lying silently on their couches. His words had sobered them.

* * *

Polybius always knew when he had the male pleasure slaves in control. He also knew that when he compared them to children in a nursery they were secretly calling him their nursemaid. But no man at Villa Orgiasta dared speak such abusive words to Polybius.

So, continuing with the tactics by which he knew how to keep the men in obeisance, and to achieve the best sexual performances from them when they were needed, he resumed his outpouring of verbal abuse.

His voice was more quiet as he said, 'I also want you to tell our newcomer about the women here at Villa Orgiasta. Not the ladies who visit you stallions. But the female slaves locked in the far wing of the villa. I want you to tell Vesuvio about the punishment he will receive if he dares makes friends with one of Druscilla's girls. But if he is so foolish as to make *love* to one of the female pleasure slaves . . . Well!' Polybius woefully shook his head. 'Well, then, you must tell him about the death he must expect.'

He smiled with pleasure as he watched the handsome young men fidget on their couches. He secretly admired their beauty but despised them for their youth. He said in a lighter vein, 'Also, there is the matter of having sex amongst yourselves. I want you to tell Vesuvio about that offence, too.'

Polybius raised his arm and pointed at one couch. 'You, Hector. You can tell Vesuvio what happened to that pretty young boy from Gaul who fell in love with you. How the guards took him out from the dormitory one night and –' He shrugged. '– What was his name? It does not matter now. He never came back.'

The man named Hector shrugged his bare shoulders. He stared down at the strip of treated doeskin moulded over his bulging groin. He mumbled, 'I could not help it if the boy fell in love with me, Master.' Hector's boyish bashfulness was inconsistent with the manly proportions of his sun-bronzed body.

'No, of course not, Hector,' Polybius said mockingly. 'Of course you can not prevent someone falling in love with you. Their own weakness is the cause, isn't it? Your skin ripples across your muscles like a mountain stream over rocks. Your body is cast like fine military armour. You stand as strong as one of the Praetorian guards. You have the stamina of a bull.'

Polybius narrowed his eyes. His voice sharpened as he continued, 'But you are wise enough to know that some day your magnificent chest will sag like an old woman's. That your prick will be softer than a sausage made with too much meal. You know this and you are smart enough to look out for your own future. You learned to appreciate the luxuries here at Villa Orgiasta. You enjoy a luxurious life. You meet people who will lavish gifts on you. Old, unattractive people who might even buy you your own villa. And for that you betrayed one of your friends to me. A mere boy professed his love to you and you tattled to me. You wanted to protect your future of luxuries. To get yourself that villa. And, so, I leave it to you, Hector, to explain to our new companion that he must never trust one of you . . . *scum!*'

Polybius faced the group and, raising his arms in mock ceremony toward the dais, he shouted, 'Behold! The cream of the Roman Empire! The finest specimens of manhood selected from all forty-two provinces! And each man looking for the same thing! A patron!'

Dropping his arms to his sides, Polybius shook his head and said, 'Poor miserable wretches. The lot of you.'

He suddenly clapped his hands. Two slaves appeared from behind the far columns. They carried a couch toward the dais.

'Set the new slave's couch here,' Polybius ordered. 'Place

it next to Rufus. They both have the same colour hair. Let us watch and see if gold . . . clashes!'

Looking at the blond slave named Rufus, Polybius teased, 'A certain gentleman from the Imperial Palace showed great interest in you, didn't he, Rufus? But will he even give you a second look tomorrow night at the banquet when he sees the new slave, Vesuvio?'

Rufus spoke in a deep-chested voice, saying, 'Tomorrow night I play the Minotaur in the drama, Master.'

'Of course! Of course!' Polybius said. 'The Minotaur! I forgot about the little theatric we are staging at tomorrow night's banquet.'

Eyeing the burly blond, Polybius teased, 'You think your performance as the Minotaur will win you the most esteemed prize which a patron can give to a pleasure slave? We'll see. We'll see.'

Looking at Vesuvio, Polybius said in his rich tone of mockery, 'Take your position on the couch, Vesuvio. Have Rufus here tell you about the patron whom he has set his eye upon. Have Rufus also tell you that when a patron is truly pleased with one of the male slaves how the patron – or patroness – has a golden replica made of the slave's phallus. A little statuette for . . . adoration. Perhaps you two can debate on who will win it first.'

Polybius turned and his sandals echoed in the vaulted room as he quickly strode across the black-and-white marble floor.

Vesuvio looked at the slave named Rufus. He saw him glaring at him. He wondered into what kind of wolf den Senator Sullus had sent him. He still did not know exactly what service he was to perform for the Senator here. He only knew that he was to act as if he were a slave – in the eyes of Rome, he still was – and wait for the Senator to contact him.

30

Vesuvio did not mind that the men did not speak to him after Polybius had left them in the *triclinium*. He lay upon his couch as they resumed speaking amongst themselves; a slave brought him a bowl of fruit, charcoaled meat, and a goblet of watered wine. He did not feel hungry but idly picked at the food and wondered if he was a fool to co-operate with Senator Sullus. He was close to home. Should he chance an escape from here and use lawyers to pursue the legal work which would establish his citizenship and innocence? Or would Senator Sullus then testify against him if he did not serve him here at Villa Orgiasta?

A hand suddenly rested on Vesuvio's shoulder. He raised his eyes and saw a household slave with a notched ear standing next to his couch.

The slave announced, 'You are to come with me to see Mistress Druscilla.'

Vesuvio could not immediately recall a woman named 'Druscilla'.

The slave explained, 'The mistress of the female slaves. She is waiting to receive you.'

* * *

Druscilla was a handsome woman, twice Vesuvio's age, he guessed, and she wore a necklace of lead replicas of breasts dangling over the front of her pale yellow *stola*. She led Vesuvio away from the iron grille to which the slave had escorted him – a grille separating the men's quarters from the main household – and calmly announced that she did not have much time to spare him but that every new male slave must be given a tour of the villa to curb his curiosity.

Druscilla spoke in a deep-throated voice, explaining to Vesuvio as they walked, 'The men at Villa Orgiasta are more curious than the females. Also, they are also more frustrated. That is primarily the fault of Polybius. He is frustrated himself. Frustrated and bitter that he is old and no longer attractive. Another reason for the men's ill-temper is the fact that it is unnatural to keep male slaves locked in a harem like women. Men become soft. Effeminate. Self-indulgent. But females become feline in these surroundings. Beguiling. Docile. But men?' She held her head erect, saying, 'Kept men grow lazy like dogs. Like she-dogs. Bitches!'

They walked down a *peristylium* which bordered a courtyard open to the blue Italian sky. Water trickled from a stone lion's head and fell into a marble font. The smell of jasmine sweetened the air. They passed from the *peristylium* into a hallway painted with murals depicting the legends of Bacchus.

Druscilla continued to speak in her hard voice, 'Knowing Polybius like I do, he probably did not tell you anything about where you are. That is, except for his little set piece about being so close to Rome yet so far.' She waved her hand disapprovingly.

'We are in Tibur,' she said, her slippers moving silently over the flooring of *pavimenta punica*. 'Some of your male colleagues are so stupid they think that Tibur means the River Tiber! But we are in the district of Tibur. North-west of Rome. The River Avio flows near here. This villa is set in a forest of pines. You can smell the pine trees when you walk in the garden. The splash one hears is the cascade of the river's waterfall. I am very fond of nature.'

'As am I,' Vesuvio said, adding for respect, '*domina*.'

Stopping in front of a hall with arched windows darkened by thick curtains, Druscilla pointed up a stretch of highly polished black marble steps. She said, 'This is the main *triclinium* where the banquets are served. There are cubicles along the left wall. We call them "love chambers". Polybius obviously told you about those.'

'Master Polybius did not mention them, *domina*.'

'And neither did his male charges.' It was not a question.

'I know nothing, *domina*, except that this is a villa in the district of Tibur. A house where pleasure slaves are kept. I do not even know if it is privately owned. Or if –'

'You do not need to know more than those few facts,' Druscilla said, lifting a ring of silver keys from her belt. She inserted one key into the lock of the brass-plated grille. She held open the gate for Vesuvio to enter in front of her, saying, 'I am showing you my charges to keep you from gawking at them when you see them at tomorrow night's banquet.'

'I will be attending the banquet? So soon after my arrival here?'

'Do not ask questions, slave. Do not anticipate what you will or will not do. Do not have expectations. Do only as you are told.'

She locked the grille behind her and passed two sober-faced guards dressed in cheetah pelts and holding spears. She and Vesuvio emerged in a small garden.

Vesuvio saw a collection of girls lying on couches. He fleetingly thought of the bordello to which he had taken his oarsmen on the island of Rhodes. The visit to Elena's seemed years ago to him. The women he now saw were as attractive as goddesses compared to the prostitutes at Elena's. Some combed their hair with ivory picks. Others were embroidering mantles. Two played knucklebone in the sand like soldiers. One girl strummed a lyre. They all momentarily interrupted their pastimes to raise their heads and look at Vesuvio.

'Do not be flattered by their attention,' Druscilla coldly said. 'They see a male only as competition. You might be vying with them for one of our guests tomorrow night.'

Vesuvio began, 'How many young ladies . . .'

He remembered Druscilla's threat about being too inquisitive and stopped.

Having anticipated the question, Druscilla answered, 'I usually have no more than fifteen girls in my charge. As agents sent you to Polybius so do agents recommend slaves to me. I have only been told about a group of five girls arriving soon from the eastern city of Petra Arabia. They are a band of acrobats. If I do decide to take them, they will swell the number to twenty.'

Druscilla's words about agents relieved Vesuvio. She did not suspect that he had been sent here by a Roman citizen. He looked at the women lounging in the yard and saw that many had returned to what they had been doing at his entry. They also saw him as only a slave.

'You now have seen the girls, slave. You realise that any advances made toward them would be quite futile as well as dangerous to your welfare.' Druscilla turned toward him and, looking him in the eye, she said, 'Remember to do as you are told. Do not ask questions. Do not try to escape. Do not form alliances with my girls. And I am sure that Polybius told you about the risk of pursuing love affairs with the other men.'

'I am not attracted to men,' Vesuvio said, 'Not as lovers.'

'Neither am I,' she said matter-of-factly. Not elaborating on her blunt statement, she turned away from Vesuvio and beckoned him to follow her across the courtyard. She said, 'There is one last thing I want you to see before you are taken back to the men's quarters which might help you better understand this house we call Villa Orgiasta.'

* * *

Druscilla stood in front of a small door lacquered dark green. She reached again to the ring of keys and, as she leaned forward to insert the key into the lock, her necklace of leaden breasts clanked against the door.

Turning the key, Druscilla stood aside and motioned for Vesuvio to peer into the small room adjoining the courtyard.

His eyes at first did not adjust to the room's darkness. But looking at a small flame flickering in the darkness, he eventually saw a young girl sitting upon a pallet with her back against the wall. The girl was completely naked and her long hair glistened red over her bare shoulders. Her breasts were large but firm, and the nipples covered by the ends of her red hair. The soles of the naked girl's feet rested on the pallet and her legs spread wide apart. She held a glistening gold object in one hand. She had been toying with the golden object in the red moisture of her vaginal lips and looked up with surprise as Vesuvio entered the room.

Druscilla remained behind Vesuvio, explaining, 'This girl is very popular with a rich merchant who lives in a palace on the Capitoline Hill. The merchant often visits her. He is devastated by her beauty. The merchant is a handsome man but men are often not always satisfied with their good looks, money, and power. Neither is this particular man excited by his attractiveness to females. To the contrary. He enjoys a woman sexually only when she is cold to him. He has chosen this girl as his . . . what? Mistress? She is very attracted to him. But to prevent her sexual tastes from interfering with our client's sexual demands, this girl must be constantly sated of all lust. She dare not even appear to desire him. The merchant visits us again tonight and this girl you see must masturbate before his arrival so that the sight of him merely makes her yawn. And that is for what that certain client pays his gold coins.'

Vesuvio stepped back from the door. He had seen and heard enough.

Locking the door, Druscilla said, 'The tool she uses on herself is a statuette made from one of the male slaves. The particular slave from whose phallus that statuette was cast is no longer with us. He tried to escape and the cast is all that is left of him. We waste nothing here at Villa Orgiasta

. . . except when a client pays for the waste. But then the waste is a thrill in itself.'

Druscilla led Vesuvio across the courtyard, saying, 'There now. I do not think we have squandered too much of what Polybius thinks of as his precious time.' The cold mockery in her voice told Vesuvio that Druscilla and Polybius were not friends, that there was a competitiveness amongst people at Villa Orgiasta other than the male and female slaves. The two free people in charge here obviously hated one another.

31

The preparations to make Vesuvio look like a pleasure slave began a few hours later. He stood stripped of his clothes on a columned pedestal in a room located in the males' section of the villa. Polybius paced around him like a potential buyer at a slave auction.

Five old men waited patiently behind Polybius, each man holding a wax tablet and a stylus to make notations of what Polybius would say about Vesuvio's appearance.

Polybius positioned one finger to his cheek as he evaluated Vesuvio's naked body. He began, 'The abdomen is flat. The shoulders are broad. No flab hangs from the waist. The legs –' He prodded Vesuvio's thighs. He looked at the bulge of his calves. '– good. Very good.'

He raised his head. He pursed his lips as he dispassionately continued to study Vesuvio. He said, 'Unfortunately, the arms have only partially been coloured by the sun. Like a field slave. Also, I see a diagonal line across his chest.'

Looking at Vesuvio, he asked, 'Did you work in a field?'

'A stableyard, *domine*.'

Polybius shook his head. He muttered, 'Waste. Waste.'

Pacing around Vesuvio again, he continued in an appraising voice, 'There is not enough time to allow the sun to colour him for tomorrow night's banquet. I do not want to dye his skin. Skin dye rubs off onto a patron's clothing.'

Polybius snapped his finger. He beckoned one of the five old men toward him, saying in a rush of inspiration, 'Valerius, make this man's tunic full enough on the shoulders to fall over his upper arms.'

'Excuse my suggestion, Master Polybius,' Valerius the

tailor said. 'But is it not a shame to cover such fine shoulders? Perhaps a bracelet on each bicep. An armlet wide enough to cover the line left unbleached by the sun.' His watery eyes eagerly waited for Polybius's nod of approval.

Polybius ordered Vesuvio, 'Flex your muscle!'

Vesuvio obediently raised one arm. He bent back his wrist. A bulge of veined muscle rose in his upper arm. His forearms strengthened with the forced knot.

Polybius stepped back from Vesuvio and returned his forefingers to his cheek. He said, 'Good biceps. Very good biceps. The triceps are fine, too. They have a natural appearance. Like a soldier's. And soldiers enjoy popularity these days.'

He shook his head. 'No, Valerius. I do not agree with your suggestion of armlets. Such adornments would detract from this slave's masculinity. I think we shall show his arms at a future banquet. By that time the sun will have coloured him naturally. He will wear a wide-shouldered tunic tomorrow night.' He motioned for Vesuvio to lower his arm.

Valerius the tailor said, 'I do not know, Master, if I can finish the tunic by . . .'

'No excuses,' Polybius snapped. 'Now pay attention to this.'

Polybius moved closer to the marble column on which Vesuvio stood. He reached toward Vesuvio's groin which the column raised to his eye level. He fluttered one hand around it, as if he were extolling the virtues of a thickly stemmed plant. He said, 'This equipment. Admirable. In any place but Villa Orgiasta it would warrant a song. An ode. It is not disproportionate to the rest of his body like so many of the bull-like pizzles we have here. The balls do not hang down to his knees like a wineskin. The cock does not look like a joke in a circus. Note the classic form of the crown. How the foreskin touches it like . . . just enough!'

Nodding approvingly, Polybius said, 'Cut his cincture from purple.'

'Purple?' the tailor gasped. 'The Imperial colour, Master?'

'I know what I'm doing,' Polybius irritably answered. 'This slave has dignity to his manhood. He is imperially sized. I want the cincture cut from purple cloth. And I want the skirt of his tunic cut short. Very short. I want it high enough to show the masculine curvature of those fine buttocks – and just a flash of the imperial purple hugging that cock!'

He beckoned the next man toward him, saying, 'Now for the hair, Gracchus. Be careful not to cut off too much. Do not clip away the bleach of the sun. Leave that tangle of curls around his neck. But there is too much in front of his ears. Trim that away. It detracts from that Etruscan profile. But whatever you do, do *not* touch-up his eyes with antimony, Gracchus. Use no facial cosmetics. None whatsoever!'

'There is a line, Master, around the slave's neck where an iron collar has recently been locked.'

'Ah, you have a good eye, Gracchus. So there is.'

'Just a touch of Sienna mud there, Master?' Gracchus the barber asked eagerly, his stylus positioned to make a note on the wax tablet.

'No!' Polybius barked. 'I know you and your Sienna mud, Gracchus. You would have him looking like a whore from Subura in no time! It will solve all problems if he is brought in late during the banquet. Keep his entry until the entertainment has begun. The guests will have had enough wine by then to forget about sunburns or white patches on skin.'

Polybius then reached forward and lifted one of Vesuvio's hands. He studied the fingers and began to shake his head. He called to the manicurist. 'Lucius. You have the most work to do. Look at the condition of these fingers! The callouses. The cuticles. The nails.'

He dropped Vesuvio's hand. It fell against his thigh with a thud. He stared down at Vesuvio's feet and lamented, 'Use a pumice stone on those feet, too. You must do something.

I don't know how you're going to make those feet presentable but somehow you must do it. He has big hands. Thick, sensual fingers. Also, I can think of two or three people at this very instant who would have sexual climaxes at the sight of his feet. Would fall down and make love to them. But not in the condition they are now. You must do something to those feet, Lucius.'

'Perfume, Master?' the fourth man asked. 'What perfume or balm do you wish stirred into the oils of his massage?'

Polybius leaned forward to sniff Vesuvio's body. He stood back and shrugged. He said, 'Strangely enough, his natural odour is not unpleasant. He smells . . . virile. We do not want to lose that quality. Perhaps put a drop – just a drop – of musk oil into his bath. But do not use oil in his massage. And under no circumstance use the oil of civet. The scent of civet is too feline for this slave.'

Beckoning the next man forward, Polybius said, 'Do you have a gold ring for him, Domitiani?'

Domitiani the jeweller stood in front of Vesuvio and eyed his genitalia. He then reached forward and, cupping it in his hand, he said, 'Good bollocks.'

Pulling back the foreskin, he said, 'A clean circumcision.'

'I do not want your opinion of his prick, you old pervert.' Polybius snapped. 'I asked if you had a gold ring for him to wear?'

Domitiani the jeweller reached into his robe and produced a wire of large golden rings. He said, 'I brought a selection of various sizes with me.' He quickly worked his way around the wire, finally unclasping the wire to free one of the round rings of gold. He said, 'I think this one will do him just fine.'

Polybius snatched the ring from the jeweller's hand and handed it toward Vesuvio. He said, 'Let him put it on himself!'

Vesuvio took the ring and studied it.

Polybius explained, 'It's a genitalia ring, slave. You put

your bollocks into the ring first, one testicle at a time. Then you push the crown of your prick into the ring. The ring surrounds the roots of your manhood.'

Vesuvio looked from the ring lying in the palm of his hand. He glanced at Polybius and then back to the ring.

'Obey, slave!' Polybius impatiently ordered. 'The ring not only makes your prick stand out over your balls but it is also the mark of your bondage to this house! Instead of wearing a collar around your neck as you did in the stable-yard you wear it around your . . . phallus!'

Polybius, the tailor, the barber, the manucurist, the perfumist, and the jeweller stood in front of Vesuvio and admired the gold ring now gripping the base of Vesuvio's manhood. And as Polybius had promised, the ring did make the phallus protrude in a thick arch over Vesuvio's scrotum.

'He is excellent, Master,' the jeweller whispered.

Polybius walked away from Vesuvio, saying blandly, 'We'll see. We'll see.'

* * *

Vesuvio spent the rest of the afternoon being fitted for his tunic, his body bathed, massaged; he was bathed a second time and his hair carefully barbered to show his profile to its best advantage. He ate with the other men that evening, again not participating in the conversation. No one approached him to offer their friendship.

The male slaves slept in a dormitory lined with mattresses slung on leather straps inside iron frames. The few objects which the men possessed set upon a wooden shelf alongside their beds. Vesuvio noticed that most of the men had a golden statuette amongst their possession, an idol made in the shape of an erect phallus.

Tired both from travel and the busy schedule of his first day at his new home, Vesuvio slept soundly that night. He was too exhausted to be troubled by dreams, nor to solve the mystery of why Senator Sullus had sent him here as a slave.

He awoke the next morning at the loud sound of a gong being struck somewhere in the distance. He began his second day with a bath and a rigorous set of physical exercises in one of the many *palestrae* built into a maze-like garden behind the stone villa. He heard the River Avio's waterfall cascading beyond the high walls. He caught the refreshing aroma of the surrounding pine forest. The sound and the aroma served as a tonic for him.

When the men met for a midday meal, they lay upon their couches and gossiped more animatedly than they had at last night's supper. Excitement was already building for tonight's banquet.

The young black man named Norax related a story he had heard whilst training with iron weights this morning in the gymnasium to keep his body trim and bulging with muscle. His voice was soft but his eyes danced with merriment.

He said, 'I went to the gymnasium and expected to have my usual exercises there. But I found the body attendants gossiping. Polybius accuses us of talking too much. He should hear how those slaves exchange stories!'

Norax motioned to Rufus and three other men to stop their conversation and to listen to him. He said, 'This story is worth hearing. The attendants, of course, swore me to secrecy –'

'As you will undoubtedly swear us,' the Sicilian named Antoninous said.

Norax shrugged and proceeded with his story. 'An old Greek in the city of Athens married a woman much younger than himself. And as often happens in situations such as that, the husband was cuckolded by a younger man, a male serving in his household as a steward. The unfaithful wife and her lover thought that they were successfully deceiving the old man. They also believed that he would die and leave all his possessions to his wife. She and her lover hoped to move to Rome and pursue their social ambitions. An old story, true.

'The old Greek was a successful physician and when he died, he left in his testament that all of his worldly effects would go to his wife only on the condition that she survived a hand-to-hand battle with her illicit lover. A woman battling a male!'

'So the old man knew?' asked Rufus.

Norax nodded. 'The old physician knew of his wife's adultery all along! But wait. That is only the first part. There is more.'

He sat on the edge of his couch, continuing, 'This story grew to be so popular in Athens over the recent months that the consul there told it to an envoy from Trajan's court. The contest between the adulterers is now going to be staged not in Athens but . . . Rome!'

Rufus asked with boredom, 'I suppose in the Flavian Amphitheatre.'

Norax shook his head. 'Not enough seats there.'

Antoninus said, 'Certainly not the Circus Maximus?'

'People would beat down the walls to get in!' Norax said. 'Anyway, it is not a spectacle for plebians.'

'So where, Norax? Where will it be held?'

Norax held his head to one side. He answered coyly, 'Some place where only the privileged classes can see it. Some place very special. Very secluded. Very . . .' He held out both hands.

Antoninous gasped. 'Not here? Not in Villa Orgiasta?'

'Why not?' Norax asked. 'What better place for a combat of . . . adulterers?'

'And when will it take place?'

Norax shook his head. 'The attendants could not tell me that.'

Vesuvio had been listening closely to the account. He asked, 'What was the old Greek physician's name?'

'Ah!' Hector interrupted. 'The volcano finally speaks!'

Laughter followed Hector's nickname for Vesuvio. One slave passed it to another but Norax leaned back on his couch and beckoned Vesuvio to bend his head toward him. He whispered, 'The Greek's name was Menecrates. He was a physician who trained medical slaves and rented out their services. His young wife is Despo. She has been brought to Villa Orgiasta with her lover, a Thracian called Cleomenes.'

*　　*　　*

Rome!

Despo cursed the Roman Empire and its laws. She cursed this city to which she had so long hoped to visit. The prophet in the cave in the Elevasian Mountains had foreseen Despo travelling to Rome but the hermaphrodite had predicted that she and Cleomenes would make a great sensation in Rome, not locked like a common criminal in a . . . cell!

Despo and Cleomenes had been placed under a civil arrest in Athens two months ago for committing adultery after Menecrates's testament had finally been taken from the Temple of Diana and read by the council. Although Menecrates accused Despo of making illicit love with his steward, he advised that she be forgiven of the crime if she met Cleomenes in hand-to-hand combat and emerged as the victor.

How long had Menecrates known about the affair? Despo had asked herself this question for the last two months in Athens and still pondered on the answer as she now sat in a guarded room in Villa Orgiasta.

Roman Law counted Despo as a criminal. She was an adulteress. A woman who had sacrileged the sacred vows of her marriage. She realised that Menecrates could have demanded her instant death. An adulterous woman was even considered to be more guilty than the male who cuckolded the husband. Menecrates had advised many men in his lifetime in how to deal with their unfaithful wives but never had he prescribed such a perverse retribution.

Hand-to-hand combat! Despo felt ashamed of the sentence. She knew that everyone in Athens had ridiculed her, even chalked obscene verses about her on the walls of the Acropolis. But now her notoriety had spread to Rome. She would have to face Cleomenes here – as amusement for Romans!

Despo did not fear death. Nor did she cower from the fact that she had to battle a man. She had been battling men – in one way or another – all her life. It was women who caused her the most trouble, females like her sister, Miranda.

She sat this late afternoon in her windowless room in Villa Orgiasta and wondered how much better her sister was faring. She wonder if Miranda by now had reached the Royal Tomb of Queen Cis-u-Ba.

Hoping that Miranda was long since dead, Despo heard a key turn in the plank door of the room. She suspected who was coming to visit her and quickly rearranged her hair and pulled at her himation.

Despo prided herself for never being without a plan, and seeing the figure of a woman enter the room with an oil lamp in her hand, Despo began to sob. She sniffed her make-believe tears and whispered, 'Why are men so awful? I was forced to marry. I was forced to make love by that obscene steward. And now look at me . . .'

Dropping her head, she ignored the woman moving closer to her and continued, 'I never really wanted to make love to a man in the first place. But what councils would understand those feelings in a woman?'

Despo dared not raise her head to look at her visitor. She only knew that her name was Druscilla and that she was in charge of the female slaves in this villa. The rest was only conjecture that this woman named Druscilla preferred to make love to females rather than males. Despo had taken this cue from the necklace of lead breasts which Druscilla wore around her neck. Her plan involved monopolising on this perverse appetite of Druscilla's.

32

The male pleasure slaves spent the remainder of the day in preparation for tonight's banquet. Vesuvio could not leave his section of the villa to search for Despo or Cleomenes; he paced the rooms and hallways like a restless animal. The idea that Despo and Cleomenes were somewhere in this very villa tortured him. They not only knew Miranda's whereabouts but were the only people who could vouch that he was not guilty of stealing coins from a temple. He did not have to stay in this villa one moment longer if he could force them to talk. He could pursue Miranda. He could go to Campania. He would be free. But whom did he have to listen to their story when he did find them? Would Polybius help him? Druscilla? Any of the slaves? Vesuvio knew that he was trapped here without a single friend. His only relief was knowing that Cleomenes and Despo were receiving some retribution for their wickedness.

Although having never met Cleomenes, Vesuvio remembered the night he and Balthazar had seen the arrogant man on the Piraean coastline. He imagined how humiliated Cleomenes must be by a sentence to battle a woman with weapons in front of sophisticated Roman spectators. Vesuvio imagined that Despo would somehow be less disturbed by this dishonourable situation.

The moment finally arrived for the body slaves to begin dressing the men for the banquet. Vesuvio's finger- and toenails were buffed one last time before the slaves wrapped the purple cincture around his groin. They followed Polybius's strict instructions to fold the loinpiece in such a way so that both the bulge of Vesuvio's crotch and the curve of his buttocks showed their full male advantages.

Next, a white linen tunic was lifted over his head and, after its hem was drawn to the proper height, the hairdresser stepped forward to make the final arrangements to Vesuvio's golden curls.

Brushing away the man's hand, Vesuvio pulled down the edges of the cincture over his buttocks and pushed the hair back from his temples. He grumbled, 'You can make me look like a whore but I don't have to feel like one.'

He angrily followed the slave who had come to escort him to the banqueting hall, trying to think whom he could use as a friend, an ally to whom he could tell his story.

* * *

The banquet was already in progress when the household slave led Vesuvio up the shiny black marble steps into the main hall and ushered him into one of the small niches called a 'love chamber'. Vesuvio caught only a fleeting glimpse of the guests at the far end of the room and saw that the actors – the pleasure slaves dressed as actors – were beginning to take their positions in the centre of the torchlit room to commence tonight's dramatic entertainment – The Birth of The Minotaur.

Vesuvio lay upon a couch inset with abalone shell in the 'love chamber' and noticed the flame of a hanging brass lamp flickering in the glistening black walls. He raised his head and saw that the ceiling – like the walls and the floor – was covered with shiny black obsidian, providing a reflection for anyone lying on the 'love couch'.

A hollow sound of musical instruments suddenly attracted Vesuvio's attention beyond the arch of the alcove. He lay forward on the couch and saw a female pleasure slave dancing in sensuous movements amongst a collection of earthen jars set upon the floor and filled with towering dried grasses. The theatric was beginning.

Vesuvio watched the dancer, listening to her clack small ivory percussion instruments called *crotala* in the palms of both hands. The ivory instruments were from the province of Hispania and the dancer continued the rapid sound – a noise of crickets on a hot afternoon – as a dark figure stalked toward her through the tall grasses set in the jars on the floor.

The dark figure was Norax, his naked black skin glistening with oil and a black bull's mask resting upon his shoulders. The mask's black hide contrasted dramatically with the smooth gloss of Norax's body; his phallus hung long and glistening from his groin. And 'Pasiphae' moved desirously around Norax – a 'bull' in this field of tall grasses.

Vesuvio watched as, first, the dancer with the clicking *crotala* swayed around Norax – she was the goddess 'Pasiphae' beguiling a bull – and, next, another figure appeared amongst the tall grasses. He wore a Greek *chalmys* wrapped around his shoulders and, after 'Pasiphae' mimed a whisper into his ear, he produced a black hide from one of the jars and wrapped it over 'Pasiphae's' body.

The second man represented the craftsman 'Daeidolos' who, according to the myths, Vesuvio knew, had constructed an image of a cow for 'Pasiphae' to enter to consummate her desires for a bull whom she had fallen in love with in the field.

'Pasiphae' danced mesmerically with the cowskin wrapped around her, approaching the 'bull' to excite his passions. They began to move together, the black body of the 'bull' slowly overpowering the 'cow'; he lay her down amongst the tall grasses, his phallus now visibly hardening.

The echoing *crotala* grew louder as Norax's slim hips began to move rapidly against the snow-white thighs of 'Pasiphae' stretching out from under the cowskin. He finally pushed himself into between her legs.

They copulated frantically on the floor until the musical instrument suddenly stopped. The 'bull' lay upon 'Pasiphae'.

Two girls ran across the floor trailing lengths of indigo-dyed silk. They represented 'night'. The dark silk gently fluttered down over the two bodies and, soon, the dancers returned trailing lengths of light blue silk behind them which represented 'dawn'.

Next, came the yellow silk meant to be the bright glow of 'day'. There was a movement amongst the thick grass standing in the earthen jars. The next length of silk was red – a violent blood red – and 'Pasiphae' began to thrash upon the floor amongst the grasses. She was in pain.

The dancers moved quickly around 'Pasiphae' as she suffered in the field, obscuring her body with more widths of red silk. A drum accompanied this new frenzied movement, becoming louder and louder until, finally – at a deafening crescendo – the red silk fell to the floor . . .

'Pasiphae' was gone. The 'bull' had also disappeared. The conception was complete and the birth pains were over. And from the midst of dried grasses rose the golden form of another man who wore nothing on his nakedness but a golden headdress of a bull. He was the 'Minotaur', the offspring of 'Pasiphae' and the black 'bull' in the field. The dancers began a worshipping dance of the Minotaur's physical magnificence as applause rose from the dining-couches at the far end of the room.

* * *

Vesuvio lay on his couch in the polished obsidian-lined alcove and listened to a harp accompany the dancers now miming their devotion to the 'Minotaur'. His mind was drifting again to the whereabouts of Despo and Cleomenes in the villa when a voice in the archway disturbed him.

Raising his eyes, Vesuvio saw a man standing in the entrance to the 'love chamber', a tall and handsomely featured man who was only a few years older than himself. He wore a toga bordered with a thin stripe of purple and, nodding his greetings toward Vesuvio, he said, 'Do sensitive translations of ancient myths bore you as much as they do me?'

Vesuvio answered without hesitation, 'Many people, I fear, would remain ignorant of myths if there were not for silks to colour them.'

The man smiled at Vesuvio's answer. He kept his eyes on him as he said, 'I never saw you here before but you look familiar.'

Vesuvio already knew the identity of this man. There were few people in Rome who did not know the Emperor's adopted heir, Hadrian, who was also reputed to be Emperor Trajan's lover. He immediately thought that, yes, he could tell Hadrian his story.

Before Vesuvio could speak, though, Hadrian quickly surveyed his recumbent body and his eyes betrayed what he wanted from him. He said, 'I will see you again,' and moved away from the alcove.

Vesuvio stared at Hadrian walking across the floor. He knew now why Senator Sullus had sent him here. The Republicans had great concern over the private life of the man who might one day control the Roman Empire. But knowing what Hadrian wanted from him in privacy, Vesuvio asked himself 'Can I live through such an experience in return for a favour? Will I emerge a sane man if another male uses my body for pleasure – or asks me to use him in an unnatural way?'

A household slave entered the alcove and, bowing more deferentially to Vesuvio than he had a short time ago, he said, 'I am instructed to escort you back to the dormitory. Your presence is no longer required at the banquet.'

Vesuvio hesitated but quickly arose from the couch. Hadrian had obviously already made his intentions clear to Polybius. Following the slave down the marble steps from the hall, Vesuvio was careful not to look over his shoulder at the guests. He did not want to be called to the dining-couches.

The house slave walked silently alongside Vesuvio as they passed through the arches which led to the males' quarter. He asked in a hushed voice, 'Did he say when he will see you again?'

The question stunned Vesuvio. He had not suspected that someone dare be so impertinent, that a household slave in Villa Orgiasta would speak to him about such an esteemed guest.

The slave whispered as they passed ornately fluted columns lit by torches, 'You will have to tell Senator Sullus all the details if you ever hope to return to Campania.'

Again, Vesuvio was stunned. He knew now that he was not the only spy whom Senator Sullus had placed in the villa. He continued walking soberly down the hallway and answered, 'The man said nothing more than he would . . . see me again.'

Chuckling, the slave said, 'You better grease yourself with bear fat! That Hadrian has a big pizzle, they say. He buggers the Emperor and he'll probably want the same from you. But at least you might get a gold statuette made of your own prizzle. But that's all you'll be using it for – as a mould for some statue!'

Vesuvio felt the nerves of his stomach tie into knots.

* * *

The horse god? Bendis? Was this imprisonment the curse of the obscure Thracian diety whom he had profaned in religious rites to gain public acclaim? Were pagan gods punishing him? Cleomenes thought about these questions as he huddled in a corner of a dark room in Villa Orgiasta. He did not know where Despo was in this house. He had heard no more about his combat with her since he had talked to the slaves in the gymnasium here who were supposed to train him for battle. Battle? Cleomenes trembled with fear at the thought of a confrontation, of being publicly pitted against Despo. She was strong. Strong-minded. Mental strength was more important than strength of the body. Despo has already defeated me, Cleomenes thought as he huddled in the corner and pushed nervously at his crotch. He reached beneath his robe and tried to shove his penis and scrotum from sight. He did not want to feel nor see his manhood between his legs. He hated his masculinity. Despo had once adored and honoured Cleomenes's manhood. She had made him proud of it, had shown him how to make a show of his unique proportions. But did he truly want that? Had the adoration of his phallus been the only way he could enjoy sexuality? He now loathed the thought of sexuality, despised the manhood of which he had once been so proud. He sat cross-legged on the stone floor of his prison room in Villa Orgiasta, pushing the palms of his hands down over his bulky penis and scrotum; he tried to remove his maleness from his sight. He did not want to see his manhood. He did not want to think about being a man. He momentarily wondered if he were losing his mind but, thinking how he might be defeated by a woman in battle, he forgot about madness and continued to shove his manhood down under his midsection. Despo had conquered him already; she had defeated him with her mind, her strength of will, her elaborate plots and ambitions. Cleomenes kept pushing his hands toward his crotch, trying to hide his penis and scrotum between his thighs. His sanity slipped further away as he sat cross-legged like this in the solitary darkness of his prison room in Villa Orgiasta.

33

Vesuvio was awoken the next morning by a violent tug. A hand gripped him on the arm. He was yanked out of bed. A man's angry voice accused, 'You did it on purpose. You set out to win him, you bastard!' The words were followed by a fist pummelling into Vesuvio's face which drove him onto the floor of the dormitory.

The blond haired slave, Rufus – who had portrayed the 'Minotaur' in last night's theatric – stood towering over Vesuvio and taunted, 'Admit it. You set out to get him. I know you did. You want him for yourself.'

Vesuvio rubbed his jaw where Rufus's fist had struck. He saw Rufus waiting with clenched fists to strike him again. His jaw was not broken. This surprised him because Rufus was a strong man.

Yanking Vesuvio up from the floor by his hair, Rufus shoved him onto the bed, shouting, 'Whore!'

Other men were beginning to gather around Vesuvio and Rufus, men who had been shaving or only awakening from their sleep. The sight of the two blond slaves fighting amused them.

Antoninus teased, 'Ah, so Rufus found out!'

'Look,' shouted another. 'The two straw-heads are brawling.'

'Too bad, Rufus. You shouldn't have had your head stuck in those bull's horns last night.'

Rufus grew more angry as the slaves goaded him. He stood over Vesuvio's body, saying, 'A man who sets out to steal my patron has to pay for it.'

Vesuvio wanted time both to gather his strength and

allow his brain to clear from sleep. He understood what Rufus was talking about, and clearly understood why he should be so upset. Hadrian would be a worthy patron for a pleasure slave.

Doubting if he was in a fit state at this moment to fight a man as angry as Rufus, Vesuvio moved to raise himself from the bed.

Rufus stepped forward; he kneed Vesuvio under the chin and again cursed him.

Vesuvio fell back onto the bed. His brains felt as if they were rattling inside his head and he saw a blurred image of Rufus standing in front of him.

As an increasing circle of men surrounded the bed, Vesuvio suddenly lunged forward, driving his head straight into Rufus's stomach, pushing him down onto the next bed and bringing both fists down in hard drives onto his face.

Vesuvio's first jab caught Rufus on the chin. The second hit his jaw. A third pummelled the side of his head. Rufus raised his arms to strike back but Vesuvio pulled to one side, hitting him again on the face, driving his other clenched fist into his stomach.

The two men rolled in a clench on the floor. Their arms were locked around one another. They pounded at each other's faces as shouts and laughter rose around them.

'The "Volcano" is a street fighter.'

'Look at the bitch fight. Like two tom-cats fighting for the cream!'

Rufus now sat astride Vesuvio's stomach and grasped his head with both hands to beat it against the stone floor. But breaking the lock with his arms, Vesuvio jerked his chest forward and sent Rufus flying backwards between his legs. He lifted his knee as Rufus fell and caught him in the groin.

'Stop!' Polybius shouted from behind the circle of men. 'Stop all this fighting!'

Vesuvio could not stop now. He was angry and, following Rufus onto the floor, he pounded his fists into his face, determined to teach him – and any other man in the room – not to start a fight with him again, especially not a fight for a lover he did not want.

'Stop!' Polybius shouted as he pushed his way through the onlookers. He bent forward to strike one hand against Vesuvio's face and ram his foot down onto Rufus's chest.

'Look at you!' he shrieked, holding Rufus to the floor with one foot. 'Look at both of you. What a bloody mess. It takes days for bruises to heal! Days! I should send you both to the whips. And I might still do it. I just might do it.'

Shoving Vesuvio aside, he demanded, 'Who started this fight?'

A voice behind him answered, 'The "Minotaur" heard about the "Volcano's" success last night with a certain . . . gentleman.'

Polybius turned to Rufus. 'Is that true? Did you start this ruckus?'

Rufus glared at Vesuvio and shouted, 'He did it on purpose! He set out to win Hadrian on purpose!'

'You stupid oaf!' Polybius said, striking Rufus across the face with the back of his hand. 'How dare you speak the name of such a great man. Silence!'

Turning from Rufus, Polybius examined Vesuvio's wounds saying, 'No skin is broken. If we tend to you carefully, no bruises will rise.'

Then glaring again at Rufus, Polybius threatened, 'If this man is marked, if this man is even slightly blemished, you will pay for each bruise or mark with fifty strokes of the whip!'

'Why do you favour him?' Rufus wailed. 'What about me? What about my chances?'

'You and your "chances" can rot for all I care!' Polybius shrieked. He looked again at Vesuvio, ordering, 'Put on some clothes. I've come for you anyway. You are to travel with me to the city.'

Vesuvio bit back his questions but Rufus blurted, 'You are

taking him to the city? Why him? Where are you taking him?'

Polybius spun around, saying in calm anger, 'One more word from your mouth and I'll have your tongue ripped out with burning pincers. Your mouth filled with salt crystals. And your lips sewn shut with wire threads.'

Beckoning Vesuvio to follow him from the dormitory, Polybius said, 'You must be quickly bathed and dressed for the journey. We shall speak further in the litter. I must now fetch Druscilla. She is coming with us.'

34

The morning was fresh, the air tainted by the piquant smell of the pines which surrounded Villa Orgiasta. Vesuvio and Polybius rode down the gravel drive of the villa in one litter, proceeding Druscilla who followed in the second conveyance borne by four husky slaves. They emerged through the stone gates which separated the villa from the outside world, the carriers trotting along the paved road which wound from Tibur toward the northern wall of Rome.

Vesuvio felt invigorated from a cold bath and he comfortably reclined on the litter's cushions as he listened to Polybius explain to him the reason for this sudden expedition into the city.

Polybius began, 'A cast is to be made of your phallus. The jeweller who creates these statuettes usually comes to us for the casting. It is then taken back to Rome and worked into metal. But a message arrived this morning that the jeweller cannot leave his home. He asks us to bring you to him. I would not normally comply to such a request but as the man who is ordering the mould is. . . .'

Pausing, Polybius nervously turned a cornelian ring on his finger and asked, 'You do know who the man is who desires a statuette to be made?'

'If I hadn't guessed last night, Rufus would have clarified the matter for me this morning.' Vesuvio thought it wise not to mention Hadrian's name and, feeling uncomfortable even discussing this subject, he asked, 'Why is Druscilla coming with us?'

Polybius continued to toy nervously with his ring, answering, 'Five female acrobats have been recommended for us to acquire.'

'The girls from Petra Arabia?'

Polybius jerked his head. 'How do you know of those girls.'

Druscilla mentioned them when she was showing me the quarters where she keeps her slaves.'

Polybius sniffed, saying, 'The bitch tells you more than she tells me.'

The litter continued to move at its gentle lilt; the sound of wooden cartwheels soon rumbled around them. Vesuvio guessed that they were nearing the Republican Gates on the north side of the city.

Momentarily halting, the litter continued through the gates and Polybius shouted to the bearers to avoid the busy traffic on Vias Sacra and Nova which crossed the main intersection of Rome's Forum. He ordered them instead to keep to the *actae*, the narrow sidestreets originally built to accommodate the width of only one cart, a way which would take them more quickly to the jeweller's house near the Janiculum.

No carts were allowed on the streets at this daytime hour but the foot traffic was thick and slaves ran ahead of the litter to make way for it to move through the crowd.

Merchants spread their wares along the sidewalks and lanes darkened by buildings which rose as high as ten and twelve storeys. Cookshops crowded against one another. Iron-mongers and sandal-makers and cloth-merchants fought for niches in these streets which entangled Rome like layers-upon-layers of spider webbing.

Vesuvio, Polybius, and Druscilla were carried deeper and deeper into this dark maze which ran up hills and around the front of promontories. The wail of mourners drifted from a passing funeral procession. The splash of a slop bucket fell from high overhead in one of the tall apartment blocks called '*insulae*'.

The litter bearers continued to edge their way over the streets often no wider than footpaths; they tried not to step in mud churned by the congestion of people; they finally stopped in front of one of the *insulae* where the guards had cleared inquisitive bystanders from the sidewalk.

Druscilla and Polybius emerged from their litters, holding cloaks over their heads as protection against garbage and buckets of excrement hurled from the upper storeys of the building – the upper floors of an *insulae* were rented by tenants poorer than those who lived on the ground level.

Vesuvio followed Polybius and Druscilla into an inner courtyard planted with dwarf palm trees. Faint shafts of daylight poured through small squares of mica embedded in a stucco wall at the far end of this *atrium*. The air was cool and tallow candles flickered in front of the household shrine. A divan set between columns of polished Phyrian marble.

A sober faced servant appeared and beckoned Polybius to one side of the courtyard. Polybius joined him and, after listening to his words, he beckoned Druscilla to come and also listen to the report.

The slave disappeared and, whilst Polybius and Druscilla whispered to one another, Vesuvio heard a rustle of garments from the other side of the courtyard. He turned and saw the servant returning with five women walking in single file behind him.

Druscilla stepped forward and clucked her tongue disapprovingly as she watched the women draw closer. The five women were not young; they were approaching middle age, their faces much harder, more severe than the faces of the female pleasure slaves kept at Villa Orgiasta.

Druscilla turned and whispered to Polybius. He nodded and beckoning Vesuvio to him, he ordered, 'You wait here. Stay with these women. An unseen situation has arisen. Druscilla and I must briefly retire to another section of this apartment.' Polybius and Druscilla hurriedly departed with the servant from the courtyard.

* * *

Vesuvio found himself alone in the *atrium* with the five females. They wore the elaborate clothing of actresses under their cloaks and their waists were bare except for the gold chains of servitude encircling their hips. Vesuvio also noticed that they were more ill at ease than himself, that they had evidently seen that Druscilla had not been pleased with them.

Not wanting to make the women more uncomfortable than they already were, Vesuvio said to the woman wearing a spangled cloth around her rouged face, 'You are entertainers, I've heard, and have only come to Rome from the distant city of Petra Arabia.'

The woman in spangles smiled at Vesuvio, pleased to be spoken to as a person and not treated like shop-worn merchandise. She answered pleasantly, 'We arrived in Petra Arabia at a very critical time. We were travelling by caravan and reached the desert city as it was being seized by the Romans.'

Stopping, the rouged woman bowed her head and announced, 'My name is Rubecula.' She stood to one side and held out her hand toward the other four women. She said, 'This is Aquila . . . and Regula . . . Phasina . . . and Passerina.'

Vesuvio listened in amazement to the five women's names. A robin . . . an eagle . . . a wren . . . a pheasant . . . and a sparrow.

He said, 'You all have the names of birds. Are you sisters?'

Rubecula shook her head. 'No, we are bound only by our profession – and slavery. We are acrobats. Tumblers. Our former master called us his aviary of flying . . . birds.' She shrugged helplessly and smiled at him.

Vesuvio pointed to the wide divan, saying, 'There is no reason for you not to rest. We do not know how long we will be kept waiting here.'

'Entertainers learn to wait,' Rubecula answered pessimistically. She looked from the couch to her colleagues, saying to Vesuvio, 'You are a kind young man. Thank you.'

When the five women settled themselves on the divan, Vesuvio squatted on the floor in front of them and asked Rubecula to explain to him about Petra Arabia. He said, 'I have never been that far east but I have heard that all the buildings in Petra Arabia are carved out of rock walls. Is that true? Does a traveller pass through a narrow passageway to enter the city and emerge in an oasis with temples and treasuries and theatres all carved from stone?'

Rubecula nodded, 'Petra Arabia is indeed magical to see but we were in no mood then to appreciate many sights.'

Pausing to take a deep breath, Rubecula said, 'It's a complicated story how we first went there but if the story will not bore you I will tell you.'

Vesuvio quickly assured her that he was interested in hearing their adventures. He saw that the woman's spirits were depressed and hoped that she would be cheered by talking about herself and her four companions.

Rubecula began, 'We had been sold by our former master to a Persian who acted as an agent for a king of a desert country beyond Petra Arabia. We were being taken by caravan from Alexandria to be attendants for a queen. Not ordinary attendants, you see. . . .'

Pausing again, she glanced at her colleagues. They nodded their consent for her to continue with the story. So, clasping her hands on her lap, Rubecula resumed, 'The king of this distant country had died. His wife was to be interred . . . alive with him in the tomb. We were meant to be her attendants, to be buried *alive* in the tomb to serve as her attendants in the next world.'

The youngest woman, Passerina, looked at Vesuvio with her large hazel eyes and said, 'It is hard to believe but what Rubecula says is all true.'

'We laugh now,' Rubecula said, leaning back on her arms

on the divan, 'but at the time we were frightened. Very frightened indeed. But what can slaves do?'

The story intrigued Vesuvio. He asked for more details, listening avidly as Rubecula explained that they had not been the only females intended to be entombed with the queen. She told Vesuvio about hairdressers, seamstresses, gardeners, all female slaves collected by Persian agents who had scoured the lands surrounding the Mediterranean for servants to wait upon the queen called Cis-u-ba in her tomb.

Passerina said, 'There was even a female doctor! Can you believe it? The dear thing was brought all the way from Italy.' Turning to Rubecula, she asked, 'Remember Miranda?'

Rubecula nodded, saying to Vesuvio, 'You see, no males are allowed to be buried with the queen. But the court chamberlain . . .'

Vesuvio no longer listened to her tale. He anxiously interrupted, 'Stop. You mention the name "Miranda". A medical slave taken from Italy.'

Rubecula fondly said, 'Yes. Miranda. She was a Greek slave whom the Persian agents had brought to Alexandria from an estate somewhere here in Italy. Miranda joined us in Alexandria, travelling in our caravan to Petra Arabia. I suppose she still is there in that city. You see, there were many soldiers wounded in the attack of that town. When the Romans seized our caravan and learned that Miranda knew about treating wounded men, they took her and she was immediately put into their service.'

Vesuvio threw his arms around Rubecula, promising, 'I will repay you for this, good woman. I will repay you and your friends for giving me this information.'

'Do you know Miranda?' Passerina asked as the other girls now pressed around Vesuvio.

'Know her?' He laughed. 'I planned – and still do plan – to make Miranda my wife.'

Looking soberly at the five women, he said, 'You told me a small part of your story. I have a story, too, an adventure which enslaved me whilst I was looking for Miranda, a long tale which has brought me here to this house today.'

'Then you are owned by the pleasure villa in Tibur,' Rubecula said. 'We were meant to be purchased by the mistress in charge there.' She shook her head, saying, 'I have seen enough prospective buyers in my life to know that she thinks we are too old. I fear we will have to go back to the slave station in the Janiculum and wait for the next person who might be interested in buying five aging . . . fowls!'

'Do not fear. Do not despair. I promise to help you and, if you do return to the Janiculum, perhaps you can help me – and Miranda – by delivering a message here in Rome.'

Passerina said, 'We would do anything for Miranda.'

Rubecula added, 'I can tell you are an honourable man. We will be glad to help you in any way that we can.'

Vesuvio profusely thanked the five women and, asking them for intricate details, he listened closely as they explained to him about Queen Cis-u-ba, the Persian agents who had scoured the Mediterranean for female attendants, and the far desert city called Petra Arabia where Miranda was still in servitude to the Roman army.

After assembling these facts in his mind, he said, 'Now here is what I would like you to do for me if you remain in the city and are not taken back to the villa with me.' He had already made the decision to travel peacefully with Polybius back to Tibur.

Rubecula laughed. 'Have no fear about us not staying in Rome. A woman learns to see when buyers are disenchanted by her age or appearance. Tell us your message. One slave can at least be useful to another. That is the only way we can survive.'

Vesuvio eagerly proceeded to discuss a plan with the five

women, a ruse which might help him not only free Miranda from Petra Arabia but also release him from his bond to Senator Sullus which held him at Villa Orgiasta. He began by telling the female acrobats about Despo and Cleomenes.

35

Polybius and Druscilla stood facing the Empress Plotina, a grim-faced woman who wore her dark hair piled into a mound of curls over her forehead. She sat upon a cushioned curule chair which was flanked by two saturnine companions.

The Empress Plotina nodded for Polybius and Druscilla to enter the tapestry hung room where she sat and, as the servant shut the door, Polybius and Druscilla dipped to their knees.

Waiting for them to rise, Plotina said, 'You have been admirable in keeping the secret that I subsidise the house in Tibur. I know that my husband's nephew, Hadrian, still visits the house. That he indeed visited it again last night. I have also learned that a new male slave there has attracted Hadrian's attention.'

Polybius wanted to ask Plotina how she had learned of this fact so soon. But checking his thoughts, he quickly said, 'The slave can easily be dispensed with, your Imperial Highness.'

Plotina raised her hand. 'No. Most certainly not. Young Hadrian is a strong-minded man. He also is very artful. He probably even suspects that I own your villa and want to keep my eye on the prurient activities there. I know that depravity is increasing in Rome and I want to keep well informed of its dangers.'

Her voice grew more quiet as she said, 'To return to the point you made, though. If this new slave were suddenly to disappear or suffer an accident, Hadrian might well blame me and I do not want to make an enemy of him.'

Polybius and Druscilla stood with their heads lowered.

They knew that the Empress was aware of her husband's illicit relationship with Hadrian. But they also knew that Plotina was clever enough to realise that Hadrian might well become the next Emperor of Rome, that the Empress was planning to marry him to her niece, a plain girl named Sabina.

The Empress Plotina held her head high as she explained, 'But Hadrian is not the reason I came here to see you at this house today. I heard that you were sending for the jeweller to commission a sculpture for my husband's . . . adopted heir. That is why I . . . arranged for you to come to Rome rather than for the jeweller to come to you. I wanted to speak to you about the matter of an Athenian woman being pitted against her lover in Tibur.'

'Your Highness has heard about the Athenian couple who . . .'

'Who has not heard of the Athenian couple by now? They are the scandal of the Empire. It is a disgrace for a woman to battle a man for public amusement. A disgrace and a serious threat to the sanctity of womanhood. I do not want such a confrontation to take place – not in Tibur, not in Rome, not any place. The provinces have threatened our empire long enough with their disorderliness and pagan attitudes.'

Druscilla stepped forward, pleading, 'But the contest has been announced, your Imperial Highness. A distinguished gentleman from your very household expects to attend.'

Closing her eyes and stubbornly shaking her head, Plotina repeated, 'I do not want the confrontation to take place. I have worked hard to raise womanhood amongst the Romans. I will not have my good works set back by one such debacle!'

Druscilla asked, 'What does your Imperial Highness suggest?'

'Nothing! That is your job. I do not want a woman fighting a man. Can you not understand that? Can you not see what history will make of me if such a thing happens?' She held back her head and mused ' "Whilst Trajan and Plotina sat upon the throne of Rome, adultery reached such depraved levels that husbands ordered their adventurous wives . . ." '

Stopping, lowering her head, she said, 'No! I will not permit it.'

Bowing her head, Druscilla said, 'Your Imperial Highness shall have her wish.'

Plotina sat forward in her chair and threatened, 'If I do not have my wish, the house in Tibur will cease to exist. As will all the people connected to it – *all* the people!'

Perspiration beaded on Polybius's bald head. He stammered, 'And what of the new slave who has won the attention of . . .' He dared not to mention Hadrian's name.

Plotina sat back in the chair. Her voice lightened as she said, 'Hadrian is an ambitious man. He will not do anything to harm his future – anyway, not until he is on the throne himself. I seriously doubt if he would create a public scandal by having an open . . . friendship with another man.'

Wagging her finger at Polybius, she warned, 'But if something were to happen to the new slave, Hadrian might suspect that I was behind it and then *you* would be in trouble.'

The Empress Plotina rose from her chair and, as her two companions lifted the ends of a white linen mantle and arranged it over her head, Druscilla and Polybius again dropped to their knees.

* * *

Polybius rose from the floor after the Empress Plotina swept from the room. He looked quizzically at Druscilla and asked, 'How could she have found out so quickly that Hadrian visited us last night? And who told her that Hadrian wanted a statuette made from the slave? He only told me last night!'

Druscilla toyed with her lead necklace, saying, 'Plotina

obviously arranged for you to come into the city. She also planned for the jeweller not to be at home. I only had the five acrobats come to this address to save me from going to the slave house. I hate slave houses and . . .' She shook her head in bewilderment.

Polybius said, 'I never had any doubts that Plotina keeps informants in the villa to spy upon us. I suspect she is even in close league with the Republicans!'

Druscilla leaned against the curule chair and said with resignation, 'One thing I *do* know for a fact is that we must immediately rid ourselves of the Athenian couple. I do not yet know how we shall do it but Plotina made it quite clear that our own positions are at stake.' She thought of Despo, remembering her supple body, the sexual interests which the young Greek woman had been showing to her. Druscilla fleetingly thought of the love which no man had even been able to give her satisfactorily, a love which she believed could only emanate from another female. Was Despo possibly that woman?

'We cannot send them back to Athens,' Polybius began but, waving his hand, he said, 'Let us not trouble ourselves about them. We are not being held responsible for their safety.'

Druscilla understood the implication.

Looking at her, Polybius said, 'We might have had our differences in the past, Druscilla, and probably will again in the future. But we must unite in this one matter or we will both be removed from the security of our positions.'

Again, Druscilla understood. She suggested, 'You dispose of Cleomenes and I will solve the problem of the girl's presence at the villa. Then we will decide what to do about Hadrian's attraction to . . . Vesuvio.'

The servant returned to escort them back to the courtyard but Druscilla told him that they were returning to Tibur and to send the five acrobats back to the slave-house in the Janiculum. She said that she was no longer interested in purchasing new slaves. Neither Druscilla nor Polybius noticed Vesuvio's newly found confidence as he followed them outside to the litters.

* * *

The jeweller's slave returned to the *atrium* after escorting Druscilla, Polybius, and Vesuvio to the litters. He announced to the five acrobats that the slave who had brought them here from the Janiculum would attend them back to the slave house, that their potential buyer was not interested in purchasing them.

The narrow streets had grown more congested with shoppers and pedlars in the last few hours; Rubecula, Aquila, Regula, Phasina, and Passerina clung closely together to avoid being separated by the press of the afternoon crowd, or shoved into pools of rancid water and sewage dotting the cobbled street. The five women quietly followed their slave escort and waited for an opportunity to commence the plan they had discussed with Vesuvio.

Rubecula finally called to their slave escort, 'Do we return by the same route by which we came?'

The man gruffly answered, 'Why? Do you have a complaint about the scenery you passed on the way here, woman?'

Forcing herself to be cheerful, Rubecula answered, 'I believed we passed a street on our way to the jeweller where our first master lives. He is a very famous man, a senator renowned for his generosity to slaves, a noble man who rewards slaves in the most unexpected ways.'

'Rewards?' the slave asked. 'What kind of rewards?'

Rubecula tried to speak casually. 'Coins. Gifts of silver. Recommendations to highly-placed friends. The noble senator bestows many small favours upon slaves who provide him with even the slightest service.'

Knowing that she now had the slave's attention, Rubecula

added disparagingly, 'The Senator would love to see us but, yes, he was an old man when we left him. He probably is no longer on this earth . . .'

The slave asked, 'You are certain this powerful . . . senator would be glad to see you five women?'

'Oh, yes,' she said as the other four acrobats joined in a chorus of agreement. Rubecula continued, 'The good senator only sold us because he knew we would be happy with our new master. Little did he know that our new master would soon die and . . . But why trouble a busy man like you with our story? Let us push through this crowd or you'll never get us back to the slave house.'

Stopping in front of a cookshop built into the ground floor of an *insula*, the guard faced the five women and asked, 'Where did you say your old master lives?'

'Oh, no, we do not have time for such an idle visit,' Rubecula insisted. 'Senator Sullus would be overjoyed at seeing us, true, but it is not a good idea for us to take this time. The Senator would want to speak to us alone. And then . . . ah, after we told him about your kindness in allowing us a brief moment to see him in his home, he would most certainly want to speak to . . . you! Oh, yes. Senator Sullus would want to find out all about you. He would ask about your past, your ambitions for the future, what you enjoy in life.'

'A senator would want to know all those things about . . . me?' the slave asked.

'All that and more,' Rubecula assured him. She tilted her head and murmured, 'I smile when I envision the dear man even trying to press money into your hand for reuniting us.'

The slave stood upright. 'I am not interested in money. But, by the gods, your old master will have the joy of seeing you five women. Why should I deprive him of that?' He looked at Rubecula again, asking, 'What did you say his name was?'

'Senator Sullus,' Passerina quickly interrupted, excited

that the ruse which they had devised with Vesuvio was working, that they had successfully appealed to the slave's greed to take them to the home of the one man in Rome who could help Vesuvio and their good friend Miranda.

The slave escort allowed Rubecula to knock on the door of a house built on the incline of the Janiculum hill; whilst Rubecula quickly urged the porter to tell his master that she bore an important message for him from Aurelius Macrinus of Campania, the other four acrobats tried to occupy the escort in conversation. They could not risk him learning quite yet that none of them knew this old man named Senator Sullus whom Vesuvio had sent them to see. They also knew that they had little time in which to speak to Senator Sullus, to impress him with the fact that the only two people in the world who could prove Vesuvio's innocence as a temple thief were at this very moment imprisoned in Villa Orgiasta in Tibur, and that Vesuvio expected the old Senator to act honourably – like a true Republican – in helping him achieve his freedom.

Looking at Rubecula speaking animatedly to the porter at the door, the escort suspiciously asked Passerina, 'Are you sure that this senator knows important people in the world?'

Aquila leaned forward, saying, 'If you are a gambling man, I will wager you right now that the Senator will send word to a man in the royal household called Hadrian. That a rider might leave this house in a few moments, only a short time after Rubecula speaks to the Senator.'

'Hadrian? The Emperor's heir? The Senator is a friend of Hadrian?'

Tugging at her ear for good luck, Passerina said, 'Let us hope the old man and Hadrian are at least on speaking terms these days. There is another . . . slave depending on it, too.'

At that moment, Rubecula beckoned them toward the door. The porter had finally agreed to take them to the Senator.

36

The gates to Villa Orgiasta opened when Polybius's and Druscilla's litters emerged from the pine forest and approached the stone gatehouse on their return from Rome. Druscilla's litter passed through the gates but Polybius shouted for his bearers to wait momentarily and he stepped from the conveyance to speak briefly to the guard standing outside the gatehouse.

The guard nodded his plumed helmet as he listened closely to Polybius's instruction and, when Polybius re-entered the litter, the guard stood watching it progress toward the villa.

Waiting until the litter disappeared, the guard closed the iron gates and went inside the gatehouse. He emerged a few seconds later. He was not wearing his helmet; another man accompanied him.

The first guard's name was Thord, a rugged Norseman who had been brought as a slave to Rome as a child. He had joined the Roman army in his youth and, by serving as a soldier to Rome, he had received both his freedom and Roman citizenship. He now worked as a soldier to private armies and had been in service to Villa Orgiasta for the last three years.

Thord's nose was broken. His hands were large like bear paws. His Latin was still marked from his childhood accent. He now explained in his broken Latin to the second guard about the command which their master, Polybius, had only given him at the gatehouse.

The second guard's name was Marcus. He came from Lombardy and had been a Roman soldier, too. A private soldier's pay was small and the owner of this villa in Tibur allowed the guards to supplement their incomes with extra work they performed on the grounds.

Thord, Marcus, and the other fourteen guards at Villa Orgiasta dragged fallen trees from the pine forest growing outside the walls. They chopped the trees into small pieces and sold them as wood fuel. They were allowed to keep all the money they received from the sales. They also were permitted to draw pitch from the pine trees in the forest surrounding the villa's walls. They sold the pitch in casks to a merchant who arrived from Rome to collect it with his wagon. The guards were allowed to keep that money.

Thord and Marcus now walked toward a shed in which the casks of pine pitch were stored. Thord entered the low-ceilinged hut whilst Marcus studied the ground covered with damp, yellowing pine needles. He next gazed overhead at the creaking spires of the tall pine trees. He moved until he found a position which suited him for building a fire.

Thord emerged from the hut carrying a black iron cauldron. They momentarily debated whether they should invite one or two more guards to help them on this job they were doing for Polybius. But after discussing the amount of money which Polybius was paying them, they decided that they themselves could do it. They could split the pay in half. Their wives would be happy.

Marcus entered the hut and returned with a spade. He went to the side of the hut to dig a trench whilst Thord gathered dry wood. He began splitting the dry wood into kindling and started a small blaze.

The fire soon grew. Thord added larger pieces of wood. He next brought a black iron tripod from the hut. He unfolded the long legs and placed it over the growing fire. He then lifted the iron cauldron and hung it from a hook in the middle of the tripod. He returned to the hut and rolled out a wooden cask toward the fire.

Marcus finished digging the trench. He left his spade by

the deep hole and went back to the hut. He himself emerged with two wooden buckets. Thord suggested that they used four buckets. That way their job would go much faster.

Marcus was returning to the hut to collect the extra buckets when he and Thord heard a horse galloping toward them through the pine trees.

Thord stood by the crackling fire. Marcus glanced from the loose skin hanging over the hut's doorway. They saw a horse emerging from the trees. The rider was Polybius. A body wrapped in a white cloth lay in front of him across the horse.

Marcus quickly disappeared behind the hide hanging from the door. Thord pointed for Polybius to ride toward the trench which Marcus had dug by the side of the hut.

The two guards now pried open the top of the cask. They lifted it between them and poured the thick, slowly-moving pitch into the cauldron. The pitch began to melt in the cauldron suspended over the fire, quickly becoming a softer, more aromatic substance.

Polybius returned to the fire on foot from the ditch. He watched silently as Thord and Marcus used hides on their hands to tip the cauldron and pour the first of the hot pitch into their wooden buckets.

Lifting the buckets, Thord asked Polybius, 'He's in the hole?'

Polybius nodded.

Marcus asked, 'He's dead?'

'The poison was strong,' Polybius assured him. 'There is no movement at all to his body.'

'Then all we have to do is –' Thord grunted as he lifted the buckets of pitch. '– get this over him quick.'

Polybius moved to mount the horse. He said, 'I'll leave you two to finish your work. Do not forget. Spread dirt over the body.'

'You won't notice a thing's been disturbed here in the forest, *domine*,' Thord called as he and Marcus moved with their buckets from the fire. 'We'll spread the needles back over the dirt and everything.'

Polybius left them, galloping through the trees back to Villa Orgiasta when he suddenly heard a scream pierce the silence of the pine forest. He reined his horse and asked himself, What has gone wrong now?

He quickly turned his animal and galloped back toward the fire.

* * *

Polybius sat on his horse and looked down into the ditch. Thord and Marcus were now tipping their next bucket of pitch into the hole, the hot yellow thickness oozing down over the corpse lying on its back on the dirt.

Polybius looked at Cleomenes's face. The pitch was transparent. He saw the expression of anguish on the Greek's face through the thick layer of pitch; he noticed one hand gripping at the dirt, its fingers now frozen into a claw.

'He wasn't dead,' Marcus said, pouring pitch over Cleomenes's feet. 'The poison hadn't taken. But this heat finished him off.'

Thord laughed. 'He's dead now, *domine*. We took care of him. Now don't you worry. This pitch will seal his flesh. There's no fear of rot attracting some wolves. No animal will come digging up this corpse for his supper. Marcus and me, we will cover him over, like I said, with needles and sticks and all kinds of brush. You won't notice a thing.'

Nodding his approval, Polybius turned toward his horse but stopped when heard the distant sound of horses. He looked toward Thord and Marcus, saying, 'Riders.'

'A full regiment it sounds like to me,' Thord said, listening.

'Soldiers, too,' Marcus said. 'You can tell by the neat military cadence of their gallop.

Polybius stared in the direction from which the riders were coming and said the name which he never allowed his men to utter. 'Hadrian . . .'

He looked quickly to the hole and ordered, 'Quickly. Cover that. You must not mention this to anyone.' He mounted his horse and disappeared quickly through the trees in the direction of the villa.

37

Druscilla opened the plank door of the upstairs room where Despo was imprisoned in Villa Orgiasta. She set the lamp she was carrying on the pine table by the door and, gently pushing the door shut behind her, she called into the darkness, 'Am I waking you?'

Lying on a narrow couch across the dark room, Despo lifted herself from a half-sleep and stared at the blurred glow of the oil lamp. She had little to do except to sleep and was now awakening from a dream about her sister, Miranda, and Vesuvio. Despo had been dreaming that she was Miranda and – whilst making love to Vesuvio – she had told him that she was pregnant with his child.

Druscilla moved toward the couch and, making a place for herself alongside Despo's reclining body, she studied her features in the faint glow from the oil lamp.

Although still heady from her dream about Vesuvio, Despo realised that she must quickly collect her wits, that she must forget about the one man she craved to be with and concentrate now on making herself desirable to this broad-shouldered woman who controlled the female slaves in the villa. Despo knew that only Druscilla could give her her freedom and, to achieve that, she must allow Druscilla to take liberties with her body. She doubted if she could be reciprocal in such love-making but she would force herself to make an attempt.

Reaching for Druscilla's shoulder, Despo began, 'You are my only friend in the world. I wish there was some way to repay a woman as kind as you . . .'

Druscilla reached to smooth Despo's hair. She said, 'You looked so frightened, my dear. Your eyes are so wide, so liquid, like the eyes of a frightened . . . kitten.'

Despo began to protest she was not frightened but then stopped. She suspected that a woman like Druscilla wanted her to be weak. She lowered her head and confessed, 'I try not to think of the ordeal that awaits me. I know you would certainly not subject me to battle a male but I also know you are a woman and your authority is limited in a world where men . . .'

'Shhh,' Druscilla urged, putting her hand on Despo's slim waist. 'You need not worry about that . . . man now. I would never let such a confrontation take place.'

'You wouldn't?'

'Of course not,' Druscilla assured her, again smoothing one hand over Despo's long hair. She said in a lighter voice, 'You seem to be shaking. Are you nervous?'

Her mind quickly racing about what she should say, how she should act, Despo answered, 'Nervous and . . . excited.' She felt Druscilla's heavy necklace of leaden breasts dangle against her.

'Why don't you relax?' Druscilla coaxed, moving her hand down Despo's legs. 'You *are* trembling. I can feel you. Poor, neglected, young girl.' She bent forward and kissed Despo gently on the forehead.

The thought of Vesuvio suddenly cut through Despo's jumbled mind. She thought of Vesuvio making love to Miranda. She compared their beautiful love to this sordid sexuality – Druscilla trying to seduce her!

But again realising that only Druscilla could arrange freedom for her, Despo quickly reached to pull her gown up her legs; she spread her knees apart on the mattress.

Druscilla sat on the edge of the couch and, looking down at Despo's passive body, she asked blandly, 'You do not think that I would take you without receiving something in . . . return?'

Despo knew what she was implying but tried not to understand. She answered, 'I do not know what to think . . . My brain is in such a turmoil . . . I am so frightened . . . Yet I feel so close to you . . .'

'But you must not make me feel like the aggressor,' Druscilla insisted as she reached to bare her breasts from her *stola*.

Despo turned her head away from Druscilla; she could not look at her large naked breasts. She could not go from a dream about Vesuvio to the reality of a woman wanting to make love to her – wanting her to make love in return.

Druscilla slowly reached toward her necklace which hung between the cleavage of her breasts. She held out of the leaden replicas in front of Despo's mouth and whispered, 'At least show me your feelings. I would do anything for you if you just show me your feelings . . .'

Pressing her eyes shut, Despo raised her head to kiss the coolness of the breast-shaped piece of lead.

'The nipple,' Druscilla urged. 'Suck the . . . nipple.'

Despo cursed herself for not having more control over herself at this moment, for not throwing herself into wild love-making with Druscilla. For some reason beyond her control, she could not force herself upon another female.

Druscilla held the lead replica of the breast closer to Despo's quivering lips, coaxing, 'Show me your feelings. Just suck the . . . nipple.'

Despo finally obeyed.

But quickly pulling back her head, she gasped, 'It's bitter.'

Druscilla dropped the necklace against her chest and studied Despo lying on the couch. She did not reply.

Reaching to inspect the lead breast which she had just sucked, Despo said, 'There is a hole in the end of the nipple!'

She examined the other breasts dangling from the chain and said, 'There is a hole in each of them!'

Druscilla answered complacently, 'You should look more

often, my dear. You will see that every breast has "a hole".'

'What do you keep inside them? What tasted so bitter?'

Druscilla ignored the hysterical question. She rose to her feet and, standing alongside the narrow couch, she said, 'Men are often fooled by women like you but not other females.'

Despo accused, 'You poisoned me!'

Druscilla turned away from the couch and moved slowly toward the table on which she had left the glowing oil lamp. She said. 'It is cruel to play with the feelings of other women, Despo. A love between women is delicate and rare, but when another woman profanes it, she must . . . suffer.'

'You poisoned me!'

Lifting the lamp from the table, Druscilla said as if speaking to herself, 'I should have learned long ago not to look for a fulfilling love. When you first came here, I foolishly thought you might be my answer. But you are ambitious. You are like all the others. You. . . .'

She stopped. She heard the thud of footsteps running in the hallway outside the room and the sound of men shouting.

* * *

Druscilla stood in front of the door and looked over her shoulder at Despo beginning to writhe on the narrow couch across the dark room: the poison was already eating into her mouth, throat, and stomach. Her protests had turned into urgent gasps for air.

Outside the room, the shouting grew louder. Druscilla backed away from the door as she heard fists pound against the thick planking.

The door was finally thrown open. A group of men pushed into the room and Druscilla saw the plumes of Praetorian helmets as well as recognising the faces of – why were they here? – Hadrian, the white-haired Republican named Senator Sullus, and the pleasure slave, Vesuvio.

Senator Sullus stood forward and said, 'Are you Druscilla, the woman in charge of the female pleasure slaves.'

Druscilla stammered, 'You must talk to . . . Polybius.'

Sullus answered, 'We want to speak to the Greeks. The two adulterers brought here to battle one another. They have proof that Aurelius Macrinus is innocent of a crime for which he was accused of committing in Athens.' He put his hand on Vesuvio's shoulder.

Druscilla looked in bewilderment from Vesuvio back to the Senator. She protested, 'But this man is a slave. His name is Vesuvio.'

Hadrian spoke for the first time, correcting Druscilla in an authoritative manner she had never before heard him use. He said, 'This man is a citizen of Rome. He was taken as a temple thief in waters east of Piraeus and sold in Antioch as a slave.'

Druscilla's mind began to spin with confusion. Why was Hadrian, the heir to Trajan, suddenly protecting Vesuvio, a man whom he desired to be his lover only last night? Why now were Hadrian and Senator Sullus at Villa Orgiasta telling her this story about Vesuvio? Druscilla knew that Sullus was a Republican, a politician as conservative in his beliefs as Empress Plotina. Up to this moment, though, she had not even been aware that Sullus knew of Plotina's involvement here. Did all of Rome know this fact?

Realising the hopelessness of her personal situation, Druscilla fell to the floor and, prostrating herself in front of Hadrian, she begged, 'Have mercy, your Excellency. Have mercy on a woman who only obeys the orders of her superiors.'

Hadrian said, 'We do not hold you responsible for . . .'

Vesuvio interrupted Hadrian, saying as he pointed into the room's darkness, 'That is the woman on the couch! There is Despo!'

Druscilla began to wail, imploring the men for understanding; Hadrian, Senator Sullus, and Vesuvio moved quickly past to inspect the now motionless body lying in darkness on the narrow cot.

BOOK SIX

THE SCARLET MANTLE

38

The weather remained unseasonably warm in Campania as the December feast days of Saturnalia drew closer; the harvesting on Villa Vesuvio was finished and, with the winter planting nearing completion, the slaves and freed people on the estate anxiously anticipated the five-day celebration to the Roman god of harvest – Saturn.

Rumours still spread amongst the workers about their master's disappearance from and his sudden return to Campania. Stories ranged from far-fetched gossip that Vesuvio had been in Rome advising the Emperor on military plans to whispered accounts about how he had travelled to Athens in search of Miranda and had found her married to the Greek doctor, Menecrates.

Nobody had personally questioned Vesuvio since his return at the end of the summer solstice, nor had they learned the truth about his mysterious absence. Vesuvio had merely returned to the estate one evening on horseback, riding up the cypress-lined drive to the villa as if he had been out for a brief ride.

The one difference which the slaves and tenant workers on the estate noticed about the *'padrone'* was that he now took his infant son everywhere with him when he rode in the fields or visited the mills and presses. Although Vesuvio did not speak of Miranda, he clung to young Aurelius as if the child were the only hope he had of re-establishing a family on this inherited land. Nor did he explain the reason for his mysterious three-month-long disappearance from the estate.

* * *

The festival of Saturnalia was less raucous in the Italian countryside than the celebrations held in the city. Whereas the urban populace went to games held in amphitheatres and received colourful gifts from their masters during this festive week, the country slaves celebrated the feast days as they had been observed in bygone days when the Saturnalia was a rustic show of gratitude to the harvest god.

Vesuvio distributed produce to his workers during this winter festival, giving them pickled fruits and dried meats to keep in their storehouse, and making presents to them of woollen cloth and thickly soled shoes to wear during the ensuing cold months of winter. Also during this holiday, a master acted as a 'slave' to his slaves.

For entertainment at this year's Saturnalia, Vesuvio had arranged for the five female tumblers – Rubecula, Aquila, Regula, Phasina, and Passerina – to travel south to Campania from the district of Transtiberina where they now lived in the city of Rome. Vesuvio had insisted that Senator Sullus help the five women find work as gymnastic instructors to young children in the public baths in Rome. He also had pressed Senator Sullus to assist the five women in applying to the *Tabularium* for their freedom, explaining to Sullus that the women had acted courageously in delivering the message about Despo and Cleomenes being held at the villa in Tibur.

Vesuvio had been impressed with the Senator's conduct in dealing with the situation when proof for Vesuvio's innocence finally presented itself. He realised that the pragmatic old man could have insisted that he wait to be cleared by a senatorial jury, that Sullus did not even have to accept Hadrian's suggestion that Vesuvio be immediately released from his bondage at Villa Orgiasta. True, Vesuvio had hoped that the Senator would be co-operative, that Sullus would send word to Hadrian as soon as Rubecula brought him the message. Vesuvio had known how undependable his own Republican uncle had been though, and his plan to be assisted by Senator Sullus had only been conjecture.

Apart from Senator Sullus's immediate co-operation in helping him, the person who had most impressed Vesuvio was Hadrian. He had listened to Vesuvio's story about Despo, Cleomenes, and the stolen temple coins. It had also been Hadrian who suggested that Empress Plotina's secret connection to Villa Orgiasta not be made public. He also proposed that Druscilla and Polybius be quietly sent away to live in obscurity in Cisalpine Gaul. Vesuvio recognised Hadrian's political acumen in arriving at such a decision, his storing-up of facts to use later against possible political adversaries.

Hadrian and Vesuvio had spoken as two patricians to one another on that afternoon in Tibur; they had both tactfully avoided any reference to Hadrian's request for a golden statuette to be made from Vesuvio's phallus. After listening to Vesuvio's report that Miranda was being held by the Roman army in Petra Arabia, Hadrian had generously promised that he would arrange for Miranda to be brought back to Vesuvio's estate in Campania, that he would send word to Petra Arabia telling the army there that they were wrongly holding a woman who was betrothed to the heir of one of Rome's oldest and most distinguished families – Aurelius Popiliano Macrinus.

That meeting in Tibur had been three months ago. Since that time the scribes in the Athenian Temple of Diana had sent word to Vesuvio in Campania that the bulk of Menecrates's estate would be officially bequeathed to Miranda – and her spouse – should the original claimant of his riches – his wife, Despo – not prove to be a true wife. Despo now lay in a grave alongside Cleomenes in the pine forest of Tibur. Miranda was Menecrates's heir.

The irony of slavery continued to perplex Vesuvio.

Miranda was now not only free but she was rich. But still – three months later – she had not yet reappeared.

Vesuvio was dressed today in the rough tunic of a slave for the Saturnalian feast. He and his bailiff, Galba, stood in the central courtyard of Villa Vesuvio. The December afternoon sun was bright and the two men worked dividing gifts for the slaves into piles.

Today was the first day of the feast; Rubecula, Regula, Aquila, Phasina, and Passerina were due to arrive soon from Rome. According to the Saturnalian custom, Vesuvio was dressed as a 'slave' to distribute the gifts of produce and clothing to his people.

Old Tia rushed into the courtyard as Vesuvio finished stacking another pile. She called excitedly to him, 'A stranger, *domine*. A strange female dressed in a red mantle approaches the house from the main road.'

Vesuvio knew that the tumblers were arriving soon from Rome. He also suspected that they would be wearing the brightly coloured clothing of entertainers. He patiently answered, 'Calm yourself, Tia. It is only my good friend, Rubecula. If you look closely you will see the other four women behind her, Regula, Aquila, Phasina, and little Passerina are coming up the drive, too.'

He put down a handful of parcels and went to the portal to welcome the five women to his home.

* * *

Vesuvio stood looking down the gravel drive.

Galba called from the courtyard behind him, 'Shall I have the entertainers escorted to the house we prepared for them, *domine?*'

Vesuvio did not reply. He stared at the woman walking over the gravel toward the house. No other females were following her as he had expected. The woman was not Rubecula.

Galba called again, 'Shall we give the acrobats refreshment here, *domine?*'

Still, Vesuvio did not reply. He continued staring at the woman now approaching the house. He recognised her as Miranda but – even in this realisation – a strange inertness overtook his body. What was this feeling? Shock or relief? And why did he suddenly possess no physical energy?

Galba called again, 'Are you there, *domine?*'

Ignoring the question, Vesuvio spoke to Miranda as if he had last seen her only a few hours ago. He casually observed, 'You are wearing the red mantle of a bride, Miranda.'

Smiling, she replied, 'And you, Vesuvio . . . you are dressed as a slave.'

He shrugged helplessly. 'It is Saturnalia.'

Continuing across the gravel toward him, Miranda said, 'I have completely forgotten about our feast days. And where I have come from this mantle means a medical attendant.' She dropped it from her head and shook her hair in the bright December sun.

'But not in Italy,' Vesuvio said as he slowly extended one hand toward her. 'Remember? Here in Italy a red mantle is worn only by brides. You should have worn such a mantle many years ago.'

Taking Vesuvio's hand, Miranda lovingly pressed it against her cheek. She kissed it and answered with equal calmness, 'Let us forget about the past, Vesuvio. Let us both promise to think only about the future.'

'A wise promise,' Vesuvio murmured. He stepped forward and, wrapping both arms around her slim body, he drew her closer to his chest. It was only at that moment – when Vesuvio held Miranda in his arms – that he began to quake with deep, manful tears.

Miranda was home.

GLOSSARY

atrium	the central courtyard of a Roman house, around which were built a series of rooms; the *atrium* was often used as a main reception area.
bandulum	a narrow cloth binding worn by Roman women over their breasts.
domine, a	form of address for the head of a Roman household or superior male personage – as 'Master'; *domina*, 'Mistress'.
gens	a Roman family, inclusive of their progenitors; a tribal conception of blood and honour.
insulae	blocks of flats in ancient Rome; housing for the lower-classes equivalent to modern day tenement buildings.
lares	domestic and, occasionally, wayside shrines dedicated to Roman household gods, a religious symbol often located in the *atrium*.
nomens	a name or family, a plaque bearing a resident's name.
peristylium	the arched colonnade surround or leading from a courtyard; see *atrium*.
portus	the formal entrance to a Roman home; hence, a haven or 'port'.
quadrigae	a team of horses for charioteering.
stola	a long garment worn by distinguished Roman ladies, usually made from bleached linen; also an outer colonnade in an open marketplace.
spina	the centre or 'spine' of a Roman race track, often decorated with statues or fountains.
triclinium	dining-room in a Roman house.